THE OLD
CAPE HOLLYWOOD
SECRET

BARBARA EPPICH STRUNA

B.E.Struna

Cover Designers: Loretta Matson, Timothy Jon Struna, Timothy Graham
Edited by Nicola Burnell

This is a work of fiction. Names, characters, places, brands, media, and incidents are either the product of the author's imagination or are used fictitiously. Any resemblance to similarly named places or to persons living or deceased is unintentional.

PRINT ISBN 978-0-9976-5663-3
EBOOK ISBN 978-0-9976-5662-6
Library of Congress Control Number: 2017905224

"Nancy Caldwell is at it again. Her new adventure takes us from coast to coast and back in time. The story is ripe with Hollywood nostalgia and develops over decades, starting in 1947 and finally meshing in present time, with Nancy putting together pieces of an intriguing puzzle. There is plenty of romance, intrigue, murder, and mystery.

A lover of old movies, I often watch Turner Classic Movies. While reading the chapters set in the old days, I could almost hear the TCM narrator describing the events of the story. If you like Barbara Eppich Struna's first two books in this series, you'll love this one. If you're new to her work, get started with *The Old Cape Hollywood Secret*. Bring some popcorn."

—Steven P. Marini, author, *Schmuel's Journey*
and *Henniker Secrets*

"What starts off as a light and breezy caper quickly turns into a dark and gripping thriller. The creepy villain, who has a taste for beautiful women and keeps a secret room lined with shoe-boxes by date and year, will keep you from sleeping until you finish!"

—Popular Thriller Writer Ray Anderson, author,
The Trail and *Sierra*

*To my mother, who always told me
how extraordinary it was to be able to
write a book*

June 1947
HOLLYWOOD

MAGGIE GRIPPED the diamond ring in her hand. Her knuckles turned white. The other hand touched the pearls on the black pouch, like prayer beads. She quickly sat on the floor of the closet to steady herself, but she couldn't stop shaking. She left the door ajar to give her a thin view of the tiny studio room. Her heart thumped against her chest as adrenaline coursed through her veins.

She watched the studio door open. Her cousin Gertie tried to stand her ground just inside the room. She sounded nervous when she asked the two men, "What do you want?"

Maggie's knees were tight against her chest. Tugging at the bottom of her cotton nightgown, she pulled it even lower to cover her bare feet. She caught her breath when she saw the men push through the doorway.

There was a quick scuffle. Gertie shouted, "Hey, you can't push me around."

Maggie could only see the back of one of the intruders. His brown suit and fedora hat loomed large, blocking most of her view. Swallowing hard, she watched him shove her cousin down onto the bed. "You're outta time, kid. Where is it?"

Gertie was defiant. "Hey, what's the idea?"

The other man was short and squat. "Let's just say we want what you stole."

Gertie tried to stand up. "I don't know what you're talking—"

The bigger man slapped her across the face with the back of his hand. She fell back on the bed.

Maggie covered her ears to block the yelling and screaming. She quickly closed her eyes and remembered her mother's parting words to her: "You're far too young to be on your own. You're only eighteen years old. That Hollywoodland is dangerous."

Maggie whispered in a prayer, "I want to go home. I just want to go home to Cape Cod."

1

One Month Earlier – May 1947
BREWSTER – CAPE COD

THE OLD FAN drove Maggie Foster crazy. For the past hour, its light green blades pushed hot air directly into her face. Sweat droplets that had formed under the floral scarf tied around her hair rolled down her forehead and stung her eyes. She wiped them away with the bottom of her cotton apron. As she stacked the last clean white dinner plate on the porcelain sink, she mumbled, "I'm so tired of cleaning up after everyone!"

Joey, the busboy, swung his mop in a slow rhythm across the narrow wooden slats of the restaurant's kitchen floor, offering no reaction to the young girl's words.

The clock struck 9 p.m. Maggie was done for the night. Her painted red fingernails, chipped and cracked from hot water and a brass scrubber, reached around to the nape of her neck and unfastened the damp knot of her kerchief.

Joey glanced over to Maggie. "Mrs. Crocker said you should tell your cousin Gertie not to come back to work here if she can't cover her shift." He returned his stare to the mop swishing back and forth across the stained wooden floorboards on his way to the other side of the kitchen.

Maggie grabbed her purse and coat from a black wrought-iron hook behind the door, hung up her apron, and then ran out the back door without a goodbye. She stopped in the middle of the dew-covered lawn, raised her arms into the night air with her palms up, her face lifted to the starlit sky. The cold salty air from the bay felt good across her young body. A deep breath passed through her.

She wondered if Eddie would be able to make it tonight, eyeing their favorite spot a few yards away under the peaked roof of the gazebo. Last summer, their clandestine meetings had been few and far between because of their long working hours. The Captain's Golf Course had kept Eddie busy and he'd made good tips caddying. She knew it was worth it, for their future together. Bad winter weather had brought snow that blanketed the Cape and covered the roads, making their rendezvous almost impossible, and now spring had produced more rain than normal. Tonight the air was warm. Summer was approaching. She had missed Eddie. Maybe he'd meet her tonight.

Her tweed skirt flipped back and forth as she ran up the gazebo's three steps and headed toward the back of the little hideaway. Maggie crouched down; her hem touching the red mahogany flooring. She felt around the wooden post for the right spot to push with her fingertips until a little door opened outward, revealing a secret hiding place. Reaching inside, she pulled out matches bearing the name of a restaurant, written in gold across its front, Tom Breneman's – Hollywood. She also retrieved a pack of Chesterfields, the chosen cigarette of movie stars. She fondly remembered the handsome customer who'd left them on the table in the inn's restaurant. The actor had left her a generous tip of twenty cents. It had been right before the Dennis Playhouse closed for the season, last fall.

Maggie returned to the edge of the canopied floor, sat down on the gazebo steps, lit a cigarette, and leaned her shoulders against the large square post that marked the entrance to the wooden structure. Her slight cough showed her naiveté for smoking, but it was just too glamorous not to try it on occasion. The moon and stars sparkled overhead. She heard the rustle of leaves in the dark and called out, "Eddie, is that you?"

"Yeah, babe. It's me." Eddie's leather bomber jacket creaked as he sauntered toward the gazebo steps, breaking the stillness of the night. He joined Maggie on the top step and gave her a quick kiss on the cheek. "Got another one for me?"

Maggie smiled and handed him a cigarette. "I missed you," she said in a whisper, putting her hand on his leg.

Eddie lit up, inhaled, and slowly let the smoke escape his lips in little white circles. "So, you goin' or what?"

Maggie took her hand away and looked down at her lap. "I think so." She couldn't look at him. She knew he didn't want her to leave. "It's only until the end of summer. Then I'll be back."

He stared at her. "Well, I'm worried about you."

"Gertie will be with me."

"That's what I'm worried about." He turned away. "She's kinda wild. You know, with the guys and stuff."

"I'll be fine. Gertie's real smart when it comes to making it on her own. She knows what to do." Maggie rubbed her cigarette out on the step and flicked the butt onto the grass. "Besides, I'm only going along for the fun, nothing serious. I'll be fine. I've got some extra money saved. I'll just be company for her in California while she finds a job and a place to live." She spoke a little more quietly. "Then I'll come home…to you." She faced Eddie and softly kissed him.

He tossed his cigarette away. "You better." Wrapping his arms around Maggie's shoulders, he pulled her across his upper thighs. "Come here, kid, I can't get enough of you."

After a long kiss, he held her with one arm and then slowly unbuttoned her coat and her blouse with his free hand.

Maggie returned a passionate kiss and let him touch her breasts.

Eddie started to move his hand down the side of her body and back up under her skirt.

The moon cast a soft light across his blond hair and square features. He looked so handsome and strong in his leather jacket. Maggie couldn't breathe and her heart pounded. "No, Eddie." She was dizzy, but she still kept kissing him. In between breaths she tried to stop him. "Eddie, please, no."

His breath was heavy and strong.

She grabbed his hand, but it kept going higher up her leg. "We can't do this. Not now." She held his hand tighter, and was able to push it down and away. "When I come back. I promise."

He stopped. "You promise?"

"Yes, I promise." Maggie sat up, straightened herself and looked right at Eddie. "We can do it when I get back from California."

"You serious?"

"Dead serious."

"You sure you don't want to seal the deal right now?" He smiled so big that the white of his teeth glowed in the moonlight.

"We'd better not."

Eddie looked for another cigarette from Maggie's stash and lit up. "You know, Mr. Gordan said they might be needing a lineman soon."

"Really?"

"Yeah, now that's a good payin' job with security."

"Oh, Eddie, that would be wonderful." Maggie stood up and leaned over to hug him once more. "I better get on home now. I have a lot of packing to do."

"How you getting to the bus on Saturday?"

"Peter Marsh is driving us in his dad's truck."

"You mean, Soaring Eagle?"

His sarcastic words hit a nerve with Maggie. She quickly shot back, "Don't you make fun of Peter. He's been my friend longer than I've known you." She turned to hide her cigarettes. Eddie stared out into the night. She remembered the day Peter showed her the secret compartment in the gazebo that he'd built for the inn. He told her it was her birthday gift and no one else knew about it. She pushed on the little door and it popped open once more for her to conceal the forbidden smokes.

"Well, I don't like no Indian coming around you for any reason." Eddie spat on the grass.

"Oh, stop it, Eddie. Besides, you said if it was nice weather on Saturday you had to work at the Captain's, so I asked Peter to drive us."

"I guess so. Mind you, after we're married, you'll have to pick your friends a little more carefully."

"What do you mean?"

"Nothing. You'd better get home. It's late."

Maggie sighed, turned away, and walked towards the road for the short walk home. She knew the time would come when she would have to say yes to Eddie.

John Foster was up late working on the Ellis's old Philco radio. Cigarette smoke filled the small borning room off the kitchen, now a workroom for John. While he worked, he bobbed his head to Rudi Blesh's radio program, *This Is Jazz*. His headphones prevented him from hearing Maggie come in the back door.

She hung her coat up and pushed open the door to the crowded room filled with wires, boxes, glass tubes, and other things Maggie couldn't name. She quietly watched the back of her father as he tested each glass tube one by one, trying to find the one that wasn't working. It was a tedious process, but one that she knew he liked to do, as long as he had his music. Besides, he enjoyed fixing things. She slowly reached for the radio's volume control to get his attention.

John looked up.

Maggie leaned over the red Bakelite radio and into his sight to wave at him.

"Hi, Sweetie," he said with a smile. He pushed one side of the headphones up above the ear that faced her.

"Hi, Daddy." Maggie sat on the edge of the table.

"Did Gertie ever show up at work?"

"No, as usual. But it was okay. The extra money was nice."

"Your Mama said that you were leaving for sure this Saturday."

"Uh huh." Maggie grew quiet. She wasn't sure how her father felt about her going to California.

John took the headset off, took one last drag on his cigarette, put it out, and then looked at his daughter. "Maggie, I want you to know that I'm okay with you going. I know your Mama doesn't like it. But if it's something that you need and want to do…then do it."

"Really? You don't mind?"

"No. I love you and want you to see as many places as you can. It's a good opportunity. Meet some new people."

Maggie got up and threw her arms around his neck. "Oh, Daddy, you're a peach."

He leaned back in his chair. "You know I always wanted to go to school to be an engineer, but things just happen."

Maggie had heard this story before, but this time it meant something more to her.

"When your grandpa died, I was the oldest, and I had to quit school and go to work. I wanted to travel too. Your uncles were too young to earn any money. So I had to do it all."

"I know, Daddy."

"I don't want you to lose your dreams." A big smile grew across his face. "Go see if there's a Coke in the fridge. We'll toast to your adventure."

Maggie scooted out the door and over to the Frigidaire. She found one bottle of Coke, opened it and reached for two glasses.

John yelled from inside the little room, "Don't forget the ice."

The metal ice tray was almost empty except for two cubes. Maggie plopped one into each glass and split the Coke between them. She stood next to her father with her glass high in the air. He did the same with his.

"To my sweet Maggie girl, may all your dreams come true." He lightly tapped her glass. "Bon voyage!"

The young girl drank the dark, fizzy liquid down in one gulp. "I love you, Daddy."

She quickly turned to leave. "Got to finish packing." She kissed him on top of his balding head. "Good night."

John smiled at her before he replaced the headphones to continue the weekly infusion of his favorite music, jazz.

2

Present Day – May
BREWSTER – CAPE COD

MY BRAND-NEW Bounty Hunter Pioneer metal detector leaned against the wall in the garage. It was a Christmas gift from my husband, Paul. He said the salesman had laughed when he'd told him it was for his wife.

I grabbed the detector and set out toward the back acre, onto a new path that now connected the other paths I'd carved out of our woods over the past years. My hiking boots avoided the deer scat that dotted the trail. I smiled and wondered if the deer appreciated my work of clearing away the brambles and thorns that grew throughout our property. This was the first time I'd walked the new path since I'd cleared it last fall. It had been a mild winter across Cape Cod and the sandy peninsula that I call home had begun to awaken. The air was brisk, ground damp, wind mild, and sun shining; perfect for exploring.

I swung the electronic wand right to left as I ventured further into the woods, my spade clanking against the ground as I dragged it behind me with my other hand. Within minutes, I'd found a few rusty nails, a broken lawn mower blade, and a #2 fishing weight. To my left, I noticed a big tree had fallen during the winter. It looked as if the old tree had grown through the boulder over the years, eventually splitting the rock into sections. I veered off the path to take a closer look. A pile of stones and clamshells were heaped together in a mound under the mangled roots. I could see a hint of the color turquoise in the dirt. I scratched at the forest floor with my work gloves and unearthed a lone coffee cup. It was a beautiful piece of Fiesta ware. There was only a small crack in it and the handle was still intact. I tried to piece together reasons why this little treasure had taken a journey into the woods. When I'd researched our circa 1880 house, I'd uncovered four distinct owners, one being a cranberry grower who'd owned the house from 1940–70. I also knew that Fiesta ware hadn't introduced the color turquoise until 1937, so it must have been the cranberry farmer who'd brought the cup so far away from the house. I sat down on one of the larger sections of the boulder that had broken away to enjoy the peace and quiet. Back in the 1940s, this area had been open farmland and would have offered a grand view of the Namskaket River. I laughed to myself and guessed that the cranberry grower wasn't drinking coffee back here. He'd probably had to hide his whiskey from his wife.

It was noon by the time I'd satisfied my adventurous spirit. Paul was painting in his studio. "Look what I found," I announced as I spread out my treasures on a piece of Kraft paper.

Paul looked them over. "Glad you like your present."

I returned the detector to its place by the garage door. "I'm going to check the mail."

The sun had ratcheted the temperature into the fifties. Most of the letters were addressed to me, Nancy Caldwell. One had a return address from the National Treasure Hunter Society. I was curious. By the time I reached the deck, I'd opened it and was reading its contents out loud.

"Ms. Caldwell, we have heard of your recent discoveries of lost treasure and would like to invite you to speak at our annual meeting, this coming June, in Hollywood, California. Airfare and hotel accommodations will be provided."

3

Saturday – 1947
MASHPEE – CAPE COD

PETER MARSH walked past his father on the way to the '38 Ford truck, his wooden toolbox in hand. "I'll be home later this afternoon."

Elwood Marsh was sanding a small wooden chest of drawers next to the barn. "You got to go back to Brewster? It's a long drive, son."

"I know, Father, but I want to make sure I measured right. Mrs. Crocker doesn't take kindly to sloppy work." Peter put his tools on the open bed of the dark grey pickup, which was also the family car.

"Well, mind your speed and watch that back tire. If it goes, it's going to be hard to find another one."

"Yes, Father."

Peter slid onto the driver's seat and started the engine. As he turned out onto Route 28, the highway dirt billowed behind him in clouds of sandy smoke. He smiled as he whispered to himself, "I'll be there soon, Maggie." Peter whistled a steady melody all the way to Brewster.

An hour later, the Ford truck drove by the Crosby Inn's stables on the Old King's Highway. Mrs. Crocker, cutting a few pussy willow branches for the inn, waved at Peter as he passed. He tooted the horn in return. Minutes later, he pulled onto Maggie Foster's clamshell driveway.

John Foster was finishing his coffee as he read the local news of last week's *Cape Codder* in the front parlor. Peter's knock stopped John in mid-sip. "I'll get it, Alice, I believe it's the Marsh boy come to take Maggie to the bus station."

Alice Foster was wiping her hands on her flowered apron when she appeared in the kitchen's doorway. She yelled up the little stairway, "Maggie! Peter's here. Get a move on."

"Okay, Mama. I'll be right down."

John opened the front door. "Peter."

"Mr. Foster, sir." The young man stood straight and tall; his wide shoulders, thick dark hair, and square-cut jaw made an impressive sight.

"How's your father?"

"Doing much better since the heart episode. The doctor said he was lucky, but he needs to stop smoking so much, sir."

"Well, you tell him that I send him my regards. He's a good and honest man. In the Pacific, we were buddies, you know. Why, he could get any radio going with his generator truck. We were a good team."

"Yes, he's often told me the stories about the Solomon Islands and such."

Maggie appeared at the top of the stairway. As she bumped her suitcase down the steps, she called out, "Daddy, let Peter be." She looked ready to travel in style. Her wide-bottomed brown slacks matched her gingham-checked sweater, which covered a crisp white blouse. The leather case landed with a thud on the polished floor of the foyer. "We've got to get going so we can pick up Gertie." Maggie took a minute to adjust a perky bow in her chestnut brown hair.

"I know, honey," her father said.

Peter used his backside to push the front door open as he carried her suitcase out to the truck. "Don't worry, Mr. Foster. I'll get her there on time."

Maggie flung her arms around her father. "I won't be gone that long."

Alice took her apron off and followed her young daughter outside. She stopped to hold Maggie's hand. They stood facing each other on the wooden porch. "You know, you're far too young to be on your own."

"Mama. Please." Maggie hugged her mother.

Alice leaned away from her. "You're only eighteen years old. That Hollywoodland is dangerous."

"I'll be fine, Mama. Remember last summer? Peter taught me how to defend myself." Maggie started to laugh.

"Oh, Maggie, really!" Alice sounded annoyed. "I'm just worried."

As Maggie flew down the porch steps and to the truck, Alice had the last word. "Behave yourself," she called out. Under her breath, she whispered, "Please, Lord, bring her home safe to us."

Maggie's white and brown saddle shoes contrasted with the dark rubber of the old Ford's running board. With a quick wave and a giddy "Goodbye" to her parents, she settled her youthful body against the cracked leather of the front seat. Taking a deep breath, she smiled at her best friend. "Let's go, Peter."

Her chauffeur for the day put it in gear and took off to Gertie's house.

"Was your father upset that you promised to drive me to Hyannis?" asked Maggie.

Peter kept his eyes on the road ahead, but his thoughts were elsewhere.

"Peter, did you hear me? Was your father mad?"

"No. He thinks I had to check measurements for a new buffet table for the Crosby Inn's dining room. I didn't tell him I was driving you."

Maggie checked her purse to see if she'd forgotten anything. Snacks and two Coke bottles were wrapped in newspaper inside a brown paper bag for the bus ride to the train station.

"Maggie?"

She looked over to Peter.

"I want you to be very careful when you get there."

"I will. You're so sweet to worry about me."

Peter's tone turned grave. "I found a newspaper from Los Angeles in the basement of the Crosby Inn."

"A newspaper?"

"Yes. I read that several women have been murdered there. One poor woman was killed…in such a horrible way…they called her the Black Dahlia. I think her name was Elizabeth Short. It made me sick to read about it."

"Do you have it? I'd love to read about what's going on there. Of course, not that article." Maggie took out her compact and applied some lipstick.

* * *

Gertie Foster was up early. The light brown suitcase she'd purchased in Orleans was already packed and decorated with labels from exotic places around the world, giving the illusion that she was well travelled. Over the last two years, Gertie had researched National Geographic magazines at the library and then sent away for advertising labels from hotels in faraway locations. She was pleased with the finished project.

She made sure her ruby-red nail polish was completely dry before slipping on her short, brown, cotton-twill skirt. Pulling a crisp, white blouse over her shoulders, she cinched it at her waist with a beige leather belt. After a quick ankle tie of her sandals and a glance in the mirror to make sure her nylon seams were straight, she dragged her luggage down the steep stairs.

Gertie's mother was heading out to work a double shift, starting at the Orleans Inn. After a quick supper in the restaurant's kitchen, she'd then sell tickets at the Orleans Theatre until 11 p.m. Ethel Foster stopped in front of her daughter. "Let me look at you." She stepped back to admire her only child, now all grown up. "Well, you certainly look the socialite. I hope you'll be happy in California."

Ethel turned to glance at herself in the mirrored hall tree. Her eyes had begun to show dark circles. At thirty-six years old, the loss of her husband and the responsibility of managing a house and raising a child by herself had started to take a toll on her body and demeanor.

Gertie squeezed her face next to her mother's image in the mirror to fix her wavy brown hair. "It's too bad Daddy couldn't be here to see me off on my first real adventure." They both stared at the mirror in silence.

Ethel broke away and mumbled under her breath, "God damn that war." She opened her small clutch bag and handed Gertie some money. "Here's a little something extra. Not much. Keep it for an emergency."

Gertie hesitated for only a moment, then folded the twenty into a hanky and stuffed it into her bra.

"Good girl. I think you'll do just fine in Los Angeles."

They hugged each other for only a few seconds before the sound of the Marsh's truck separated them.

Maggie waved her arm out the window when she saw the two women exit the old house. "Hi, Aunt Ethel."

"Hello, Mrs. Foster." Peter got out and lifted Gertie's suitcase from the dirt driveway into the back of the pickup.

Mother and daughter followed the well-worn path of weedy grass that led to the street. The passenger door flew open. Maggie slid closer to Peter as Gertie squeezed herself onto the bench seat. When she was settled, Ethel stuck her head close to the open window, a few inches from her daughter's face, and looked straight at the cousins. "I trust that you two will take care of each other?"

"Mother, please don't worry," Gertie said as she straightened her skirt.

Maggie tilted her head to the side to see her aunt. "Don't worry, Aunt Ethel, I'll watch her for you."

Ethel tapped the car window's metal trim with her fingertips. She took a step back. "Be safe. Call me collect at one of the stops along the way. I've only one shift tomorrow...I'll be home after 8 p.m."

Gertie touched up her lipstick. Maggie yelled goodbye as Peter shifted into gear.

The girls giggled for almost the entire ride to Hyannis.

Gertie finally spoke up. "Hey, Peter. We need to make a stop at the Hyannis Pharmacy, on Main Street, before we get to the bus station."

"I don't know if we have time." Peter stared at the road ahead.

"We've got to stop. I need my nail polish and they're the only store on the Cape with such a big selection of cosmetics. I insist we stop!" Gertie pushed her hand against the dashboard, as if she could stop the truck herself.

Maggie could see that her cousin would not take no for an answer. "It's okay, Peter. She'll be quick." She glared at her cousin. "You'd better be."

Peter stopped in front of the drug store. Gertie grabbed her coin purse and jumped out.

Maggie stayed in the truck and noticed that Peter's eyes were fixed on his feet.

"What's wrong, Peter?" She touched his arm.

He turned towards her. "I'm going to miss you."

"I know, but it's so exciting for me. Remember when we were little? We talked all the time about going on adventures; me in the movies and you a pilot, flying all over the world."

He finally broke a smile. "You're right. My time will come. Our time will come. And I hope when you come back, we can talk…"

Before he could finish his sentence, Gertie scrambled onto the seat and stuffed a small paper bag into her cosmetic case.

"Maggie…about our future together?"

Maggie never heard Peter's words. She was too nervous about missing the last bus to Providence. "Let's go. Our bus leaves soon." She waited for Peter to pull onto the road. "Did you ask me something?"

He sighed. "No. I just said that I hope you two don't kill each other. A week is a long time to be cooped up on a train together."

The old Ford disappeared around the corner in a cloud of dirt as it headed towards the bus depot.

4

Present Day – May
CAPE COD

THE KITCHEN was hot and the floors slick as Nancy Caldwell's oldest son, Jim, did his dance from stove to sink to pick up counter. He read the mint green paper clipped to a wire that was strung across the opening: *Chick parm, garlic bread, house salad.* "God, it's hot!" he whispered.

Jim was pacified by the thought that he could put up with the final hour before closing his Cape Cod bistro for the night. He stuffed his hand into the pocket of his shorts and felt for the crumpled paper on which he'd earlier scrawled a phone number. *Don't forget to make the call*, he reminded himself.

His head was swimming with everything he had to do before he left for Hollywood. At twenty-seven years old, his decision to move out west and leave the restaurant in his partners' able hands was a good one. All of his hard work to get the place profitable was finally paying off. The partners promised they'd take over the business and send him his share of the profits each month. After all, Jim had been the one to put in the long hours and tons of his own cash, and had piled up a huge personal debt. He deserved this opportunity to follow a dream to Hollywood that he'd had since high school.

He picked up his cell phone to call his mom.

"Hello?" Nancy's voice was soft, but sounded tired.

"How ya' doing?"

"Hanging in there. What time is it?"

"Almost 10 p.m. It's not very crowded. It'll be a quick cleanup tonight."

"That's good. I'll probably be up late anyway."

"Well, hopefully you'll be asleep by the time I come home. I'll be quiet."

"Be careful driving."

"Love you, Mom."

Jim checked his email and then punched in the number from the crumpled paper. No answer. He left a message. Within minutes, *Easy Ship Anywhere* was calling him back. After some quick words, the deal was set; his dune buggy would be picked up from his family's home in ten days and delivered to his rented apartment in Venice Beach, California. He'd been fortunate to find two girls for roommates to share the new place. The rent wasn't too high; it was being split three ways. In one week he'd be in L.A., living just like the old sitcom, *Three's Company*.

That night, on his drive home to Brewster, he coached himself out loud; his voice blending with the beat of the music and the cool wind. "If this works out, my partners will be sending me money from the profits in about a month." Straightening the rearview mirror and then adjusting the bass on the radio, he took a sip of his drink and grinned. "I have enough money saved to be all right for a while."

*   *   *

Jim's new apartment sat just off the Pacific Coast Highway, or the PCH, as the locals called it, and within minutes of the Venice Beach Boardwalk in Southern California. The dune buggy arrived as scheduled and was stored in one of the two parking spaces allotted for each apartment. After a couple of days exploring, Jim landed a job as a waiter in an upscale restaurant nearby in Santa Monica. Not exactly his dream, but serving people from every venue of the entertainment business was part of his plan to reach his goals. Networking was a big element of the Hollywood game and schmoozing was the way to go. He also found another job bartending, part-time, down the street on the boardwalk.

Jim was a good son, who faithfully called home on the weekends to tell everyone, especially his mom, about all the movie star sightings from the beach, street, or restaurant. His latest call started with some good news. "Mom, I think I could get a reduction on my rent if I built a patio deck next to my apartment for the landlord."

"That's great," Nancy said, with encouragement in her voice.

"I'm going to start in a few days and hope to be done by the time you get here for that Treasure Hunter Conference. I'll be sure to call you if I find any jewels or gold."

She gave out a laugh on the other end of the phone, "Yeah, right. I love you. See you soon."

* * *

Jim was eager to finish his patio project before his mother's arrival. He woke around 6 a.m. After inserting his contact lenses and taking a couple of blinks to focus, he was ready to start digging the first of four holes for the posts of the new deck, to be located on the side of the two-story apartment. Pursuing his dream of becoming a movie star in L.A. had only just begun and he was on a tight budget. After all, he thought, what's a little manual labor? The whole project was only 10 x 10 feet square.

He jammed the point of his shovel into the unkempt side yard that bordered the alleyway leading to the beach. The grass was sparse; mostly pebbles and sand. After reaching a depth of almost a foot, a small piece of stained gingham material appeared at the bottom of the hole. Jim leaned down to give it a tug. The cotton stretched a little and then separated from the soil. He threw it onto the cement walkway that edged the area for the new patio. Eying a straight line across the yard, Jim continued to dig a second hole.

After several more minutes of digging, he picked up one of the posts and placed it inside the hole to measure how far down he still needed to dig. He dug deeper, exposing another piece of dirty gingham, this time about ten inches square. He bent over to claw at the dirt and tried to see where the fabric was coming from. Then his fingertips brushed against something hard and tan-colored. He quickly pushed away the loose soil only to flinch backwards.

After a few cautious seconds, his curiosity peaked higher. He reached for the small trowel to carefully pick at what looked like the partial skeletal remains of someone's arm wrapped in the patterned cotton fabric. He called the police.

* * *

While the police worked on their investigation outside his apartment, Jim tried to call home, but had no luck. He assumed his dad was driving his mom to the airport so he left a message for him to call back. Finding the remains of a dead body was something that needed more of an explanation than a quick sentence or two.

As the police sifted the dirt in a hunt for clues as to who or what was buried there, a few more bones, similar to the one Jim had unearthed, were removed from the hole. Jim couldn't stop watching through his tiny kitchen window. By noon, the whole side yard was still cordoned off with yellow tape. At 1:20 p.m., the police uncovered one final item: a small metal mesh purse. He could see the officer remove something from inside of it and his imagination took off. As he walked towards the kitchen door to head outside, he wondered if the purse was sterling silver and worth any money.

"Excuse me. Excuse me. What did you find inside that purse?"

The officer turned. "Sir. You shouldn't be out here."

"I'm just interested to know what you found. It was me who called the police this morning."

The policeman stood up. With white-gloved hands he placed a faded, sepia-toned photograph of two young women on one of the small boxes that he was using to collect evidence. "Here. You can take a look, but don't touch."

The year 1947 was written at the bottom of the old photo that featured two women, all smiles. One had light-colored hair with a bow in it. She was dressed in a dark skirt and dark blouse. The other girl had mid-length hair that was smooth and rounded at the bottom, just like a movie star from Old Hollywood. Her ring finger was looped through a top circle ring attached to the chain handle of a mesh purse. It dangled low on her leg, next to her ankle-wrapped sandals.

Jim recognized where the two women were standing – right in front of Grauman's Chinese Theatre. "Say, this is a Polaroid." He'd taken a class about the old photography technique in college. He pointed to the purse in the picture. "Doesn't this look like the one you just found in the dirt?"

The policeman leaned toward Jim for a better view. "Yeah, maybe you're right." He stepped back and opened a clear plastic bag. "We'll take everything back to the lab and run some tests."

"You know," Jim added as he nodded at the photo, "Polaroid first came out in 1947. That connects to the date on the picture." Jim returned his stare to one of the girls in the picture. "This one girl looks familiar to me."

The sergeant ignored Jim's comment and slid the dirt-encrusted purse and the photo inside the bag. "Here's my card if you have any questions."

"When am I going to be able to finish my patio?"

"We'll let you know, sir. Just hang tight. We'll be in touch." The policeman left the yellow tape in place. "Don't touch a thing. This could be a crime scene."

Jim checked his watch. It was getting close to 2 p.m. He texted his mom to tell her he was going to be late to the airport.

As he showered, Jim couldn't stop thinking about how much fun it was going to be when he explained to his mother about the unexpected discovery of the bones, an old, maybe sterling, mesh purse, and a faded photograph. She wasn't like other mothers. She'd been known to get involved in anything mysterious, whether she wanted to or not. Jim knew his mom would be very interested in his story. He stopped for a moment and cocked his head...who did the girl in the old photograph remind him of?

5

1947
LOS ANGELES

THE TRAIN pulled into Southern California's Union Station, the largest train terminal in the Western United States. Maggie and Gertie gathered their belongings and, with suitcases in hand, the two cousins walked through the beautiful southern garden. Both girls gaped at the sheer size of the elegant waiting area.

Maggie couldn't resist the urge to feel the luxury of the brown leather chairs that filled the cavernous room as she chose her seat about midway in. Her saddle shoes looked too casual for the shiny brown terra cotta tile floor with its center strip of patterned inlaid marble. Above her head, six circular chandeliers lit up the ceiling and its massive, exposed beams. Maggie felt like she was in an old hunting lodge.

Gertie threw her things across one of the seats. The huge chairs had armrests of thick carved wood that connected two or three together in rows. She glanced over to Maggie. "Here, you watch my things. I'm goin' to powder my nose." She grabbed her purse and disappeared into a restroom.

Maggie didn't mind; she was content to just sit and take in all of her surroundings.

Once inside the bathroom, Gertie noticed an attractive young woman appear in the mirror behind her as she powdered her nose. Both smiled at their reflections.

Blonde and fashionably dressed, the woman in the mirror began to wash her hands and coyly asked, "Visiting, or on your way to somewhere mysterious?"

"Oh no, I'm here to stay. What about you?" Gertie dabbed a final pat of powder and closed the clasp on her cosmetic bag.

"Well, I work at RKO. You know, the movies," the blonde said with an air of pride.

Gertie perked up. "Really? That must be so exciting." She too washed her hands. "I was hoping I could do the same."

The woman stepped back and gave the new kid in town a once over. "Hike your skirt up a little."

Gertie did so without hesitation.

"Now turn around slowly."

Gertie projected the classic pin-up look.

"Maybe I can help you. You certainly know how to dress...and I love your nails."

"Could you really get me into the movies?" Gertie asked.

"I think so. Where ya' stayin'?"

"Nowhere yet. I'm here with a friend. We're hoping to find something small...not too expensive."

"I know just the place. Got a piece of paper?"

"I think so." Gertie fumbled in her purse and found a small notebook and pencil.

The woman grabbed it. "I'll write it down for you. Say, what's your name?"

"Gertie Foster. I'm from Cape Cod."

"Where?"

"Near Boston."

"Oh, yeah. I know where that is." The woman twisted her bleached blonde hair around one finger and wrote down the address with her free hand. She handed it back to Gertie and then proceeded to slather on red lipstick.

"This is just swell. I gotta tell Maggie."

Turning, the stranger introduced herself. "I'm Blanche Jones, but my stage name is Bebe Jones. Mr. Dirkson tells all his girls that they should have a stage name...for privacy."

"Oh," Gertie said with admiration. "How are we going to get to this place?" She straightened her skirt and began to study the address.

Blanche laughed. "Hey. Don't worry, honey. Why don't you just come with us? Gaylord is picking me up in a few minutes. He's my boyfriend, you know." She blotted her lips in the mirror.

Gertie tore out the paper, folded it in half and stuffed it into her blouse.

"We'll show you around and then drop you off." Blanche looked to see if the seams in her stockings were straight. "Whatta' you say, kid?"

"I'll do it. Give me a few minutes so I can tell my friend."

"Meet you outside in ten." Blanche twirled around and within seconds she was out the door. The image of her polka-dotted halter-top stayed with Gertie. It was exactly what she wanted to wear and could hardly wait to buy one.

Maggie saw Gertie hustling towards her. "Anything wrong?"

"Absolutely nothing is wrong. In fact, everything is just peachy." Gertie quickly sat down on the leather seat that was attached to Maggie's seat.

"What do you mean?"

Gertie leaned in closer over the wooden armrest. "I met a movie star in the bathroom. She's going to help us find a place to live and maybe even a job." Breathless, she began to gather up her things. "We're supposed to meet them outside right now!"

"Who is this person? Can we trust her?"

"Oh, Maggie, don't be such a baby. I've got a chance to really make a go of it here and I'm not going to lose it. Get a move on!"

Maggie stood up and put her hands on her hips. "Gertie! We can't just go off with some stranger."

Gertie ignored her words and started for the door. "Come on. She's Blanche and he's Gaylord."

Maggie grabbed her luggage and followed her cousin out the door.

It was a beautiful California day as the girls stood outside in the warm seventy-four degrees that partnered with a soft ocean breeze.

"Who are we looking for?" asked Maggie as she swiveled her head back and forth.

"Blanche, or Bebe, that's her stage name. Isn't that wonderful, Maggie? A real movie star."

"What's she look like?"

"A beautiful blonde. Real glamorous."

Maggie's hand shielded her eyes from the strong sun. To her left, a gorgeous mint green convertible pulled alongside the curb.

Gertie squealed, "That's them!" She began waving high and wild, trying to get the attention of Blanche and Gaylord. The car came to a halt right in front of them.

Blanche stood up and leaned her back against the top of the windshield. "Girls. This is Gaylord Cannon. He's my boyfriend!"

Gaylord looked them over. A big curl of dark brown hair fell across his forehead. He brushed it back to reveal a handsome face with sparkling green eyes. "Greetings," he said with a beautiful smile. "Welcome to sunny California."

6

Present Day – Thursday
LOS ANGELES

MY PLANE from Boston landed safely around noon. I was eager to get off. The L.A. terminal was crowded as usual. My gum found its way into the nearest trashcan and then I located the rest room. I checked phone messages. Jim's name appeared at the top. *Something came up explain later going to be late ...maybe 2:30.*

I texted back: *Okay. I'll wait.*

I thought about taking a cab, but the extra wait time would give me a chance to call Paul at home to let him know I'd arrived safely. I settled in with a cup of tea at a small café table.

"Paul?"

"Hi, honey. Everything okay?" Paul sounded relieved that I was on the ground.

"All is well, just waiting for Jim." My herbal tea tasted comforting.

"Danny and Molly want you to get some pictures of anything Hollywood."

I laughed. "Give them some good hugs for me, will you?"

"Sure. Hey, Jim called and said to call him back, but he's not answering."

"It's probably nothing. I'll see him soon. Gotta go. Jim may be texting or calling soon. We'll talk later. Love you."

As soon as Jim's call came through to say that he was finally outside, I gathered my luggage and hurried through the sliding glass doors into the steamy heat of L.A.

Jim got out to give me a hug, grabbed my bag, and threw it into the back of his car.

I quickly asked, "So, what's going on?"

Jim pulled away and joined the other cars that were leaving the airport. "Remember I told you that I struck a deal with my landlord to dig a patio for a month's rent?"

"Yes. How did it turn out?"

"Well, I never finished it. Something came up."

I noticed his lips slowly change into a smirk. When he was little, he'd fine-tuned this expression whenever he teased his other brothers and sisters. Evidently, he hadn't outgrown his penchant for joking.

"Come up? What'd you do...find a dead body?" I laughed as I rolled up the window to hear Jim better. His car had no air conditioning.

"Yup." Jim stared ahead at the road, waiting for my reaction.

"What? You found a dead body?"

"That's what I said. No joke."

I shook my head in disbelief. "I honestly think our family needs to curtail our desire to dig things up." My fingers found their way into my graying hair. "Okay. Tell me all about it."

After a detailed explanation of what he'd uncovered, Jim finally pulled into a parking space near his street; his allotted space at the apartment was occupied by his dune buggy. We sat for a moment in silence, taking in the Pacific Ocean view, which was magnificent from the lot's high location.

I took a deep breath of the salty air. "It's beautiful. Looks and smells good, just like back home."

Jim seemed preoccupied. "It's Natalie," he blurted out.

"What?"

"Natalie. She's the girl who resembles the one in the old Polaroid. Natalie's a waitress from the Clamshell Café, on the boardwalk."

"You mean she looks like the girl in the old picture from the purse?"

"Yeah."

* * *

We decided to leave my suitcase in the car. Jim would drive me over to my hotel later. Checking out his home away from home and meeting his new roommates were high on my priority list. But what was going on under the dirt of the new patio was right next to them. We talked as we walked along the alleyways and streets of Venice Beach, passing a mix of small gate entrances made of wrought iron, wood, and plastic.

"So tell me, Jim, are you happy?"

"Yup. It's a little different out here, but it's where I should be. It's what I want."

"I guess that's all that matters." The air was getting a little warmer and the pace to keep up with my tall son was wearing me out. I was in great shape, but jet lag slowed me up a little. I stopped to admire the flowers nestled among the houses and the red bougainvillea vines and bushes that divided each person's property, giving me a chance to catch my breath. Jim stopped to wait for me.

"Do you feel safe?"

"Oh, yeah, Mom. It's fine."

"But you found a dead body. And who's Natalie?"

"I met her about a week after I arrived. We sort of hit it off. Not romantically or anything."

"Oh?"

"Some of her relatives are from the Cape and she grew up in New Hampshire. Whenever we have a shift together, we commiserate about the cold and all the nor'easters that we don't get in L.A."

As we approached Jim's apartment, yellow tape was evident through the vine-covered fence. We walked around to the front door, then stepped across the cement pavement that was bordered with a chain link fence protecting pedestrians from the highway or the PCH.

After entering Jim's place, the traffic noise lessened, which was a relief, because I wanted my son to be comfortable in his new home. I followed Jim to the rear of the apartment, through the kitchen and then out to the side yard.

It looked like an official crime scene. "Oh, my goodness! This is really something."

Jim walked over to the far side. "Here's where I found the first piece of material and then the bone."

"Are they sure it's a human bone?"

"They have to do some tests first, but I have a feeling it's human."

"What about the picture? I'd really like to see it."

"I don't have it. The police took it with them. I suppose we could go down to the station and ask."

"Maybe we could get a copy of it. I can explain that I know a few things about digging up mysteries and solving them, too."

"I don't know, Mom. Let's wait."

"I'd also like to meet Natalie. If we had the picture, we could show it to her and then ask—"

"Mom. Slow down. Let's get you settled into your hotel. I've got a few errands to do for work tonight, but I could show you around tomorrow. I'm also working a double shift on the weekend."

"Sounds good. I can explore on my own. My hotel is right on Ocean Boulevard, across from the Santa Monica Pier. I would have liked to stay at the Georgian Hotel, but it was beyond the budget I was allotted from the Treasure Hunter Society. I can't complain. An all-expenses paid trip just to talk about my adventures in finding treasure is simply awesome."

"So when is your presentation at the meeting?" Jim grabbed a soda from the fridge.

"Monday afternoon." I poured myself a glass of water.

"Then I can come by to visit with you again on Monday morning?"

"Absolutely. Will I get a chance to meet your roommates?"

"Probably not, they both work crazy hours, but they're real nice." The soda can gave a quick burst. "I still can't believe you found pirate treasure... and not once, but twice."

My face lit up. "It is pretty amazing, isn't it?"

After Jim locked up, we headed back to the car.

"Did you know that the Georgian Hotel was built in 1933?" I asked.

"No. But it sure stands out on Ocean Boulevard. It's the only one painted turquoise."

"It still maintains that old Hollywood look, you know, very art deco. They say it makes you feel like you've stepped back in time. If I can't stay there, maybe I'll just snoop around in the lobby."

Jim laughed. "You're too funny. I'm glad you're here, Mom."

I could see the Georgian Hotel on Ocean Boulevard. It was down a few yards from where Jim had parked his twenty-year-old, rusted Rodeo. My hotel, the Oceanspray, which had been booked by the Treasure Hunter Society, looked a little too modern for my taste, but would serve nicely for a few nights. Unsure of what the young bellman would think about Jim's grungy car, I was surprised that he still did his job with flair and flew over to the curb to greet us.

Jim quickly pulled the suitcase from the back of his car. "I'm just dropping off," he called out to the friendly man.

I stepped onto the curb with my backpack and a smile.

"May I take that for you?" the bellman asked.

"Sure."

He grabbed the suitcase from Jim.

After a big hug for Jim, I said, "See you tomorrow." I followed the bellman closer to the glassed entrance.

As we stepped over the open-door threshold, my eyes glanced down to the marble tiled floor. That was a mistake. The biggest cockroach I'd ever seen was trying to decide whether to go inside or out. After a nervous giggle, I directed a comment to the bellman and the doorman. "Is that a cockroach?" All three of us kept a stare on it.

The doorman said, "Oh, they come in from the gardens."

"Aren't you going to get it?" I asked, hoping it would go away on its own.

He replied, "When you leave."

"Why don't you check in?" the other man added.

Living in old houses and near the ocean, I knew those particular bugs do not like to live in gardens. So instead, I walked up to the desk clerk and asked if they could find me another hotel. In my mind, there were witnesses, so a refund on my reservation would be justified. Surprisingly, it worked.

The pleasant woman behind the counter said they work in tandem with other hotels when they overbook. The problem was that the only hotel available was the Georgian and there would be an extra $150/night.

After only a few moments of hesitation, I said, "Yes." It was fate, I decided. That's where I'd originally wanted to stay.

I pulled my red suitcase and carried a backpack down the street; not exactly the look of a sophisticated traveler on Ocean Boulevard, but I didn't care.

The Georgian Hotel had an impressive, arched stone entrance flanked with carved lion heads, and café tables that dotted the large porch. The bellman ran out to assist me up the seven old stone steps and into the classy lobby. I noticed that the shiny terra cotta tiles that greeted weary travelers, along with the high ceilings, created a soft echo with each person's voice or movements. An offering of fresh lemon water was neatly arranged on a side table across from the front desk. After a quick check-in, my luggage was carried up a few steps and into a small elevator by the bellman, Carlos.

The door opened to the eighth floor. I followed behind the rolling luggage, down the carpeted hallway.

"If you need anything else, just let me know," Carlos said as he opened the curtains and started to exit my room.

A $5.00 tip was handed over. "Okay. I will."

To my delight, the room was on the top floor and had a view of the ocean to the left. And what a view it was…palm trees, blue skies, and rolling waves. The L.A. skyline, Santa Monica Mountains, and a faint image in the distance of the famous Hollywood sign were to the right. The king-sized bed and soft hotel robes rounded out the ambiance into something I could get used to and wouldn't soon forget. But first things first; a nap and maybe something light to eat on the porch out front.

The old elevator inside the Georgian Hotel measured only about four feet square and was lined in dark wood from top to bottom. Next to the door was a small black wrought-iron seat folded up against the wall. I knew that's where a bellboy would have sat, years ago, when he operated the elevator for hotel guests. I wanted to flip it down to see what it looked like, but by the time I'd mustered enough courage to do it, the door opened to the lobby.

I headed down six marble steps towards an eagerly awaited dinner on the porch. The air was soft and warm as I tasted my bowl of vegetable soup, which smoothed the edges of my hunger. The ocean was magnificent to look at and the historic Santa Monica Pier beckoned me for a walk across its old boards. I caught Carlos's attention as he waited to greet new arrivals at the hotel. He came right over to my table.

"How far is it to walk to Venice Beach?" I asked, as I ate the last bite of crusty bread.

"About two miles, along the boardwalk."

"Is there a bus?"

"Yes, the #1. You can get it down a block and across the street. It's a big blue bus."

"Thank you." I pulled out my phone to call home.

"The Caldwell Gallery. May I help you?" Paul's voice made me smile. He sounded so welcoming.

"You'll never guess where I am right now."

"No, I don't think I will," he answered with a laugh.

"At the Georgian Hotel! Exactly where I should've been from the beginning."

"That's great. Did Jim tell you what he found?'

"Yes, it's really weird. I'm so curious about what the police will find in their investigation."

"Please be careful, Nancy."

"Now, don't worry about me." I gave him a quick description of the old hotel's art deco style. Our conversation finally ended with, "Maybe I could do some exploring after dinner. But if it gets too late, I'll probably stay put. I'll check in with you later. Love you."

As I finished my meal, I got a text from Jim. He asked how I was doing.

I texted back I was feeling tired and on my way up to the room for the night. I also told him about the change of hotels. The Georgian was now my home away from home.

Friday

The next morning I was eager to visit with my son. I found him waiting by the curb in his car. I hopped in.

Jim craned his neck up to admire the old hotel. "It sure looks pretty."

"It's fabulous! Before I leave, you've got to come inside."

"No problem. What do you want to see first? You want to walk down the Third Street Promenade?"

"Maybe, but not yet. I'm sure it's nice with all the fancy stores. What I really want to do is go to the police station to see if we could get a copy of that old photo."

Jim laughed. "You sure you want to drive all that way? I'm not that familiar with the roads yet."

"Can we GPS it?" I asked.

"I guess so." He began to look for the directions. "That's all the way over on Culver Boulevard. There'll be a lot of traffic."

"But I really want to go."

Jim was right, the drive was horrendous; the three-mile trip took almost an hour and I was getting a little carsick reading his GPS screen. "Sorry it's taking so long. I guess I could've just called the station. But sometimes I think it's easier for a grey-haired lady to get information in person from a business or store, than through a phone call. I remind them of their mother..."

We pulled into the parking lot off Culver Street. After a short walk, we entered the plain concrete building.

A policeman sat behind a glass enclosure. "What can I do for you?"

Jim leaned toward the circular opening cut out of the glass window. "The police have been doing an investigation of some bones that I found in my backyard." He leaned in closer. "They also found an old photograph. I was wondering if we could get a copy of it?"

I stood behind Jim, waiting for an answer.

"I'm afraid not. You'll have to take that up with the investigating officer."

Jim turned to me and whispered, "I forgot the policeman's card at home and don't remember his name."

I squeezed in next to Jim. "My son here," I placed my hand on Jim's shoulder, "thinks he knows someone that resembles the person in the photo that he dug up."

He looked over to Jim. "What's your name?"

"Jim Caldwell."

"Where did you find the bones?"

"20th Avenue, Venice Beach."

"Not sure what I can do for you today. Fill this form out and someone will get back to you." He handed the paper to Jim.

Disappointed, but not deterred, I found a pen for Jim to fill in the needed information. He handed the form back through the window opening.

7

1947
HOLLYWOOD

MAGGIE COULD FEEL the sun on her face as Gaylord pulled the Chrysler New Yorker convertible away from Union Station onto North Alameda, and then towards Hollywood Boulevard. The wind whipped her hair in circles as they sped past the Pantages Theatre, the Broadway Building with its giant neon sign that said, "Hollywood", Musso & Frank's Restaurant, the Brown Derby, and the famous Chateau Elysee. It was all there, every place that Maggie had read and dreamed about. As the two girls sat in the open back seat of the fancy car, the glitz and glamour of Hollywood surrounded them with the possibility of a chance meeting or glimpse of a famous movie star.

Grauman's Chinese Theatre came up on their right. Blanche yelled to them, "Did you know that my Gaylord knows everyone in Hollywoodland?" She stroked the back of his neck with red polished fingertips.

With a quick turn left, the stylish mint-green vehicle took Maggie and Gertie to their new home. North Sycamore Avenue was lined with stately old houses. Almost all of them had signs in their windows advertising: *Rooms to Rent; Rooming House; Clean Rooms for Rent: Inquire Within.*

"Miss Sylvia is real nice. Wait until you meet her. You'll see." Blanche grinned at the girls. "Gaylord, pull up right here."

The car stopped in front of a triple-decker with two turrets attached to each side of its roofline. Fifteen stone steps led up to a carved wooden door.

"Oh, it's perfect," squealed Gertie.

Maggie could hardly wait to see inside.

Blanche stood and leaned back against the windshield. She looked up and down the street. "Well, I've come a long way, haven't I, Gaylord?"

Her boyfriend looked into the rearview mirror to slick his hair down and then smiled. "You sure have, Doll."

"Come on, let me introduce you to your new landlady." Blanche sailed up the steps and walked right into the old house with the girls close behind her.

Gaylord waited in the car to smoke a cigarette.

"Miss Sylvia!" Blanche called out, as she hustled over to the round newel post attached to a lovely wooden staircase. She looked up toward the top floors and called again. "Miss Sylvia?" She wiggled her way down a long, carpeted hall that ran alongside the stairs and through a swinging door to the rear of the house. Turning around, she waved her hand. "Come on. She's around here somewhere."

The girls followed. Maggie took in quick glances as she walked past ornate paintings, large palm plants, and beautiful wood paneling. The floors had a comfortable squeak.

A stout woman in her fifties walked out of a spacious pantry and into the main kitchen. "Blanche! Or should I call you Bebe?" She laughed and proceeded to bear-hug her former tenant. "You look so stylish." Her large hands held onto Blanche's shoulders. "What have you been doing? What movies have you been cast in?"

"Nothing real big yet, but I know it'll happen." Blanche broke away from Miss Sylvia and adjusted her halter-top. She gestured to her two new friends. "These two are looking for a place to stay. I told them Miss Sylvia's was the best rooming house on North Sycamore."

"I'm pretty full right now, but I do have a small room, up on the third floor, for $5 a week. It's tiny, but you'll probably have a little more privacy for the bathroom. No one wants to stay way up there."

Gertie looked over to Maggie, but didn't wait for her cousin to answer, "We'll take it."

Their new landlady folded her hands across her waist under a huge bosom that hung low. A silver monocle dangled from a delicate necklace. "There's only one bed up there. I have a cot I'll throw in, for no charge, since you're friends with my Blanche."

"Thank you." Maggie smiled.

Gertie beamed. "Shall we pay you now?"

"Well, let's go upstairs first so you can see the accommodations."

As Miss Sylvia passed Maggie, the unpleasant smell of alcohol mixed with "Evening in Paris" perfume drifted into the air. The young girl placed her fingertips over her nose.

It didn't seem to bother Gertie, who closed her purse and said, "Swell."

Blanche started towards the front door. "Say, there's a get-together tonight at the Roosevelt. Gaylord said there would be some movie people there. Why don't you gals come as my guests?"

Gertie's eyes popped open. "That's a wonderful idea. We'll be there."

"Just tell the doorman that you're guests of Gaylord Cannon." Blanche threw a kiss to all and flew out the door. She was gone in seconds.

As the three women made their way up the old steps, Maggie noticed that each floor was decorated in a similar manner as the entryway. Not even the Crosby Inn, back on Cape Cod, was as extravagantly adorned. The hallway on the top floor was smaller and had a single painting hanging to one side of the wall. There were two doors; the first opened into a small bathroom, the second to their room. It contained a single bed, dresser and mirror, closet, one chair, and a window.

Maggie went over to get a better view of how the house was situated within the California landscape. She opened one side of the divided window and gasped at the Hollywoodland sign in the distance. It was nestled in the scrub and brush of the Santa Monica Mountains. "This is so beautiful. I can't believe I'm actually here." She plopped down onto the bed. "It sure was swell of you to invite me to come along with you, Gertie." Maggie leaned forward on her elbows and glanced out to the hallway.

Miss Sylvia rested against the wall at the top of the stairs, trying to catch her breath. "Dinner...is...at...6 o'clock... I'll see you downstairs." With a wave of her hand, she turned to leave. Gripping the railing, she began to pant, "Mercy me. I shan't be coming up here again." After a few more steps, she groaned, "Ohhh...Mercy!"

Gertie and Maggie looked at each other, quickly closed the door and burst into a fit of giggles.

Gertie lay back onto the bed. "Oh gee, I've never been so thrilled in all my life. We haven't even been in Hollywoodland for a day and I've already got a place to live and an invitation to – maybe – be in pictures."

Maggie returned her gaze to the mountains. "I wish Peter could see what I see. I bet one day he's going to fly right outside this window and maybe buzz the Hollywoodland sign."

"Peter?" Gertie sounded surprised. "You're thinking of that Indian?" She stood to fix her hair in the mirror. "What would Eddie think?"

"Honestly, Gertie. Peter's just a good friend." Maggie's ruby red lips slowly went from a soft smile to an irritated frown. She continued staring at the Santa Monica Mountains in the distance, trying to ignore Gertie's rude comments about Peter.

"I'm going to freshen up before we go sightseeing." Gertie slipped out the door and headed for the bathroom.

"Why does she care who I think about?" Maggie whispered under her breath. After all, Peter was her best friend. Even before Gertie's family moved to Brewster, he and Maggie were already pals. She glanced at her nails and hoped to borrow some of Gertie's polish for the party. A dreamy-eyed look came over her as Eddie's handsome face popped into her head and she recalled his passionate kisses.

The sound of a toilet flush through the paper-thin walls of the third floor quickly transported Maggie back to reality. She turned to grab her coin purse, walked into the hallway and rapped on the bathroom door. "Gertie. I'm going downstairs to call my parents."

A high-pitched voice came from behind the paneled door. "Would you ask if they could call my mother and tell her I'm doing fine?"

"Of course."

As Maggie descended the grand stairway, she felt like the heiress to a great fortune. From one of the rooms, she could hear someone playing a quiet jazz melody on a saxophone. She didn't recognize the tune. Her father would have guessed it right away. A black phone rested on a dark mahogany table at the foot of the stair. She sat down on the chair next to the phone. A sign taped to the tapestry-covered wall read: *Collect Calls Only!*

Maggie grabbed the receiver, listened for a dial tone, then spun the 'O' for operator. "I'd like to make a collect call to anyone at Brewster 63, in Brewster, Massachusetts."

A distant voice asked, "Who may I say is calling?"

"Maggie Foster."

"One moment, please."

Maggie heard three rings, the signal for their party line, and then…"Hello?"

She waited to hear the conversation between the operator and one of her parents.

"I have a collect call to anyone from a Maggie Foster. Will you accept the charges?"

"Oh yes. Put her on."

"Momma?"

"Maggie. Your father and I have been so worried."

"Sorry. I've been…"

"Tell me, where are you and are you and Gertie safe?"

"Oh, Momma. Of course we're safe. We found a room in a house right near Hollywood Boulevard."

"A rooming house? Is it proper?" There was a cautionary tone in her mother's voice.

"Now don't worry. Miss Sylvia, the lady who owns it, is very nice and genteel." Maggie could hear a slight rustling in the background through the earpiece. "Mom. Are you still there?"

"It's me. Poppa."

"Poppa, it's wonderful here. You'd love it. And they have jazz, too. I can hear it in the hallway."

"That's good, honey."

"I won't talk very long, it's expensive for you. Would you please call Aunt Ethel and tell her that Gertie's doing just fine?"

"Sure."

"Gotta run now. We're going to see some of the sights."

"Maggie, be careful and watch your money. Love you."

There was a pause and then her mother's voice shouted, "Maggie, this is your momma again. Stay out of trouble and behave yourself."

Within the hour, the two girls were walking along Hollywood Boulevard. They looked for the inscriptions of their favorite movie star or starlet in front of Grauman's Chinese Theatre. Famous celebrities were known for cementing imprints of their hands, shoes, autograph, or favorite saying into squares along the sidewalk. Gertie favored Betty Grable and Maggie adored Frank Sinatra. They then hopped on the orange line trolley to Chinatown, an exotic location that Gertie insisted on seeing.

The Lotus Blossom Gift and Antique Shop caught their attention with its outside display of Buddha statues and beautiful dark oriental tables, bureaus, and chairs. Once they stood among the deep, rich images of dragons and serpents that were carved into the old pieces of furniture, they stepped closer. Large picture windows flanked the doorway and overflowed with ornate jewelry, brass bowls, ivory figurines, and green jade vases.

Gertie whispered, as if they were about to do something they shouldn't, "Come on, Maggie. Let's go in." She reached for the brass filigreed door handle.

The pungent smells of incense wafted over the two visitors. Gertie stepped gingerly inside. Maggie took a step back; she could hardly breathe. It didn't seem to bother Gertie, who was familiar with strong perfume because she wore it every day. Maggie remained cautious and stayed by the closed door. Soft melodious chimes drifted through the heady air in the old shop. Gauze curtains hung in front of the windows and replaced bright sunshine with a murky yellow glow. From behind a glass-topped counter, a middle-aged Chinese woman appeared. Startled, Maggie took a quick breath, positive there had been no one there a few seconds ago. She continued to hold her ground near the exit.

Gertie danced her way up and down the crowded aisles, fawning over all the intriguing objects. She stopped at the counter to greet the petite woman. "Hello."

The proprietor simply smiled.

A purse inside the glass cabinet caught Gertie's eye. She pointed to it. "That's so pretty. May I see it?"

The woman took a key that dangled from a black silk cord around her neck and slowly opened the back of the glass case.

Maggie was curious and crept closer. The small, sterling-mesh evening purse created a gentle flutter as it was placed against the glass counter.

"Oh," chirped Gertie. "It's absolutely stunning."

"Yes, my dear. It's very elegant," the proprietor cooed. "From the turn of the century."

Gertie leaned closer. "May I touch it?"

Maggie approached the counter.

As Gertie fondled the sterling silver beads that hung from the bottom of the delicate piece, Maggie listened to its description.

"This Chatelaine Sterling Silver Mesh Purse has a lovely finger ring attached to its chain." The proprietor's long painted nails twirled inside the circle. "If you look closely, you will see its markings, French Mercury, and the sterling hallmark of London."

Maggie had never seen such a beautiful fashion accent.

The woman smiled. "It has lovely detail."

Gertie motioned for Maggie to touch it.

As Maggie reached out, a spark of electricity flew through her fingertips. She flinched back with a small cry.

The woman whispered and shook her head. "It seems the purse does not like you."

"I guess it doesn't," Gertie said. "Then I would like to buy it. How much?"

"Ten dollars."

Gertie looked disappointed. "That's more than our rent at Miss Sylvia's."

Maggie had had enough excitement for one afternoon. "We should be leaving. It's getting late."

"Wait." Now the woman seemed more animated. "Because I like you and your young friend, you may have it for $5.00."

Gertie thought for only a few seconds before deciding. "I'll take it."

A sly grin grew across the face behind the counter. "You will not be sad when you wear this alongside your favorite beau."

Gertie swung her new purse with an air of sophistication as she and Maggie left the store and disappeared from the shopkeeper's view.

Su Lee Cheung hurried to the backroom. "It is done."

Margaret Cheung, her daughter, looked puzzled as she finished her homework on a small wooden table.

"The purse has transferred to another woman."

Margaret understood her mother's comment and casually opened another textbook. Without looking up, she said, "Did you tell her about its past?"

"I'm afraid it slipped my mind." Su Lee began to brew fresh tea. "The important thing is...that it is gone from the shop." She sat down at her desk to open a brown ledger and dipped a sharp pen point into black ink. "I will never forget the previous owner who sold this to me. I sensed she was eager to be rid of the purse. Her whole body shook and her hands had trembled when I paid her. I'd assumed she was in trouble and needed money." She began to inscribe onto the last page of entries the name of the purse and its date of sale. "It is possible the purse may have had a dark history, none of which I was ever privy to. I am happy it is gone."

"I feel sorry for the young woman who bought it today," said Margaret. She was studying for her final tests before graduating high school. "I hope nothing unfortunate happens to her."

Her mother took a sip of tea. "Sometimes it is best for a person to not know their future."

8

1947
LOS ANGELES

IT WAS A little past four o'clock when the girls got off the bus on Hollywood Boulevard. Gertie swung her new purse so everyone would notice her sophisticated taste. Maggie enjoyed all the sights and glamour of everything and everyone they encountered. A familiar mint-green convertible pulled in across the street, in front of a restaurant called the Pig & Whistle.

Gertie stopped. "That's Blanche and Gaylord. It must be, I recognize the car." She started to cross over to the other side of the street. "Come on, Maggie. Let's go talk to them."

Blanche saw them. "Yoo-hoo!" She got up to kneel on the front seat so the girls could see her. She waved and called out as Gaylord finished parking, "Gertie! Maggie!"

Gertie hustled over to the car. "Blanche! Gaylord!"

Blanche pushed a thick blonde curl away from her eyes. "Want to join us? You won't mind, will you honey?" She touched his shoulder.

He agreed with a smile.

"Wonderful. Come on." She waved the girls closer to the car.

"Oh, this is swell," said Gertie. I was just telling Maggie how hungry I am. You rescued us from starvation."

Maggie never remembered anything about Gertie being hungry, but a bite to eat sounded good. Maybe they wouldn't have to pay for their meal.

Gaylord jumped out over the door of the car. He looked quite athletic to the girls and definitely handsome. "A friend of mine is joining us, Harry Gibson. He's a great guy." He led the girls up a tiled inclined entrance and into the Pig & Whistle. "My treat today, ladies."

The girls waited while Gaylord talked to the waiter.

Blanche looked around. "You know, all the movie stars come here after their performances or after a premier of their new movies." She held her head high and pushed her bosom out as far as possible. "Maybe we'll see someone famous. You never know." She kept turning her head, looking for anyone important.

The ornately carved, wooden beams across the whole ceiling held Maggie's gaze. They were beautiful and so unusual.

Gertie pulled on Maggie's arm. "Maggie! Let's go."

The group was led past the counter, which ran the length of the room, to a center table. One seat was reserved for Harry.

Within a few minutes, a short young man with wire-rimmed glasses came bounding through the doors and approached their table.

Gaylord held his arm out. "Ladies, I want you to meet Harold Gibson. The best pal a guy could ever have. Everyone calls him Harry."

Each person returned a smile as Gaylord's guest sat down. Then they quickly ordered their food.

Maggie sipped her water and directed her question to the new guy. "How did you and Gaylord become such good friends?"

Harry laughed, "Gaylord and I grew up together in Texas. About a year after his family moved out to Los Angeles, I followed him."

Gaylord leaned back in his chair and took a cigarette out of a flat gold case that he'd retrieved from his jacket pocket. "Harry here is one heck of a guy." He tapped the cigarette against the closed case a few times, lit up, and blew out a perfect ring of smoke. "He used to do trick horseback riding."

"Not so much since my injury." Harry rubbed the back of his neck in an almost automated response.

"Oh my," said Gertie.

"Enough of that," Harry said, "I'm sure these gorgeous girls don't want to hear about broken bones." He looked over to Maggie as if he favored her looks over the other women.

Maggie could feel his stare. Her face reddened. She quickly returned her gaze to the table.

Harry looked over to his best friend. "Gaylord! I have great news."

"What? Did you find oil down there on Venice Beach?"

He laughed. "No. Something better. I got a job."

"Congratulations."

Blanche piped up. "Don't tell me." She tapped a finger on her lips and said, "Will you be starring in the next mysterious drama at RKO?"

"No. Not that glamorous. But I will be talking to a lot of Hollywood stars and producers."

"Tell us all about it," Gertie squealed.

"It's at the Georgian Hotel, in Santa Monica. I'll be starting out as a bellhop and running the elevator."

Everyone grew quiet.

Harry looked around the table at four disenchanted people, then tried to justify his new job. "There are plenty of opportunities for advancement." He sipped his beer. "You know, all the bigwigs go there to get away from the craziness of Los Angeles. The hotel is quite a sight on Ocean Boulevard, surrounded by all those woods."

Maggie and Gaylord quickly came to Harry's rescue with encouraging words. Maggie spoke first. "I just want to say that it sounds quite fascinating. Besides, I bet you'll have a steady paycheck and lots of tips."

Gaylord took another drag on his cigarette. "Harry, I got to hand it to you. You're going to be fine. You never know what could come of any connections you'll make there. I think it's grand."

During dinner, Gertie and Blanche took over the conversation with their insistence that the man sitting with two pretty women near the back wall was Clark Gable. Gaylord ignored them and concentrated on his smoke, steak, and beer. Harry kept staring at Maggie and trying to make small talk with her.

Maggie grew fond of his attention and wondered why she felt attracted to him. He was a bit odd, a short cowboy with glasses. He looked more like a professor.

"Where you from?" Harry cleaned his lenses with the cloth napkin.

"Cape Cod, near Boston." Maggie thought he looked handsome without his glasses.

Harry adjusted the wire stems over his ears. "Never been East."

"It's very nice."

"Are you going to stay out here?"

"Oh, I don't think so. I know that Gertie, she's my cousin, wants to stay. She'll probably find a job with some movie studio." Maggie covered her mouth and whispered with a smile, "She's rather pushy."

"I'd like it if you decided to stay." Harry leaned back to gaze at Maggie.

She could feel her face flush again.

After dinner, they stood outside talking and laughing.

"Hey, everyone, I've got a new gadget. Just bought it yesterday." Gaylord leaned over his car on the passenger side, opened the glove compartment, and pulled out a rectangular metal box. Letters spelled POLAROID across its bottom. "This is such a new camera that I don't even know how it works. Give me a minute." After a few seconds, he said, "Oh, the heck with it. Come on. Let's give it a try. Everybody, line up in front of my car. It'll make a great picture."

They all did as they were told, still laughing.

He clicked the camera. "Great. Now hold on." He started counting.

Blanche said, "What're you doing?"

"Hold on," he replied, then he opened up the back of the camera and slowly pulled out a thick, square piece of paper.

They all waited in silence as they stood around Gaylord and the paper negative he was holding. After another minute, he peeled it apart. Soon Blanche, Gertie, Maggie, and Harry's images slowly appeared on the paper, all standing in front of the convertible. There was a jagged white line edging the entire picture. It had a few fuzzy blotches on one side. "Maybe I didn't wait long enough."

Harry whistled in astonishment. "I can't believe it."

The girls couldn't believe their eyes either. It was like magic.

"Let's take some more. Line up again. How about Gertie and Maggie? Then Harry and Maggie? Harry, take some of me with the girls."

Gertie sidled up to Gaylord. "Do you think you could take a couple of shots of Maggie and me over there, in front of Grauman's Theatre?"

"Sure. Let's go."

They all ran across the street to Grauman's. As they crossed over, Harry pocketed two pictures, one of Maggie and himself, and the extra one of the group in front of Gaylord's car.

Blanche said, "Don't forget me. Maybe Harry could take one of Gaylord and me?"

The new camera fascinated Maggie. "I feel like it's Christmas morning and I'm opening up a secret present."

With all the laughter and squeals of delight, Gaylord never noticed that he was almost out of film. "I guess I'll have to figure out where to get more. What a hoot."

After a while, Gertie finally spoke up. "It's late. I need to get ready for the party tonight. Let's go, Maggie."

Harry turned to Maggie. "Will you be there tonight?"

"Sure will."

"Great. I'll see you later."

By the time the girls returned from the restaurant to Miss Sylvia's, it was close to 6 p.m. Maggie's cot was set up next to the single bed in the cramped room. She lay back on its cool sheets and pillow. "Oh, this is small, but nice."

Gertie sat down on her bed to untie her sandals. "Don't stay there for too long. I want to get going." She changed into a long, striped skirt with a short-sleeved white blouse, a string of pearls, and a black cinch belt around her tiny waist. "The party doesn't start until 8 p.m. If we leave for the Roosevelt Hotel a little early, we can stop by that dress shop we passed earlier. Maybe I can find a sexy peasant blouse instead of this old one."

* * *

Maggie thought Gertie looked great. She certainly didn't need a new blouse at this moment. Of course, she knew what she was going to wear: a dress she'd bought at Puritan's, back on Cape Cod. The three-quarter-length pink floral cotton dress with cap sleeves, scooped neckline, and matching belt fit her young figure like a glove. She looked down at Gertie's beige sandals. "Are you going to wear these or the black ones tonight?"

Gertie hollered over her shoulder as she left for the bathroom, "You can wear the beige."

"Thanks." Maggie slid her feet into them and began to tie the straps over her ankles. Soon she was dressed and waiting by the window, scanning the sunny California landscape. It always took Gertie twice as long as Maggie to get ready. She didn't mind today; she felt very grown up in her new dress and began to think of Harry Gibson.

It wasn't long before they were on Hollywood Boulevard and walking past Grauman's Chinese Theatre, the Pig & Whistle, and then into Bette's – Designer Clothes for the Stars.

Both girls were enthralled with the dazzling array of dresses and tops on display, but the price tags took them by surprise.

Gertie whispered to Maggie, "There's nothing here I can afford. I really wanted a blouse like Carmen Miranda wears, you know, low and sexy, off the shoulder."

A middle-aged woman with an up-do of finger waves on top of her head appeared from behind a curtain in the back of the store. "May I help you young ladies?"

"I'm looking for something to go with the skirt I'm wearing. Maybe a peasant blouse?"

"Well, let me see." She walked to the back to a rack of clothes marked with a SALE sign. "Here's one." The store clerk thought to herself, poor Carmen Miranda, not a very popular movie star anymore. She hoped to get rid of this style to make room for her newer fashions. "I can let you have this for $1.00."

Gertie flew over to the saleslady. "Let me try it on." She giggled all the way into the dressing room. "It fits! It's perfect. I'll take it. May I wear it out?"

"Certainly."

Within seconds Gertie reappeared. She looked quite the alluring movie star. "Do you think you could keep my other blouse here at the store until tomorrow? We live in the area. Just moved here to be in the movies."

"Sure, why not. Maybe someday you'll start a fashion trend when you become famous." The saleslady was laughing as she took Gertie's money along with the extra blouse, which she placed in a bag under the counter. "What's your name?"

"Gertie Foster," she replied while she waited. "I'll probably have to get a stage name soon." Gertie refolded two dollars back into her new mesh purse. There was just enough room next to the picture of her and Maggie, a social security card, operator's license, lipstick, and a mirrored compact.

9

1947
ROOSEVELT HOTEL – LOS ANGELES

THE ECHO OF gentle water bubbling from the lobby's circular fountain added to the exotic ambience of the Roosevelt Hotel. Maggie tilted her head up to the grand ceiling as she walked around the pillars and through the Moorish stone arches that surrounded the perimeter of the main room. She delicately stepped across the shiny tiles and admired the potted palms that dotted the luxurious lobby.

Gertie walked right up to the man behind the front desk. "Could you tell me where the Cannon party is being held?" She haughtily added, "We're guests of Gaylord Cannon."

"They're in the Blossom Room." He pointed behind Gertie's head to the other side of the lobby.

"Thank you!" She could hear the music and headed straight for the room's entrance. "Maggie, quit your gawking. Let's go."

Through the arches, the two girls proceeded to their first social event as hopeful ingénues. Maggie's hands began to perspire. She wiped them on her dress before she grabbed the black wrought-iron handle of the massive wooden door that led into the famous Blossom Room.

Laughter echoed across the cavernous party room where an orchestra on the balcony played *Peg O' My Heart*.

A tall, stocky man shoved his arm in front of Gertie to block her way. "Sorry, this is a private party."

"Say, wait a minute," Gertie roared in her defense. "I'll have you know that we're guests of Gaylord Cannon."

"Let's see about that." The man's face contorted into a quizzical expression as he stared at Gertie. He ordered them, "Wait here." He signaled to a short man. "Hey, Jeff, watch these two for me."

Jeff made his way in front of the girls while the other guard went to find the boss's son. He growled. "You gals stay right here."

Maggie stepped back while Gertie tried to stand even taller than she actually was to get a better view. "This is silly. I can't believe they won't let us in."

"Maybe we should leave," Maggie suggested and started to go.

"Wait!" Gertie grabbed her cousin's arm. "I see Gaylord." She waved at him with her free hand.

"Hi, girls!" Gaylord gestured for Jeff to move aside. "It's okay." He looked over to the taller man. "Listen, Big Paulie, these girls are with me."

Big Paulie Kowalski solemnly resumed his post at the door.

Gaylord took hold of both girls' arms and led them into the party. "Don't let Kowalski and Snider bother you. They work for my father. Isn't it a hoot, though, they look just like those comic strip characters, Mutt and Jeff."

The three of them made their way through the crowd to the open bar. "What'll you have, ladies?"

"Ginger ale with a cherry, please," Maggie answered.

"I'll have a martini," said Gertie.

Maggie glanced over her shoulder to the guards and then turned to Gaylord. "Those two guys kinda scare me."

"They're not as lovable as cartoon Mutt and Jeff...best to keep your distance from them. They're a bit rough around the edges." He leaned against the bar with his drink. "There's no love lost between me and them. Never could figure out why my father hired them on. Hollywood is pretty tame and such fun. Not like back in Texas."

Blanche joined them at the bar. She was dressed in a sleek, haltered black dress.

Gertie took note of a large yellow diamond on Blanche's finger. The ring stood out against the stark ebony color of the sexy dress. "Blanche, where did you get that fabulous ring?"

"I asked my honey here if he could convince his father to let me wear it tonight." She stroked the back of Gaylord's head with the hand that wore the ring.

Gaylord's dreamy look implied that he would probably do anything for Blanche. "It was no problem. My father just wants it returned tonight. No excuses."

He saw his father about ten feet away. "Come on, you two. I want you to meet him."

Franklin Cannon wore the finest of tailored clothes, hiding his double-X-sized body. Maggie couldn't help but notice him. He stood out among all the faces in the room. His laugh boomed as several starlets fawned around him. As he raised a hand to slick his dyed hair flat, she noticed a large gold, diamond-encrusted ring covered half of his little finger. He was nothing like her father, or any man back on Cape Cod that she knew.

"Father, I want you to meet Gertie and Maggie. They're from back east, Boston."

Cannon seemed to eye the girls as a new opportunity for some fun. "Aren't you two the prettiest girls here?"

The women near him stopped their smiling and gave the intruders a quick once-over. Some of them left, but a few still clung to Cannon's arms.

In one quick movement, he lifted his huge arm to encircle Gertie's shoulders. "Honey, you look luscious in that little blouse. What's your story, my sweet thing?"

Gertie beamed. "I want to be in pictures."

"You've come to the right person." Cannon swept his free arm across the room. "You see all these faces?'

Gertie nodded. "I sure do, Mr. Cannon."

"Some of them will eventually be famous, and some will fall by the wayside. You want to know why?"

"Oh, yes, Mr. Cannon." Gertie nodded again.

"Because they don't want it bad enough...and they may or may not do as I ask...I mean, suggest."

Gertie kept smiling, but Maggie's face turned serious.

A reporter with a camera approached them. "Mr. Cannon, how about a picture for the *L.A. Times* social scene?"

"Sure." Mr. Cannon slicked his hair again and tried to suck in his gut.

The reporter pointed to Gertie. "How about that cutie next to you, let's get her in too?"

"Sure." The crowd backed away. Cannon whispered in Gertie's ear, "Now what's your name again, honey?"

"Gertie! Gertie Foster!" She pulled her blouse even lower across her shoulders.

The flash exploded in everyone's eyes. The reporter asked how to spell Gertie's name, which she excitedly repeated for him.

"Thanks again, Mr. Cannon. Look for it in the next edition."

Cannon leaned closer to Gertie. "See what I mean, my dear? Stick with me, and you might have something to write home about."

They walked together to the bar for another drink. Gertie looked over her shoulder at Maggie with a wide grin on her face.

The party quickly lost its luster for Maggie when several drunk people started to fall over tables. Maggie caught Gaylord's attention. "I'm feeling a little tired. Tell Gertie I'll be waiting for her outside."

"Sure enough." Gaylord continued jitterbugging with Blanche. The yellow diamond flickered across the dance floor as Blanche waved her arms to the rhythm of Gene Krupa's *Sing! Sing! Sing!*

Maggie left the Blossom Room and walked only a few feet to a massive wooden bench inside a red velvet-curtained alcove. She took a seat and leaned against its high back. Relief came over her as she recalled how Big Paulie Kowalski hadn't noticed her leave the party. He'd been too occupied cleaning his nails with the point of a pocketknife. She closed her eyes just as the music returned to a fast-paced melody, and everyone started hollering. Despite all the noise she managed to stay calm, imagining herself back home on Crosby Landing Beach, where the soothing rhythm of the tidal waves moved back and forth along the wrack line. The memory made her feel homesick.

A gentle voice broke into her thoughts, "Say, what're you doing sittin' out here all by yourself?" Harry Gibson sat down beside her.

Maggie flinched. "Oh! You startled me."

"I'm sorry. I didn't mean to scare you." Harry leaned back next to her.

She gave a little sigh.

After a few seconds, he eased forward to look at her. "You look real pretty tonight, Maggie."

She smiled, straightened up and smoothed her dress. "Thanks. It was getting a little too wild in there for me."

"I see." His face was soft, as if he understood Maggie's feelings.

"I told Gaylord to tell my cousin I'd be waiting for her out here."

Harry stood up. "Since you're not having such a great time, how about I take you for a drive? I know a real nice view of the city."

She hesitated before she took hold of his hand. "Wait. I should tell my cousin that I'm leaving."

"Okay. I'll go in with you."

The party was still going strong when Maggie and Harry attempted to return.

This time, Big Paulie did notice them. "Where are you two going?"

"Just looking for Gertie. Have you seen her?" Maggie stretched her neck high to see any familiar faces.

Big Paulie snarled. "You mean that pushy dame who came in here with you?"

"Yes. Do you know where she is?"

"Naw. I ain't seen her for a while now."

Jeff Snider came over to them.

"Hey Jeff, you seen the dame that came in here with her?" Big Paulie thumbed in the direction of Maggie.

"Yeah. She left with Mr. Cannon." Jeff straightened his suit coat as if it would make him taller.

Big Paulie stared into Maggie's face. "Well, you heard him. What else do you want?"

"Left? With Mr. Cannon?"

"That's what I said." Big Paulie turned away to break up a fight between two men by the bar.

Maggie touched Harry's arm. "I don't like this crowd. Should we call the police?"

"The police?" Harry laughed. "They won't do anything. Cannon's got them all under his control. If you're ever in trouble, just call me. Remember, the police aren't going to help you."

Maggie turned to look for Gertie again. "I really don't like Gaylord's father."

Harry took her arm. "I don't take too kindly to him either. Let's find Gaylord, and get out of here."

It didn't take long before they spotted Gaylord sprawled across a chair holding his head.

Harry lifted him upright. "Don't you think you've had enough?"

Gaylord sputtered, "Harry! You old son of a gun you! Where've ya' been all night?"

"Around. Say, where's Gertie?"

"Who?" Gaylord said between hiccups.

Maggie piped up. "My cousin, Gertie?"

"I think she's with my father." With his head in his hand he added, "Don't worry. He'll see to it she gets home."

"You sure?" Maggie asked, her voice nervous.

"Yeah. I'm sure. She'll be fine." Gaylord continued nursing his gin and tonic. "Wonder where my Blanche went?" He tried to focus his attention on the people around him, then took another sip of his drink. "Oh well. I'll find her later."

Harry pulled Maggie's arm towards the door. "I'm sure she'll be okay. Let's go."

Maggie stayed put. "I don't know. You think it's okay to leave?"

"Definitely. I may not like the old guy's business doings, but I'm sure he wouldn't hurt her."

"I guess you're right. I know Gertie can take care of herself. She's no dummy."

"Come on. Let's go." Harry ushered Maggie out into the starry night.

Harry had parked his 1946 Woodie Sportsman convertible on a side street near the hotel. He opened the car door with a flourish. "Your chariot awaits."

Maggie smiled and, for the moment, forgot all about Gertie. The air was still warm as they left the lights of the city. Soon the heavens exploded into clusters of blinking stars. By the time they reached the top of Mulholland Drive, Maggie was laughing, and Harry was tapping the steering wheel to the rhythm of *Pennsylvania 6–5000* coming from the car radio.

Harry parked at the edge of the road while Maggie stood up in the open car and leaned over the front window. "Wow. It's so beautiful."

He sat back behind the wheel and admired Maggie's simple beauty. He wanted to wrap his hands around her tiny waist, feel the softness of her body against his and kiss her ruby red lips.

She sat down next to him. "This was such a swell idea, Harry. Thanks!" Her head fell back against the seat. "I wonder if we can find the Milky Way?"

Harry stretched his arm up and across the seat, barely touching her shoulders. "Maybe." He wanted to grab her, but he stopped. She seemed like a real lady – not like her cousin Gertie. He tried to think of something to say, but all he thought of was, "Maggie, I could get used to this." The second he'd said it, he hoped Maggie hadn't heard it.

They stayed up on the hill for another hour, mostly in silence, enjoying the light show in the sky. Maggie felt comfortable with Harry. He reminded her of Peter.

All of a sudden Harry winced. His arm was numb from being stretched across the back of the seat. "I guess I'd better get you back to Miss Sylvia's." He slowly lifted his tingling arm and brought it down to his side. His desire to be as close to Maggie as possible was cut short.

Maggie straightened herself in the seat. "Okay. Let's go." She noticed Harry was massaging his shoulder and gave him a peck on the cheek. "You're so nice."

He started the car to begin the return drive down the hill. From the radio, Frank Sinatra crooned *Someone to Watch Over Me*.

By the time they arrived on North Sycamore, it was past midnight. Maggie got out of the car and turned to Harry. "Thanks again. I hope we'll see each other soon?"

Harry smiled. "I'm sure of it."

She thought Harry's idea for a drive was definitely a beautiful end to an awkward beginning.

* * *

Maggie thought she heard something and woke up to see the face on the little white alarm clock read 3 a.m. She rolled over to catch a glimpse of Gertie sitting on the other bed, removing her sandals. "Are you just getting in?" she asked, rubbing her eyes.

"Shhh. I'm fine. Go back to sleep," Gertie whispered.

"How'd you get here?"

Gertie stood to take off her blouse. "That stupid Jeff Snider drove me home."

"Well, I'm glad you're safe." Maggie rolled over to face the wall.

"I'm going to take a bath," Gertie said as she grabbed a robe from the back of the door.

Maggie rolled back again. "At this time of the night?"

"Yeah. I just need to clean myself up." She started to leave for the bathroom, but turned. "We've been invited to another party tomorrow afternoon, at Cannon's estate."

"I really don't want to go, Gertie."

"Well, you have to." Her voice sounded angry. "You need to go with me."

"Okay. Okay." Maggie closed her eyes.

10

Present Day – Saturday and Sunday
LOS ANGELES

I HAD BREAKFAST on the Georgian Hotel's patio with views of the ocean in the distance. Jim had to work through the weekend, so I was looking forward to doing some exploring by myself. Within the hour, I started to walk the two blocks to catch the #1 bus to Venice Beach. The old picture that Jim had uncovered in the dirt next to his apartment was still on my mind. Somehow I had to get a copy of it.

As soon as I got off the bus I found a little coffee shop, and then made my way along the two-mile ocean walk back to my hotel and the Santa Monica Pier. The boardwalk of Venice Beach hadn't changed much since the last time I'd visited. I was sixteen and on a cross-country trip with my older sister. She had a new teaching job and wanted company for the long ride from Ohio. It was an exciting adventure for a young girl. This time I was on my own.

People were rollerblading, jogging, skateboarding, and strolling along the paved boardwalk. Stores and honky-tonk vendors were setting up their wares for the daily stream of tourists who visited from all over the world. I didn't buy anything: it was simply fun for me to observe all the antics of so many characters. I passed a man with a big white snake around his shoulders. He offered people the opportunity to hold the six-foot creature so that they could take a souvenir picture. I stopped to listen to a piano player plunking out a classic Beatles tune on an old upright with wheels. I peered into the

Clamshell, where Jim worked part time as a bartender. It hadn't opened yet. I remembered that was where Natalie worked and decided to go back later. Maybe I'd have a copy of the old photo by then.

By 2 p.m., my air-conditioned room was a welcome retreat after my long excursion in the hot sun. I fell asleep on the cool sheets of the king-sized bed. My phone woke me up a little before three. It was Paul. I was half-asleep. "Hello?"

"Nancy? Hi, honey."

"It's good to hear your voice. Just taking a nap. Had fun exploring down the boardwalk, but it got too warm for me."

"I've been painting most of the day; thought I'd check in with you." He sounded lonely. "Casey and Danny said hi."

"Tell them that I love them." I sat on the edge of the bed. "Wish you could have come with me to L.A." The beautiful blue ocean created a breathtaking view out the window.

Paul's voice was calm. "I miss you, too. When do you have to go to the Society's meeting?"

"They have an opening reception on Sunday. I'm not much for networking, but I guess I have to go."

"Oh, you'll have a good time."

"I suppose I will. It's always exciting to talk about all the crazy things that have happened to me." An adventurous feeling came over me as I thought of the treasure I'd already found over the last few years.

"I'm getting another call," Paul said. "I gotta go, have a good night. Call me tomorrow. Don't forget the time difference. You know me, I'll probably be in bed before 11."

"Okay. Love you." I hung up and looked over the information packet explaining the Annual Treasure Hunter Society's upcoming program.

Sunday

The cab driver seemed pleasant when he picked me up to take me to the reception. "The Roosevelt Hotel, please."

"Right on it," the elderly man said. He made a U-turn and headed over to Hollywood Boulevard.

I pinned my I.D. badge onto my blouse and sat back to text Paul that I was on my way to the function. At 3:30 p.m., traffic wasn't too bad for a Sunday afternoon. The events were going to start soon, with a meet-and-greet, then a formal introduction by the president of the society. Hopefully, I'd be back at the Georgian before 8 p.m.

The Roosevelt was another grand hotel in Hollywood. The tiled floors in the Moorish-decorated lobby were beautiful. There was a fountain in the middle, but it didn't appear to have seen any water for years. To the rear of where I came in was a bar. The front desk was on another level below. I noticed a large sign on an easel over to the side depicting gold doubloons, pieces of eight, and a compass rose with *Welcome National Treasure Hunter Society* across the top. I headed towards the entrance. The room's exterior door had a gold inlaid plaque that read *Blossom Room*.

I checked in at the welcome table wearing my I.D badge. The room was filled with rugged-looking men, some with tiny diamonds in their pierced ears and others wearing large gold chains around their necks. Not surprisingly, there were few women. Of the females present, most looked like they were paid escorts or possibly girlfriends of some of the older men. I felt a little awkward and decided not to stay very long. I'd just make an appearance and then go back to my hotel. After ordering ginger ale in a wine glass, I smiled a lot and pretended to read the extra information that the greeter had given me on check-in. After several minutes, I left to take a stroll around the lobby. I could see framed pictures up on the balcony. They looked interesting, so I went up to investigate. To my pleasant surprise, they were images of the Roosevelt's storied Hollywood past.

Mary Pickford, Douglas Fairbanks, and Clark Gable stared back at me in gorgeous headshots. Marilyn Monroe posed on the diving board of the hotel's swimming pool in the first ever ad for suntan lotion. I sidestepped down the carpeted hallway, taking note of the old movie stars I remembered. I marveled at a picture taken on May 19, 1929. It was the first Academy Awards Ceremony in none other than the Blossom Room. I leaned in closer to see who the people were at one of the tables in the picture. As I took a step back to view the next picture, I bumped into someone. "Oops, sorry," I said as I turned around.

"No problem." A silver-haired man brushed off drops of liquid that had spilled onto his navy-blue sport coat from his drink.

"Wow. I'm really sorry. These pictures caught my interest so much...I guess I wasn't thinking. I love Old Hollywood." I couldn't help but notice his light blue, button- down shirt was so striking against his white hair and deep tan.

He looked at me and then at my badge. "You're Nancy Caldwell, one of the people on the panel for the Treasure Hunters?"

"Yes." He wasn't wearing a badge. "Are you attending the event?"

"That I am." He walked up to the same picture that I was looking at. "See that guy there?" He pointed to a rotund man at a circular table. "That's Fatty Arbuckle. You know who he was?"

"Sure. An old-fashioned Chris Farley." I smiled and walked over to another picture.

He followed behind me. "So, what's your favorite time period in Hollywood?" he asked as he came closer.

I took a sip of my ginger ale. "I actually prefer the '40s and before."

"Yeah, me too. That Golden Age was phenomenal." He eyed a picture of Greta Garbo.

I went in the opposite direction to look at a framed *L.A. Times* newspaper headline, and sensed him staring at me. It felt uncomfortable, and yet, it was flattering.

He came over to study the same news clipping. "That's awesome."

I read the caption aloud. "Hollywoodland's newest producer, Franklin Cannon." I laughed. "Why do they call it Hollywoodland?"

"Back in 1923, the land was supposed to be turned into an exclusive housing development that was going to be called Hollywoodland. When the project failed, the sign stayed until 1949. That's when the 'land' was dropped and the sign repaired."

"I'm impressed: you seem to know a lot about Old Hollywood." I studied the headline and picture again. "Look at the girl next to this guy. Gertie...that's a name you don't hear anymore."

He returned his focus to the suited guy in the frame. "This guy here in the clipping, Franklin Cannon. I wonder if he's related to that recluse, Gaylord Cannon, in Hollywood Hills? They say he's about eighty now, filthy rich. His family was in the business, back in the '30s and '40s, but he shies away from publicity and is very secretive about his past."

"I've always loved the old stars and their stories." I focused on the next picture. The conversation was turning into a lot of fun. He checked his watch.

"It's almost 5 p.m. I guess we'd better get downstairs. The presentations are going to start in a few minutes."

"Sure." I headed for the stairs.

He followed behind me again. "Maybe we'll meet up sometime over the next few days?"

"We'll see," I answered, thinking to myself...probably not.

11

Present Day
HOLLYWOOD – LOS ANGELES

THE PRESIDENT OF the Treasure Hunter Society, an older gentleman named Jake Billings, gave the introduction to the opening of their annual gathering. After talking about himself for over fifteen minutes, he gave a short tribute to the godfather of treasure hunters, Mel Fisher. I'd heard of him before. News reports stated that his illustrious career became more notable after he'd discovered the remains of the 1622 Spanish galleon, *Nuestra Senora de Atocha,* near the Florida Keys on July 20, 1985. Fisher, along with his family, had continued to find artifacts from the deep seas and established a Maritime Museum in Florida.

After heaping praises upon Mel by the president, several of the attendees raised their arms in a wave to salute their famous colleague and brought an end to the formal speech. At that point, I was ready to go back to the hotel to look over my notes for the next day's panel discussion. After a few more minutes of socializing, I left to call for an Uber ride.

There was an interesting alcove with a regal-looking settee to my right, just outside the Blossom Room. I sat down and ordered the car, only to discover there had been some kind of accident on Hollywood Boulevard, so nothing was available for at least an hour. I closed my eyes and thought of Paul and the kids back at home.

"Hello." A gentle voice quietly spoke near me.

I opened my eyes to see the man from the balcony. "Hello," I answered back.

He sat next to me. "Need a ride?"

I'm not getting into a stranger's car, I thought. "No, I'm waiting for an Uber. I guess there's been an accident and the road is blocked off."

"Do you mind if I sit here with you for a while?"

He had a gentle smile. Nice white teeth. After a few seconds, I decided he looked harmless. "Of course not."

He held his hand out. "My name is Stephen Boudreaux, private investigator and treasure hunter. That's why I'm here. How did you get involved with the society?"

I returned his handshake and glanced up to his face. He was really good-looking. "I was invited. I'm what you call an amateur sleuth." I leaned back against the leather-cushioned seat. "I've found treasure. Actually, my two discoveries of pirate treasure were really just by accident. I never intended to seek anything on purpose. Then again, I'm a naturally curious person, and I love a good historical mystery." I checked my phone for the time; only ten minutes had passed since I began waiting. "When clues pop out at me, I can't resist finding the answers. You probably understand my inquisitiveness, based on what you do for a living."

Stephen leaned back. "Yeah. I was a policeman in New York City before I retired and got into the private investigation business."

"How did you land in treasure hunting?"

"I resettled in Florida and met Mel Fisher. Did some work for him, and decided I liked it. Being a PI was a logical solution for my free time."

"So you're not with him anymore?"

"No. But my involvement with Fisher proved to be very profitable for me. It gave me the opportunity to open my own firm here, in L.A. I guess I like the warm, dry weather and the big money that flows here."

Another five minutes passed; I stood up. "Maybe I should go and see if my ride is outside."

Stephen followed me. "Care if I come with you?"

"No. I don't mind." He seemed like such a nice gentleman and cautious of not offending me. I appreciated it.

Hollywood Boulevard was cordoned off for several blocks on both sides of the Roosevelt Hotel. Police were walking in the middle of the street, and there were no moving cars.

Stephen surveyed the scene with a casual but procedural posture; his hands in his pants pockets, his head turning from side to side, then up and down the street. He stepped closer to me. "I know a great little place to grab a coffee or drink. Want to join me? It looks like I won't be going anywhere too soon either."

"Oh, I don't know if I should." I adjusted the strap of my purse over a shoulder. "Maybe it'll clear up. I should stay here."

"The Pig & Whistle is just down a few blocks. The décor is beautiful inside. It's also where a lot of movie stars frequented, back in the day. I think you'd like it. The restaurant has been there since 1927."

I couldn't resist his invitation. There's absolutely no harm in walking to an interesting place for coffee. "You talked me into it. I'd love to see it." The walk was eerily quiet because of no traffic and, being a Sunday night, not many people walking around.

The second I entered the place; I loved it. The ceiling was wonderful; its dark, carved wood ran the length and width of the narrow eatery. We got a table near the front so we could look out the window to see when the traffic started moving. "Just decaf coffee, please."

"No wine?'

"Nope, not a drinker, never have been." I noticed a few tables had couples at them. One man, by himself, sat in the middle of the room holding his cell phone. I could hear every word of his side of the conversation. I shook my head and laughed. "It's funny, he's talking on one phone about business or something, and he's got a second phone on the table in front of him." The lone customer was getting louder and more animated in his tone.

Stephen leaned on one elbow to observe the rude guy. "That's L.A. for you. A character on every corner."

The waitress brought my coffee and a glass of wine for Stephen. The man's loud voice took over the whole restaurant. He yelled into the phone, "Yeah, but the guy said he would be there with the cameras." There were a few seconds of silence, and then he continued with extra energy, "If she thinks she can get away with it, she's crazy. I'll find someone else." The guy looked like he hadn't ordered anything, because only a glass of water was on the table, along with an open menu.

Stephen and I smiled at each other, and we both sensed we were thinking the same thing. Either it's all fake, to impress whoever is listening, or it's some kind of deal that's actually going down. I kept watching and listening to the man rant, trying to make sense of what he was talking about.

Stephen waited until there was a break in the noise before he spoke. "Where did you say you lived?" He sipped his drink.

"My husband, Paul, and I are from Ohio. In the late '80s, we moved our three teenagers and a five-year-old to Cape Cod, to further Paul's career as an artist. I wanted to write my first novel."

"What kind of an artist is he?"

"Watercolor and acrylic. He's very good. He's also been supporting the family with his art for almost twenty-five years."

"That's quite an accomplishment. How many children did you say you have?"

"When we moved, we had four children, then we had one more; total of three boys and two girls. In fact, I'm visiting our oldest, Jim, who recently moved to Venice Beach to try his luck in show business."

"Wow! You certainly have your hands full. Who's minding the children now?"

"We hired Martha. She's been with us since I found the treasure. She was a real luxury for me. We had kids ranging from toddlers to twenty–seven so I needed all the help I could get. She's actually more than a nanny; she's become a great friend."

"Sounds like a nice life."

"I'm very fortunate. Just like you with your relationship with Mel Fisher, there were finder's fees and jewelry, lots of it. Some of the treasure couldn't be sold because I have a strong respect for history, and I would never think of selling the silver or gold that I found, only to have it melted down for profit by some businessman." I gave Stephen a mischievous grin. "Almost got killed a few times, but I've come out okay in the end."

"What do you mean? Got killed?"

The traffic started to move on the boulevard outside. "I bet my ride isn't going to wait for very long." I gathered my purse and scarf to leave.

"Wait. Let me walk back with you." Stephen pulled out his wallet to pay.

I fumbled through my purse for some cash. "Here, let me split the bill."

"My treat." He tossed a twenty-dollar bill on the table and gave a wave to the waitress that we were leaving.

As we walked, we talked some more. Now I was curious about him. "Boudreaux is such a mysterious name. What's your history?'

"My father was also a career policeman in New York. After working a case about someone's background and DNA he grew inquisitive about his own French heritage, so he took a vacation to Paris in search of his ancestors. While he was there he met my mother. They married, came back to the states, and I was born. That's pretty much it."

"Do you have any children?"

"I have a son who's a sophomore in college. My wife and I are divorced. I guess she couldn't take the fact that I could get killed whenever I left for work. It's a common scenario for anyone who puts their life in danger for their job."

"I'm sorry to hear that."

"She's remarried now."

By the time we reached the hotel, traffic was definitely moving, but there was no sign of a red Toyota Camry, my Uber ride, parked out front. I started to go inside to wait. Stephen opened the hotel's door for me. Once in the lobby, I extended my hand to say goodbye. "Well, it's been very nice, Stephen."

"Let's not do any goodbyes. Maybe we can talk more tomorrow, at the end of the day's events?"

"Maybe." I turned to look for the red car out front.

He smiled at me. "Talk later."

I watched him leave for the lower level and the parking lot, and then I headed outside in the opposite direction. The Uber finally pulled up. Too late to call Paul; he'd already be in bed. On the ride back to the hotel, I wondered if Stephen could help me get a copy of that old picture. I bet he had connections at the local police station.

12

Present Day – Monday
HOLLYWOOD – LOS ANGELES

MY ROLE IN the panel discussion on Monday was to enlighten the professional treasure hunters about how I managed to find 300-year-old pirate treasure, not once, but twice. "It was pure luck..." I began, "...coupled with a strong sense of curiosity and always questioning."

Everyone in the audience seemed to nod their heads in agreement that being naturally curious was the key to success. I explained that I had intended to dig a simple garden behind our Cape Cod barn, but had instead found an old root cellar. At its bottom, evidence was uncovered that linked our land to the 1717 pirate legend of Sam Bellamy, his lover Maria Hallett, and the *Whydah* pirate ship. People looked very interested in my story.

I went on to convey some of the details from my second encounter with what I prefer to call 'fluky' discoveries. "Several years later, on a trip to visit our Peace Corps son on Antigua, I ran into a descendant from one of the pirate survivors of the *Whydah* wreck. Then, with the help of an old map, a broken teapot, and a bit of danger and conspiracy, I found another cache of riches."

The next two people who spoke about their experience mentioned their keen observation skills. One had found a hoard of trinkets and gold from Roman times, as they dug up their fields in Great Britain, and the other panelist was just walking his dog on his land in the Western United States when he discovered cans of silver dollars.

By 4 p.m., my part in the annual meeting was over. I was tired and hungry. I could see Stephen in the back row. He stood to give me a thumbs-up and a smile. I returned his greeting with a wave.

As I gathered my notes, he came over to me. "That was awesome. I really enjoyed hearing all the stories, especially yours."

"Thanks."

"How about coming to dinner with me? Nothing serious. We're just a couple of colleagues, who have the same interests, getting together."

"I'm a little tired," I protested, but then recalled that he may have a connection with the local police department. "You know what? I may take you up on that offer. Do you know another old Hollywood place where we could go?"

"Well, why don't we try the Pig & Whistle again? You never actually ate any food there."

"Okay," I said as we left the Blossom Room. "Let's go."

I ordered a BLT and a cup of herbal tea while Stephen picked the Rugged Shepherd's Pie and a light beer.

He settled himself in his chair. "Everyone in L.A. is so obsessed with diet. Sometimes I like to live on the wild side with some good old-fashioned meat and potatoes."

"Funny. That's what my husband says whenever we have a chance to eat out." I poured my tea from a small porcelain teapot.

"How long have you been married?"

"It will be thirty years this summer."

He gave a low whistle. "That's a rarity out here, in fact, anywhere. I guess some people can't seem to find happiness, and they give up on relationships too easily." He placed his napkin across his lap. "Sometimes I think I could've tried harder in my marriage. Maybe left the force or requested a desk job."

He looked sad to me.

"I'm sure you did your best. We're not all perfect in our choices in life." I didn't know what more to say. It felt awkward, but only for a few seconds.

Stephen leaned in over the table. "So tell me, how did you almost get killed?"

"Well...the first time I was in a precarious situation, but probably not in danger of death. I know I felt like I was going to die." I grew quiet for a moment, thinking about that night. I touched my cup for its warmth. It grounded me, and I felt safe again. "Two men had heard about the discovery of the root cellar in our backyard and decided there was more to be found besides the three gold coins that had already been dug up. The local newspaper leaked the information, even though it wasn't supposed to."

He looked concerned. "What did they do, break in?"

"Yes. It was storming outside. I was pregnant and home alone, watching a movie."

"What'd you do?"

The waitress brought our food. "Well, let's just say that I made it out okay." We began eating and settled into conversation about our kids.

Stephen was almost finished with his meal when he asked, "What about the second time?"

I finished the last triangle of my BLT sandwich. "As you may remember, from my talk, I was visiting my second son in the Peace Corps. After finding the old map in the family bible of the relative of pirate John Julian, I returned to Cape Cod to decipher the map and what it meant in terms of more riches."

"Jeesh. You can't stay out of trouble, can you?"

I smiled at Stephen's remark, realizing I could laugh now, but also remembering that it wasn't funny at the time. "I'm really not that helpless, you know. Of course, eventually my husband encouraged me to take a self-defense course."

"Well, I would have done the same thing. You seem to be quite a treasure yourself."

His words took me by surprise. I didn't think of myself as a treasure, but graciously accepted his compliment.

He signaled the waitress for our check.

"How about you?" I asked. "Have you had any near-death experiences?"

Stephen rubbed his shoulder, not in pain, but more of an achy reflex. "I was shot on a drug-related stakeout. I'd called for back-up right before my partner went down. I proceeded to go after the dealer, but it took a turn for the worse, and I got it, right above the heart, and a second bullet in my shoulder."

"Oh, my goodness."

"I remember waking up in the hospital to see my wife and thirteen-year-old son in tears, looking down on me."

"It must have been difficult for you and them."

"It was. After that incident, my marriage began to break apart." He repeated under his breath, "I should've asked for a desk job."

"I'm so sorry."

He looked as if he was going to cry. "I didn't make a good choice. To this day, I can't get their faces out of my head; how frightened they'd both looked, thinking they might lose me." He took out his wallet to pay the bill and seemed to breathe a sigh of acceptance. "Enough of this sadness," he said quietly. "Nancy, I've really enjoyed our time together. It's not often that I meet an attractive woman who's genuine and enjoys a good mystery."

Stephen kept his stare on me. It felt like a long time, and yet I didn't feel uncomfortable. He finally fumbled for some cash. "It's been fun talking with you and learning more about you. You're very interesting."

I stood up to leave, but remembered that I wanted to ask him about getting a copy of the old photo. "Stephen, would you be able to get a copy of a piece of evidence from the local police?"

"Now what are you up to?"

"It just so happens that my son, Jim, found the remains of a body next to his apartment in Venice Beach, right before I arrived."

He opened his eyes wide. "You've got to be kidding. A body?"

"No, the *remains* of one. He also unearthed a silver mesh purse with a photo inside it. Jim thinks one of the people in the image resembles a girl he works with. I want a copy of it so we can show it to her."

Stephen stayed seated as he listened.

"Are you still with me?" I asked, hoping I had his attention.

"Yes. Go on." He pushed his chair away from the table to get up.

"I'd like to follow up on the fact that there's a possibility we could identify the person in the picture. Could you help me out?"

He rubbed the back of his neck. "Now you're asking me this? When were you going to tell me about what your son found?" He started to laugh. "How could you keep this to yourself?"

"I really didn't know you. Now I do. Can you get me a copy?"

"I'll see what I can find out. What's the name of the person down at the force I need to contact?"

I pulled out my phone. "I don't know off-hand. Let me see if Jim is available. I know he's off work soon. He's got a card with the investigating officer's information on it." I waited for Jim to answer. No luck. I left a voicemail and turned to Stephen. "What's your email address so I can send you the name of the officer?"

He handed me his business card.

"I really appreciate this, Stephen. Thank you!"

We started to leave for the door. "Do you trust me yet?" he asked.

His question made me laugh out loud.

"I take it that's a yes? Now can I give you a ride to your hotel?"

We laughed as we walked down Hollywood Boulevard toward his car.

13

Present Day – Tuesday
LOS ANGELES

I WAS UP EARLY. I noticed Jim had texted the officer's name and email address to me. I forwarded it to Stephen and then dressed for an early morning walk. With coffee in hand, my destination was the Third Street Promenade. Most of the stores were closed at 8 a.m., and there were not many people around. It was nice and meditative. Following Danny's birth, my regimen had been to walk two to three miles every other day, followed by a thirty-minute workout. I was back, after several years, to my college weight and feeling wonderful. I returned to the Georgian by around 10 a.m. and ran up the stairs to the lobby.

I heard my name as I poured a glass of lemon-flavored water from the complimentary refreshment. "Mrs. Caldwell?"

I turned towards the front desk. "Yes, that's me."

"Someone delivered this for you." A pleasant young woman placed a yellow 8x10 envelope on the dark green counter.

"Thank you," I said, hoping it might be from Stephen. If it was, that was pretty fast service. My hunch proved to be correct. The return address was stamped Stephen Boudreaux, Private Investigator. By the time I got into the elevator, I had it opened and was looking at the image. Once back in my room, I read Stephen's handwritten message:

Hope this helps. If you need anything else, don't hesitate to call me.

It was a pleasure to meet you.

Fondly, Stephen

I called Jim. This time he answered. "Hi Mom."

"Hi, honey. When can we meet Natalie? You wouldn't believe what I've got in front of me."

"What?"

I stared at the image of two young girls. "It's a long story, but I've got a copy of the photo that was in that old mesh purse."

"How'd you get it?"

"I'll explain later. When can we meet Natalie?"

"I guess within the hour. I'm off until 2 p.m. today, but I know she's working on the early prep shift. She's at the Clamshell now."

"Great. I'll be ready in about thirty minutes. I'll be downstairs waiting for you."

After a quick shower, I threw on some jeans and a cotton top and waited outside for Jim with the yellow envelope in my hand. I opened it several times to look at the photo. Each time I studied it, something felt familiar to me. It wasn't Grauman's Theatre, but a connection, or a memory, to whatever was in the picture. He was late. I started pacing.

Jim finally pulled up and opened the door for me from inside his car. "You look nice, Mom. Doing your regimen while you're here in L.A.?"

"Thanks for noticing. I try to walk as much as I can." I buckled in.

"Can I see the picture?" Jim idled the car, waiting to see the old photo.

I pulled it out to show him. "You know, something's been bothering me. I'm not actually worried about anything, just stumped."

"What's wrong?" He kept his stare on the two girls in the photo.

"Every time I look at it, I feel like I should remember something about it." I leaned in close to see the photocopy.

Jim pointed to the girl holding the purse. "This one really looks like Natalie."

By the time we arrived at the Clamshell, I'd explained how I'd met Stephen Boudreaux and that he was an ex-cop turned PI. The bar was empty of patrons and only a few workers were buzzing about. Natalie stood behind the bar. Her brown hair was clipped up on top of her head with a few tendrils hanging down the sides of her face. She was very attractive and trim.

Jim led the way across the newly-mopped floor. "Hey, Natalie. This is my mom. She's visiting from the Cape."

"Hi, Natalie." I followed Jim, careful not to slip on the wet floor, while clutching the yellow envelope. "So you're a New Englander. Whereabouts?"

"Near Portsmouth, New Hampshire. That's where I grew up." Natalie took out a knife and began gathering limes in front of her.

"I was wondering if you could take a look at this picture. Do you recognize anyone?" I pulled the photo out and laid it onto the shiny shellacked bar. "Jim thought you looked like one of the girls in this old picture that he unearthed next to his apartment."

Natalie stopped cutting and dried her hands. "He did tell me that he'd found some bones or something, along with an old purse." She leaned over to see it. "My mom once mentioned that my grandmother was from the Cape." She took the photo over to the side of the bar near the window.

I joined her and pointed to the girl holding the metal purse. "You resemble this one."

"I don't know," Natalie laughed. "I don't think so."

Jim walked over. He looked at the girl's face and then to Natalie's. "Look at the smile. That's you, Natalie. Even the eyes resemble yours."

"Maybe." Natalie still looked puzzled.

I agreed with Jim. "Natalie, you could definitely be a distant relative to the girl in the picture." All three of us craned our necks to look at it again. "Do you know anything else about your family back a few generations?"

"Nope. I'd have to call home to see if my mom remembers."

"Would you mind?" I was so curious.

Jim quickly spoke up. "Mom, take it easy." He looked over to Natalie. "You'll have to excuse my mom, she's always asking too many questions."

Natalie laughed. "I don't mind. My mom should be up and around by my break. She'll be happy to get my phone call."

"Thanks so much," I said as I placed the paper back into the envelope. "Jim, we should leave Natalie to her work so she can have a chance to call home."

Jim raised his hands in the air and shrugged his shoulders, as if everyone should humor me and my quirky tendencies to know everything. I ignored his reaction to my inquisitiveness and chalked it up as something a kid would lovingly do to their parents.

"See you later, Natalie," he called out. "You got my cell?"

She nodded and waved goodbye to us.

Once back at the Georgian, Jim parked his car in the hotel's garage so he could come up to see my room.

"Wow! This is awesome." He bounced on the bed, just like when he was little.

I left him for a bathroom break. When I came out he was appreciating the fantastic view out the window while he held Stephen's note.

He turned around to me. "What's with the 'fondly' that he signed the note with?"

"Huh? What do you mean?"

"He signed the note 'Fondly, Stephen'."

I looked at the signed note again. "I didn't give it much thought. I don't know."

"What's he look like?"

"Nice looking. Like your father."

Jim smiled at me.

"For heaven's sake, Jim. There's nothing going on between us. Remember, he helped us in getting the copy of the photo. Don't be silly."

We strolled down to the boardwalk to watch the locals, tourists, and the waves. It grew cloudy, and people began to leave.

We stayed put on the beach, relishing the lack of voices and enjoying the soft cawing of the seagulls. I closed my eyes. The two of us didn't need conversation; the ocean echoed familiar sounds from our home on Cape Cod and reminded us of when we'd all go to the beach. It always seemed to comfort and placate any tendencies that we had to feel at odds in a strange place. In fact, I often found my time at the beach to be one of my favorite places to be creative. It was when my mind would clear so that I could concentrate on only one or two ideas at a time. Today, I zeroed in on the old faded picture. What was it about that picture? Why couldn't I figure it out?

My phone went off. It was only a robo call. I disconnected and noticed the time. "We should get back. When do you have to go to work?"

"In a few hours. No problem." Jim stood up and extended a hand to me.

"Oh, you're such a gentleman," I said, standing to brush off the sand. "Must have been your fine upbringing." We laughed as we walked over the sand to the steps that led up to the pier.

As I climbed the stairs, it came to me. "I know what's bugging me." I stopped and turned to Jim. "I saw the face of that girl in a framed picture at the Roosevelt Hotel...and the purse, too."

"What?"

"The afternoon of the reception. I went upstairs on the balcony to look at frames of old movie stars connected to the hotel, and there was an *L.A. Times* news article from 1947. It was the social scene and featured a movie producer named Cannon. I think the girl next to him could be the same girl in the old photo, and she was also holding onto a mesh purse."

"Are you sure?"

"Positive. In fact, that's when I met Stephen, the PI guy, who helped me get this copy."

I wanted to get another look at the old pictures. Jim's work schedule only allowed enough time to drive me over to the Roosevelt Hotel. I would need a cab on my return to the Georgian. I was desperate to compare the faces of the two girls. "Thanks, Jim," I yelled as I exited his car. The streets were busy and stores crowded. I made my way through the Roosevelt's door and up to the balcony.

To my disappointment, all the pictures were gone. The outlines of where they once hung were the only evidence that they'd ever existed. I hurried down to the lower level of the lobby and waited in line to talk to the young man behind the desk. Finally I stepped forward. "Can you please tell me where the pictures of the old movie stars went from the balcony?"

He gave me an all-knowing smile. "Unfortunately, we had to remove them. The new owners of the hotel officially took over yesterday. It's been almost a year in negotiations and now they'll be doing some renovations."

"Are they stored somewhere close? Can I see them? I need to see one in particular." I quickly thought of an excuse. "I'm doing research about Old Hollywood."

"Let me see what I can do." The receptionist picked up a phone and pressed a button. "Can you tell me where the old frames are from the balcony? I have someone here who wants to look at them."

I waited patiently for his answer.

"Yes. I see. Thanks." He hung up. "You're in luck. If you go up the stairs to the old main lobby, they're being stored in the Blossom Room."

"Thank you so very much." My heart sped up, my whole body filled with excitement at the thought that I was on a hunt again.

The frames were stacked against each other, not very smart of whoever did it, I thought. The wires and hooks were making small indentations on the fronts of several of the gold frames. Within the third stack, halfway down the wall, I found the news clipping I was looking for. I picked the frame up and laid it on the floor so that I could see it better. When the copy of the photo was laid next to the girl's face in the newspaper, I could see it was the same person and the purses looked identical.

I wrote the names of both people in my notebook and took a picture of the news clipping with my cell phone. I replaced the frame against the wall, making sure it was safe. I then stood back to study the picture once more and repeated the names out loud of the so-called celebrities: "Franklin Cannon and Gertie Foster."

14

1947
HOLLYWOOD – LOS ANGELES

MAGGIE FELT someone shaking her shoulder. "Maggie, wake up! Get dressed. It's almost noon." The voice sounded familiar.

The sleepy girl mumbled, "Mom, cut it out," then rolled over onto her back.

"It's me, Gertie. Come on, Jeff will be here in a half hour." Gertie hurried out the door to the bathroom.

Maggie quickly realized that she was in California and not back home on Cape Cod. She rubbed her eyes and stretched her arms above her head. *Why is that guy picking us up? Oh...the party,* she remembered. *It's not that she didn't enjoy going places, but she knew it would probably end up with everyone being drunk but her. If this was Hollywood, she didn't care for it.* She picked her clothes out and waited for her turn in the bathroom.

At 11:30 a.m., they stood outside on the stone steps of Miss Sylvia's. The tall building, with its turrets behind them, offered shade to the girls while they waited for Jeff to pick them up.

Maggie watched the cars and people pass by. Finally she asked, "So, how was your evening with Mr. Cannon?"

Gertie checked her makeup in a small mirror. "Okay."

"Just okay? You seemed to be a little disheveled when you came in last night."

"I'm fine."

"You want to tell me about it?"

"Not really." Gertie closed her compact. "Nothing happened. Cannon passed out before he could do anything to me." She smiled at Maggie, hinting that all was well. "You know what I mean?"

"I understand." Maggie sat on the top step.

Gertie joined her. "Of course, I made sure I was in bed next to him before he woke up. He thinks we did it!" She began to laugh.

Maggie wagged her finger at her cousin in a friendly jest. "I'm going to tell your mother."

Gertie laughed even harder. "She won't believe you."

At 11:45, Jeff pulled up in a burgundy Plymouth Sedan. He got out on the street side, stood up on the running board, and yelled, "Let's go, ladies. The party's already started."

The girls got into the back seat. Maggie admired the dark grey pinstriped cloth covers that matched the inside roof of the car. Within seconds, they were on their way to Hollywood Hills and the Cannon House.

As Jeff turned onto the gated driveway, Maggie and Gertie stared out the window at the luxuriant landscaping. "This is swell," Maggie said. "I'm curious to see what the house looks like inside."

The Cannon residence stretched over five acres with lush palm trees, gardens, and three putting greens. Franklin Cannon liked his privacy, but when he did socialize he spared nothing. He insisted that everything should be fun and sexy; drugs and liquor flowed freely.

A large stone entranceway graced the white marbled front of the mansion. Palm fronds and red birds of paradise colorfully grew out of the planters that greeted guests upon entering. Gertie was out of the sedan first and intent on getting inside. Maggie followed her up the stairs and through the doorway flanked by vibrant multi-hued stained glass windows, past the winding stairway and then out to the patio in the rear of the house. An Olympic-sized pool stretched to her left, and on her right, marker flags waved to her from the closest of the golf course holes.

Gertie wiggled her way across the patio to the open bar, where she promptly ordered a margarita, the latest drink of the stars.

"A little early, isn't it, cuz?" Maggie grabbed a cold Coke from a large ice chest to the side of the ornate turquoise-tiled bar.

"You do what you need to do. I'll do what I want." Gertie adjusted her sunglasses, turned to face the crowd, and zeroed in on Franklin Cannon. She lifted her hand in the air and called out over the beat of the four-piece jazz band. "Oh, Franklin dear, here I am." She walked the walk of a Hollywood starlet.

Maggie was taken aback at the brashness of her cousin. It was over the top even for Gertie. But she seemed to get the attention she wanted. Everyone noticed her.

Franklin left the circle of wanna-be's surrounding him for Gertie. He put his arm around her waist.

Maggie drifted over to the pool where Esther Williams, who'd recently returned from Mexico after filming *Fiesta*, was swimming laps to the encouragement of the crowd. How many could she complete in five minutes was the question on everyone's lips. She spotted handsome Johnny Weissmuller, famous for his role as Tarzan. He was waiting for his turn in the pool. It was all in fun and Maggie enjoyed watching every splash that fell on those who stood poolside.

"Maggie!" Harry Gibson stood next to her with a cold drink in his hand.

"Harry, so glad you're here." She shielded her eyes from the bright sun with her hand.

"Whenever the Cannons have a bash, I plan to be here," Harry laughed. "You never know who'll show up."

She glanced back to the competition. "Those two are so glamorous, and they can really swim."

Harry stared at Miss Williams. "I've always wondered if a beautiful tall woman would ever be interested in a short guy like me."

"You never know in Hollywoodland," Maggie quipped as she looked over at the muscular Weissmuller.

Before the name of the fastest swimmer could be officially announced, Franklin took to the microphone near the steps leading down to the rolling green lawn. "May I have your attention, please?"

Everyone turned to face Franklin. His arm cradled Gertie's shapely waist. "My good friends and those of you who are not such good friends." There were a few snickers to one side of the pool. "As you know, I will be producing a new film about murder and mayhem...a little on the dark side." There was a smattering of applause throughout the partygoers. "It will be partnered with the great RKO movie studio—" Loud clapping interrupted him, "...and production will be starting within the year."

A uniformed waiter brought him a martini. He drank it in one gulp. Guests toasted with their drinks and cheered. Franklin threw his glass over his head, onto the grass, then raised his arm to quiet the noise. "Now, I have one more thing I want to tell all of you." He looked at Gertie. She took off her sunglasses and posed her head to the side, her smile wide.

Gaylord and Blanche appeared, wearing white terry cloth robes, from behind the French doors of the pool house. "Now what's the old man going to do?" Gaylord looked angry as he tied his robe tighter around his naked body.

Blanche adjusted her blonde hair, but let her robe stay loose around her shapely curves.

Maggie elbowed Harry as they watched the spectacle that Franklin Cannon was creating. "What has my cousin gotten herself into now?"

Franklin continued, "This beautiful girl is Gertie Foster...my new leading lady!"

Gertie waved and squealed at hearing her sudden celebrity status. She kissed him on the cheek.

Glasses were refilled and another toast was given to the latest ingénue.

Gaylord uttered, "Shit! What about my Blanche?"

Blanche looked stunned. "Yeah, what about me?"

Maggie was shocked. "I can't believe it. Gertie did it. She actually did it!"

Harry gave out a low whistle.

The two friends made their way closer to where Gertie was standing. People crowded around her, trying to introduce themselves.

Harry held onto Maggie's arm. "They seem eager to touch her. Maybe they think some of her luck will rub off on them. Who knows?"

"Goodness, I hope she's making the right decision." Maggie looked concerned. "I told her mom I'd watch out for her. But then again, it's Gertie, she's a force to be reckoned with."

Within the hour, Gertie and Franklin had disappeared into the main house. Maggie and Harry, looking for something to do other than drink, walked the edges of the golf course. By the time they returned to the party it was 4 p.m. Gertie was sitting outside, on top of the piano, with a large yellow diamond ring on her finger.

Maggie came over to her. "Gertie! Where'd you get that?"

"From Franklin. He said I could wear it for a while, just like Blanche did the other night." She held her hand away from her to admire the sparkling yellow stone in the fading sunlight.

Maggie took a seat near the bar next to Harry. "This whole thing makes me nervous. It's too fast. And I don't like Gaylord's father." She made her way back to her cousin. "Gertie, isn't it time we leave?"

"I can't leave yet. The party's just starting."

"I think we should go."

"Well, Maggie, you can go. I'm staying."

"So you want me to leave you here again by yourself?"

"That's what I said." Gertie whispered in Maggie's ear, "I'm going to take this old guy for as much as he'll give me, and that includes the opportunity to be famous."

"But Gertie—"

"Cannon told me himself." Gertie grabbed another drink from the waiter. "If you want to get ahead...then do as he asks...and I'm going to do just that."

Gertie called out over the din of the voices at the party, "Johnny, have you seen Franklin?" She hustled over to Weissmuller.

Blanche came from behind her. With a sarcastic twang, she said, "Nice ring."

Gertie held it up for all to see. "It certainly is, isn't it?" She turned on her heels and headed toward the house as her white and navy blue, polka-dotted skirt swayed back and forth.

Blanche was livid. She gathered the edges of her robe closer to her neck, then hurried back to the bathhouse.

After another twenty minutes, Maggie had had enough of the party. "Harry. Do you mind driving me back to Miss Sylvia's?"

"Not at all." He pulled out his keys.

Maggie glanced over to the crowd gathering around the house where a waiter was handing out some small envelopes on a silver tray. "I need to use the ladies room, but not in the house. I'll be right back." She hoped to avoid the crowd.

The bathhouse had one large main room with two bedrooms toward the rear and a kitchen and bathroom down a hallway. It was long and narrow, almost the length of the pool. Maggie entered through the glass doors.

Blanche was furiously filing her nails while she sat on a white tufted couch near the front windows.

"Where's Gaylord?" Maggie asked.

"How should I know?" Blanche scowled. "Why don't you take that bitch, Gertie, and go back to where you came from?"

"Where's the ladies room?"

"Down the hallway." Blanche thumbed over her shoulder.

The bathroom was nothing out of the ordinary except for one thing – there were two loose razor blades and a dusting of fine white powder on a flat mirror. A hypodermic needle lay next to it on the sink's counter. It took Maggie aback, but she soon realized what was going on. Her fears of the Cannons and for the safety of Gertie grew stronger. All she wanted to do was get out of there and warn her cousin.

At the far end of the patio, Gertie entered the main house. "Franklin? Where are you?" She wandered into the living room, past the winding staircase and stopped in front of the library when she heard the mention of her name coming from behind a door that was half closed.

A loud, anxious voice interrupted Franklin's words. "You can't be serious Franklin. She's a nobody. The studio won't stand for it, I tell you."

"Now don't get your shorts up all over your ears." She recognized Franklin's voice. "Gertie Foster will not be starring in the picture. You have my word on that."

The nervous man continued, "But you announced it to everyone."

"I do a lot of crazy things, Thompson. She's sort of my plaything right now and I like her."

"Well, I trust you, Franklin," said Thompson. "We at RKO have always enjoyed and profited from your backing...let's keep it that way."

Gertie leaned back against the tapestry-covered wall. Her hand covered her mouth to muffle her sobs as tears streamed down her cheeks. She couldn't breathe. She quickly turned and ran into the guest bathroom under the stairs. She hung her head over the sink to vomit. The after-taste of too many margaritas stung the inside of her mouth. Within seconds, dark angry feelings rose up inside of her. She looked at her pale face in the mirror. He can't do this to me, she thought, he promised me that part in his movie.

The sparkle of the yellow diamond ring contrasted with the sinister notions that now swelled to a peak in her head. She wouldn't let him get away with this. She didn't deserve to be brushed aside. An image of another side of herself slowly took shape in her reflection and she liked who she saw. She saw a smart girl now; someone who was going to win. She'd teach Franklin not to treat her like a second-rate actress. She was going to be a star, no matter what.

The ring. That's it! It must be very special to the old bastard. It was only fair that she got compensated for her disappointment. Gertie smiled, then washed her face and straightened her skirt. After a quick makeup refresh, she grabbed her silver mesh purse and went in pursuit of the black pearl pouch that the ring was always stored in. Voices were still talking behind the door as she crept upstairs to Franklin's bedroom.

Within minutes, Gertie descended the stairway carrying in her silver purse what she thought was due to her.

Franklin was on his way out of the library. "My dear Gertie, where've you been hiding that luscious body of yours?"

"Oh, I'm not feeling well. Too many margaritas. My head is spinning with all the excitement from today. I was resting upstairs on your bed."

He took hold of her hand on the last step. "Now where is my ring, darling?"

"The ring?" She looked down at her finger. "I put it back into that lovely little pearl pouch you keep it in. Don't worry, it's safe in your jewel box." She smiled sweetly at him.

"Thank you, my dear."

Gertie put her arms around his shoulders and tugged on his shirt collar. "Will you mind very much, Franklin sweetie, if I call it a night? I'm really not feeling well."

"Go run along. I have plenty to keep myself amused. Do you need a lift somewhere?"

"No. Harry Gibson will drive me home."

He kissed her on the cheek. "Shall I send a car around for you tomorrow afternoon?"

"Of course," Gertie turned to leave and forced one last smile.

Franklin grabbed a quick feel on her well-shaped rear and winked. "See you tomorrow, my little peach."

Maggie and Harry were about to get into the car when Gertie came running towards them in the circular driveway. "Wait! Wait for me," she called out to her friends.

Maggie turned around. "Gertie! I'm so happy you've decided to leave with us."

"I changed my mind." She climbed into the back seat of Harry's convertible.

Maggie settled herself in the front seat next to Harry. She turned around to face Gertie, "Everything okay?"

"Everything is just fine."

15

1947
HOLLYWOOD – LOS ANGELES

ON THE WAY BACK to Miss Sylvia's, Harry stopped at Carpenters on Five Points in Hollywood. The girls were treated to chicken-fried steak sandwiches and the drive-in's famous deep-fried onion rings.

Harry was smiling about Maggie and how she was just so swell. He took a quick left onto Ocean Boulevard. "Do you mind if I show you where I work?"

Maggie turned to him. "Sure. It's a real nice evening. There's time." She looked to the back at Gertie. "You don't care, do you, Gertie?"

"Not at all."

Harry pulled up to the front of the Georgian Hotel. "Isn't it gorgeous?" They all looked out the windows of the car.

Maggie craned her neck to see the top of the building. "The color is so exotic."

"I have a great idea. How about we take a picture of the three of us out front?" Harry waited with a big grin on his face for them to answer.

"Sure," Maggie said. "Come on, Gertie, it won't take but a minute."

As they scrambled out of the car, Harry grabbed his new Brownie camera from the glove box, and pulled out his bellhop's jacket and hat from the trunk. "This'll be fun," he said as he slipped his uniform on. "There's my buddy, Tommy, he'll take the picture." He waved his friend over to the car, then handed the camera to him. "Here. Take our picture? Please?"

Tommy stood in front of Harry's car, ready to shoot.

Maggie, Harry, and Gertie lined up on the steps of the hotel. They were quite a sight, with Harry's arms around the two laughing girls, his bell cap cocked to one side, and his gold-braided jacket open.

Harry yelled out, "What a hoot!"

By the time the girls returned to their small studio, it was almost 8 p.m. Gertie went in first, while Maggie stayed behind to talk to Harry.

"Thank you so much for buying us dinner." Maggie smiled. "We don't get that kind of food back home...and I loved the carhops on roller skates."

Harry pulled a pack of Chesterfields out and lit one up. "L.A. is a fun place, that's for sure."

The air was cool and one star shone in the sky. They sat for a few moments in silence.

Maggie avoided looking at him. "Harry, I think I'm leaving for Cape Cod tomorrow."

He threw his cigarette into the street and turned towards her. "Do you have to go so soon?"

"I'm afraid so. At least I'm going to leave – I don't know about Gertie."

"It seemed like we were going to become, you know, a thing." Harry's arm went across the back seat and around Maggie's shoulders.

She stared at the floor. "I'm just not comfortable here. Don't get me wrong, I really like you, Harry."

He placed his free hand over Maggie's. "Can't you stay a little longer?"

"Things would be different if I didn't have a boyfriend back home." Maggie twisted the edges of her skirt. "We've even talked about getting married."

He took his arm away and held onto the steering wheel. "Maggie, you never mentioned you were sweet on someone else."

She straightened herself on the seat. "I'm sorry, Harry. It's just the way it is. I really miss Cape Cod and my family." There was an awkward silence. "It's getting late. I need to pack."

As she started to open the door, Harry took hold of her arm. "Would it be okay if I drove you to the train station tomorrow?"

"I don't see why not." She gave him a quick peck on the cheek. "Maybe you could come by around noon?"

Harry quickly added, "You never gave me your home address? I'd like to send you a copy of those pictures we took."

Maggie pulled out a small brown bag that held postcards she'd bought at the new Owl Rexall Drug Store on Hollywood Boulevard. She took out the cards and wrote her Brewster address on the bag.

"Thanks, Maggie. I'll miss you."

She watched him drive away into the night and thought, if only I had met you earlier, my sweet Harry, things might be different.

Maggie reached the top floor of the triple–decker to see the bathroom door was closed. She began laying her clothes out to pack.

Gertie came in. "You leaving?"

"I'm afraid so. I want to go home." Maggie continued folding her clothes. "You coming with me?"

Gertie towel dried her hair. "I don't know. Franklin hinted that maybe the part he promised me wasn't right for my career."

Maggie started for the bathroom to collect her toiletries. "I'm sorry to hear that, Gertie. So you think you'll come home with me then?"

Gertie hung her towel over the bedpost. "I'm going to go out for a while. The cool night air will clear my head." She picked out a gingham dress that hung in the back of the closet.

"I'll probably be in bed soon," Maggie said. "I'm tired. Got a big day tomorrow." She left the small room and headed into the hallway.

After Gertie finished dressing, she hid the pearl pouch with the ring next to her undergarments in the bottom drawer of the dresser. As she passed the bathroom, she knocked on the door and yelled to Maggie, "Don't wait up for me."

Gertie was hungry for chocolate. She headed for the Pig & Whistle and a big chocolate sundae with whipped cream. The restaurant was not very crowded so she sat at the counter and ordered her sweet dessert. As she was about to pay for it, she noticed that her operator's license and social security card were missing from the silver purse. Then she remembered taking them out to get to the pearl pouch and the ring. She quickly recalled seeing the papers on the bed, back in her room. Inspecting the purse one more time, the Polaroid picture of her and Maggie alongside two-dollar bills were the only things that remained.

* * *

As the Cannon estate grew quiet, Franklin retired to his bedroom. The party guests slowly moved on to the new Café Trocadero nightclub over on Sunset Boulevard. What a grand party, he thought, removing his linen sport coat, shirt, and white trousers; nothing but the best. His diamond-encrusted pinky ring was a little tighter than usual. With a few extra twists, it finally slid off. He opened the lid of his jewel box with one hand and tossed the ring inside with the other. It made a hollow sound as it fell into the box. He lifted the lid once more and his eyes opened wide. He yelled, "Where's the pouch?" His heart began to race. Little beads of sweat dripped down his red puffy cheeks. "Where's my ring?" he roared. Pulling a velvet cord to summon help, he hustled out the door in his shorts and undershirt. "Gaylord!" he hollered. "Big Paulie! Where is everybody?"

By the time Franklin found his silk dressing gown, everyone was present and wondering what all the commotion was about.

Franklin poured a big glass of Johnnie Walker Black to calm himself. He disliked his heart pills and favored scotch as his preferred medicinal treatment for a bad heart. He settled into a large wingback chair beside the massive stone fireplace to face Gaylord, Big Paulie, and Jeff. "Where's my ring?" He demanded.

No one answered.

"You're nothing but a bunch of idiots. My ring and pearl pouch have been stolen." Franklin wiped his brow with a white linen handkerchief. "Did any of you see anything suspicious today?"

All three shook their heads no.

Franklin blew his nose into his handkerchief then wiped it using the corner bearing a delicately embroidered letter C. "You!" He glowered at his only son. "That Gertie was the last one to wear it. You must know where she lives? You brought her to my party."

Gaylord stammered, "I don't think she took it."

"Well, you don't think very well," Franklin sputtered, "do you?"

The three men stood in silence.

"Listen, Big Paulie, take that sniveling son of mine and get my ring back." White spittle seeped from the corners of his lips. "Jeff, you go with them."

"Let's look around the house first. No need to get crazy," Gaylord protested.

"You think I'm crazy, you son of a bitch?"

"No Father, I was only saying that—"

"Shut up! Get out of here. All three of you! And don't come back without that pouch!"

As they were leaving, Franklin signaled Big Paulie to come closer. "Teach that gutless boy of mine what it means to be a man. His mother raised him too soft. If that girl has my property, teach her a lesson too!" He lit a cigar. "Do you understand me?"

Big Paulie pulled his shoulders back to stand taller. "Don't worry, boss, I can handle it."

Franklin blew a puffy cloud of smoke towards Big Paulie's face. "You'd better."

When he heard the downstairs door shut, Franklin poured himself another drink, leaned his head back and closed his eyes. He didn't care about the ring. He only wanted the black pearl pouch. He thought about his trip last year to Paris, in the spring of 1946, when the jewelry had been acquired. With a heavy sigh, his thoughts drifted to Paris and the luxurious Hotel Meurice. The scotch slowly took effect and calmed his mind and body as he relaxed into the memory.

He'd entered the regal lobby of the grand hotel with a gift for his wife. Guilty of regular indiscretions, this purchase of an exquisite yellow diamond ring had been warranted. The diamond lay nestled within a beaded velvet pouch that he'd concealed inside the breast pocket of his custom-tailored suit coat.

Franklin's hands stroked the silk robe around his bulging stomach. He reached for another sip of his drink, then let his head fall back as he succumbed to a mild stupor.

Thanks to the discovery of oil on his 2000-acre Texas ranch twenty years ago, his fortune had allowed him to be a guest at the splendid Hotel Meurice, which had been THE place to stay among the travelling wealthy. Each year thereafter, on trips to the famous landmark, Franklin had encountered kings, sultans, presidents, and movie stars.

A sleepy grin grew across his face as he recalled his first visit to Paris, years earlier, in 1938, when he'd met Salvador Dali. Franklin rearranged his body into a more comfortable position in the fireside chair. The unusual artist, Dali, had been on his way to Coco Chanel's house on the French Riviera, to paint for a forthcoming exhibition in New York at the Julien Levy Gallery. Franklin recalled the artist's quirkiness and the many notorious parties Dali had hosted: extravagant and always scandalous. He snickered under his breath at the pleasant thoughts of the many women he'd partied with. They were quickly interrupted with a stinging memory that took him back, once more, to the same night he'd purchased the ring, in 1946.

He had thought his evening was going well until a disturbing telegram from Roscoe Hogan, his idiot foreman back in Texas, had been delivered to him. The message stated that four of his seven oil well fields had gone dry and a fifth was on fire. Franklin held his stomach, feeling nauseous again, even a year later, thinking of the devastating losses he'd incurred. His face moved in nervous twitches, then he snarled, "That incompetent Roscoe." Under his breath, he mumbled, "Idiot!"

He pulled the collar of his silken robe closer around his neck as he relived that fateful evening. Rain had pummeled the city of Paris and with the tragic news of his wells, he'd been forced to return to the jewelry shop. Cold raindrops, from the edge of the hotel's overhang, had fallen through a gap in his collar and run down his back as he'd entered a taxi. Monsieur Clevell, owner of the shop where he'd purchased the ring, was an old acquaintance and owed him a big favor. It was time to collect a debt from a reluctant business partner that might save him from ruin.

Cannon's body contorted and slumped even further as he reclined by the fire on his estate in Hollywood Hills. Half asleep, he raised his arm, extending it out and pointing across the room, as if directing the taxi driver back in Paris. "17 Le Chanteuse. Vite! Vite!" His breaths grew labored. Sweat beads appeared across his forehead as he yelled out from the safety of his mansion, "Clevell, you owe me. I want more diamonds…NOW!"

16

1947
HOLLYWOOD – LOS ANGELES

THE PIG & WHISTLE'S old clock struck 10 p.m. Gertie grabbed her silver purse and said goodnight to Eugene as he washed the glasses behind the counter. He had been very nice to her. There must be more people in Hollywoodland like him, she thought, and she was going to find them. It may take a little longer than she'd planned, but she'd stay where she was and become a star. Gertie smiled, thinking of the jewelry she'd stolen. She could sell it. The extra money would tide her over until she made better connections in the movie industry. Maybe even the woman from Chinatown, who'd sold her the silver mesh purse, would want to buy that back.

Gertie rounded the corner onto North Sycamore Street and stopped dead in her tracks when she saw Jeff's sedan making a U-turn under the streetlight by Miss Sylvia's. The car came to a stop in front of the stone steps. Panicked, she ducked in between the houses to the rear and hugged the fence line that separated the backyards from the alley. The wooden gate surrounding the rooming house creaked, but only for a second, as she moved as fast and as silently as she could.

Gertie flew up the back-porch stairs, into the kitchen and down the hallway. She noticed that Miss Sylvia was passed out in a parlor chair, an empty bottle of liquor lying on the floor beside her. The front door was still unlocked, as usual, for late guests. Gertie fumbled with the deadbolt trying to lock the door, hoping to delay the men who were no doubt looking for her and the ring. With no luck, she ran up to the third floor and found Maggie asleep. "Maggie, wake up!" she yelled.

The young girl moaned. "Gertie?"

"Get dressed. Maggie!"

"What?"

"Get dressed. Something awful is going to happen if we don't leave, now!" Gertie bent down to retrieve the pearl pouch from the bottom drawer.

"I don't understand." Maggie sat on the edge of the cot and rubbed her eyes.

Gertie sat next to her and placed the pouch in Maggie's hand. "Take it. Don't tell anyone I gave it to you."

Maggie's hand trembled as she took the ring out of the little bag and placed it in the palm of her hand. She stared at the yellow stone flanked by rows of beautiful diamond baguettes. "What should I do with it?"

There was a knock on the door.

Gertie whispered, "Take it back to the Cape, Maggie. Hide it. It's worth a fortune." She cupped her hands around Maggie's. "I've decided to go home with you after all. I'll follow you as soon as I can. Don't worry." She looked over to the door then back to her cousin. "Get in the closet. Keep quiet! Don't come out until I tell you to."

Confused, Maggie did as she was told.

Gertie smoothed the covers on the cot and looked around for anything that would hint that Maggie was still in the room. "Just a minute," she called out as she grabbed her identification papers from her bed and hid them in a drawer. Finally she pushed the suitcases under the bed.

The next knock was louder.

When Gertie opened the door, Big Paulie burst in with Jeff close behind. Big Paulie slapped her and then shoved her onto the bed. Within seconds, Gertie realized that the only way to save herself would be to admit to Cannon's henchmen that she took the ring and pouch, then convince them she could show them where the jewelry was hidden and somehow, try to escape.

They believed her.

Big Paulie held onto Gertie's elbow with gusto, practically pulling her down the stairway. "You better be taking us to where the boss's stuff is, girlie."

When Gertie's shoe landed on the last step, in the entranceway of the rooming house, she could see Miss Sylvia was still in the parlor. Now her landlady's arm hung down to the floor, her head tilted back, her mouth open. That doesn't look right, she thought. "What'd you do to Miss Sylvia?"

"Shut up." Big Paulie led her through the massive front door.

Once outside, they hurried down the stone steps towards Jeff's sedan.

Gertie could see someone in the backseat of his car. Maybe she could make a run for it. Eugene might still be at the Pig & Whistle. She pretended to trip and bent over, causing Big Paulie to lose his grip on her. She took off like a runner at the start of a race. Out of the corner of her eye, she recognized Gaylord, running alongside her by the curb.

"Gertie! Stop!" he yelled. By the time he'd caught up with her, he was out of breath. He grabbed her arm. "Stop! It'll be okay. Don't run! Just tell them where you hid it."

Gertie stopped and turned to her friend, panting. "Gaylord! You have to help me. You have to call the police. They're going to kill me."

Gaylord held her shoulders so she could see him. "Look at me. I won't let them hurt you."

Gertie could see Big Paulie rumbling closer. "Please help me."

"I will. Now come with me before they get angrier. We don't need the police."

Gertie reluctantly headed for the car with Gaylord.

Big Paulie intercepted their slow pace and with a gruff voice, he yelled, "Get out of the way, you pansy." He pushed Gaylord to the sidewalk and grabbed Gertie's elbow, dragging her more forcefully than before.

Jeff held the passenger door open on the sedan. Gertie leaned forward to climb into the back. Big Paulie lifted his foot and, with an angry kick, jammed it onto Gertie's backside. She lost her balance. Her body flew across the seat. Her forehead landed with such force against the chrome trim and glass plated window that her skull cracked. The young girl bounced back against the rear seat. Her head fell forward then lay to the side. Dark blood trickled down her face and cheek, onto the luxurious gray pinstriped material of Jeff's new car.

The three men stood on the street, trying to figure out what exactly had just happened to the girl.

Big Paulie wiped his brow with a white handkerchief. "Mr. Cannon ain't gonna like this."

Jeff cursed. "God damn it. My car is ruined."

Gaylord slid onto the backseat, next to Gertie. Her face was covered in blood. He felt for a pulse. There was none. He backed out of the car to the curb and turned to the two men. "You stupid idiots. Look what you've done. She's dead! My father will go crazy."

"What've we done?" Big Paulie stared at Jeff. "We didn't do nuttin'."

Jeff chimed in with, "Yeah, I saw YOU push her in the car. We didn't want to hurt her, only wanted her to show us where she put the jewelry."

Gaylord was stunned. "You can't do this to me!"

Jeff straightened himself. "Oh, yes, we can. Your father trusts us more than you."

"That's right. You know, little man," Big Paulie hurled a sarcastic grin at Gaylord, "I think your father'll be proud of you. We'll tell him that the girl tried to get away from us and you took care of it. You know, to get his property back."

"But I..." Gaylord started sweating.

Big Paulie put an arm around his boss's son. "Don't worry. We'll take care of everything."

Jeff questioned Gaylord, "Say, where's that friend of hers? The quiet one? Maybe she'll know where her pal hid the stuff."

Gaylord grew nervous. "Wasn't she up in the room?"

Big Paulie scratched his head. "Naw. I didn't see anyone else."

Gaylord liked Maggie and didn't want anyone to harm her. "I'll go in and find her for you," he offered, hoping to delay them until he figured out how to keep Maggie safe.

"Listen. Forget her. We gotta figure out what to do with that one." Big Paulie pointed at Gertie in the car.

"Let's take her over to Venice Beach," Jeff suggested. "No one will ever find her there."

"You mean that 'Slum of the Sea'?" Big Paulie laughed. "Got a shovel?"

Jeff opened the trunk to check. "Yep."

"Okay. Let's go." Big Paulie thumbed over his shoulder to Gaylord as he got in the front seat. "Get in the back with her."

* * *

The stench of oil and sewage hit the three men as they drove down Ocean Boulevard towards the Kinney Pier in Venice. Oil wells dotted the shoreline and pipes carrying sewage emptied out onto the beach and into the Pacific. At midnight, there was hardly any traffic or people around. The moon was out and the air stagnant.

"God, it stinks!" Big Paulie rolled his window up.

Gaylord held a silk handkerchief up to his nose. "What if we get stopped by the police?"

"Doesn't matter," Jeff said. "Your father has the Chief of Police in the palm of his hand."

"That's right," Big Paulie added. "Mr. Cannon will take care of it."

Jeff's car pulled off the road and onto the open field of sand dotted with tufts of grass and garbage. "This looks about right."

Big Paulie surveyed the area. "Yeah, looks good."

Jeff got out first and opened the trunk. He handed the shovel to Gaylord.

"What?! Me?"

"Yup, you!"

"But...I can't do this."

"My daddy won't like this." Jeff used a whiny voice. "He'll cut off my allowance. Boo-hoo."

"Oh, I can't get my fancy clothes dirty," Big Paulie mocked before he spat onto the ground.

"You'd better get started." Jeff leaned against the side of the car and offered a cigarette to Big Paulie. "We'll help you with the body when it's deep enough."

They waited for the boss's son to do their job. They thought the whole scene was amusing. They were in control tonight.

Gaylord took off his jacket and reluctantly began digging. He hated the two bullies. His father preferred them to his own son. With every shovelful, he grudgingly convinced himself to keep digging so that his monthly allowance of money for drugs would continue. Within the hour, his clothes went from soft white to ashen gray in the damp night air.

Now stripped down to his undershirt and pants, Gaylord finally stopped digging and hoped he'd gone deep enough. He crawled out of the hole and found Jeff asleep in the front seat. Big Paulie was finishing up his flask of bourbon.

"Got any left?" Gaylord's dehydrated lips were dotted with white blotches.

"Sorry kid. I'm all out. Almost done? It's getting late." Big Paulie got out of the car. "Well, looks like you're doing a good job. Your Daddy will be right proud of you." He slapped Gaylord on the back. "Let's get the body."

17

Present Day – Tuesday Afternoon
HOLLYWOOD HILLS – LOS ANGELES

I EXITED THE Roosevelt Hotel and hailed a cab back to the Georgian. When I landed in the back seat, I texted Jim: *Ask Natalie if Gertie Foster means anything to her.*

The streets of Los Angeles were hot and crowded. As the cab driver maneuvered through traffic, I kept glancing at my phone, impatient for Jim to respond. I decided he must be busy at the bar and thought about calling Stephen. He'd mentioned that he knew of an old recluse, Gaylord Cannon, who lived in Hollywood Hills. I wondered if Franklin Cannon was his father.

Jim finally responded: *Natalie has day off. I'll text her.*

When I got back to my room, I called Paul. "Just checking in. How's everything going?"

"Holding down the fort. No problems. Sold a big watercolor this morning." He sounded rushed. "Someone's pulling in. Might be a customer. Gotta go."

"Okay. It's just that I've been uncovering a lot of interesting information about who might've been buried next to Jim's apartment."

"Sorry honey. Call me later?"

"Sure."

"Never mind, it was just a turn–around. Nancy, what did you say?"

"Actually not much, when I think about it. Just some coincidences that I can't seem to ignore."

"Don't let your curiosity get the better of you. You're still having a pretty good time, aren't you?"

I laughed. "Of course I am. You know me so well. Now I'm getting another call. Love you and miss you."

"I miss you, too."

By the time I hung up, I saw someone had left a voice mail. It was Jim.

He said he was sorry, but he was really busy and didn't have time to text Natalie about knowing a Gertie Foster.

I only had a few more days in L.A. I called Stephen.

Within the hour, Stephen was out front in his blue BMW sports convertible. I slid in next to him. The last time I was in his car, it had been at night; now in the daylight, the wood-grained details across the dashboard looked luxurious. I greeted Stephen with a big smile. "Wow, P.I. work must be very profitable."

"Nancy, I'm so glad you called me." He slowly pulled away from the curb and headed towards the 405. "I woke up this morning hoping for an adventure, and sure enough, you called." Adjusting his sunglasses, he accelerated onto the highway.

The wind took my breath away and tore into my hair, but I didn't mind. We stopped dead after about a mile in the 4 p.m. traffic.

I used the stillness in the air to talk. "Like I said on the phone, I'm curious about the Cannon family. What did you find out?"

He turned to me. "Before I left my office, I did some searching and found the address of Gaylord Cannon."

"That's great!" After a few seconds, I added, "But how are we going to get in to see him? You said he doesn't talk to anyone."

"I've got an idea that should work. We're reporters from *USA Today*—"

"But you said he won't—"

"Let me finish." He laughed. "That's what I like about you Nancy, always curious." The cars moved at a crawl. He opened the glove compartment and pulled out two ID badges with *USA Today* on them. "Photoshop is like magic, isn't it?"

I smiled as I admired the professional look of the badge with my name on it.

"Okay, here's some backstory. This Gaylord character collects cars, and not just any car, but rare ones. It's his passion, according to a radio interview he gave about ten years ago. He's got a rare 1956 Austin Healey 100M."

"What's so special about that?"

"They made 640 of them and only 190 survived. It's news if someone has one in good condition."

"You did all this in forty-five minutes?"

"I do have an assistant, you know."

"Now I understand why you're so successful."

He flashed me a handsome smile. "I work hard because I love it."

"I hope I don't screw it up. I've never gone incognito before."

He touched my hand. "You'll do just fine."

*   *   *

At 5 p.m. we stopped in front of a large wrought-iron gate. Stephen pushed the white intercom button. "*USA Today*. Stephen Parker to see Mr. Gaylord Cannon."

I started to question the last name. Stephen held my hand, so I stayed quiet. The gate opened and we drove onto the winding driveway.

"Goodness, this is really nice," I said, taking in the sprawling estate. The grounds on either side of the car were a little unkempt, but still beautiful.

"Just remember, you can still call me Stephen, but my last name is Parker. Okay?"

"No problem." I grinned at the thought that I was going to be a part of this exciting charade.

I noticed huge empty planters flanked the once-white marbled entrance and a few of the steps had cracks running across them. "It must have been beautiful back in the day."

We stopped at the top of the steps in front of stained glass windows that graced each side of the grand door. A large green section at the bottom of one window had a missing piece.

Stephen looked at me. "You okay?" His eyes were a soft blue, just like Paul's.

"Absolutely," I answered with confidence. I figured that Stephen would do all the talking. I'd pretend I was his secretary and not say anything.

We took a few steps forward and Stephen rang the doorbell. We waited several minutes before the door finally opened.

A short, dark-complexioned, elderly gentleman stood before us. "May I help you?"

Stephen quickly responded. "Yes, we have an appointment with Mr. Gaylord Cannon. We're from..."

The door closed. We looked at each other with quizzical expressions. The door opened again. "You may come in. Follow me."

The butler took us past a magnificent curved stairway and into what looked like a library. He turned and left us standing there and then closed the doors behind him.

The room felt stuffy, as if it hadn't been used in years. "So now what?" I asked, catching glimpses of framed photos across the top of a small bookcase featuring people from the '40s. I went over to look at them more closely. The clothes and poses were very glamorous. As I studied the faces in the frames, I noticed there was something strange about their eyes. Some of the women looked docile, even sad. A few of the men wore stern expressions. As I wandered toward a mahogany desk I felt a chill, yet no windows were open. "This place gives me the creeps."

Stephen was looking at a painting above the fireplace. He read the nameplate: "Franklin Cannon."

I hurried over to where he was standing. "Wait! What'd you say?"

"Franklin Cannon."

I stared at the portrait. The man pictured in front was dressed in a white suit with a red ascot tied around his bulbous neck. To his side was a small gold eagle atop a shiny black walking stick. His sausage-like fingers held onto the bird replica, its wings spread as if in flight. Behind him, in the background, on a baby grand piano, were three Motion Picture statuettes and one trophy with a gramophone on it.

"That's the guy in the old newspaper," I whispered. "Look at the movie paraphernalia around him." I stepped back to view it again. "People liked to depict their favorite things in their portraits as far back as the Middle Ages."

Stephen started to talk, but was interrupted by the door opening.

Gaylord Cannon held a black cane and walked with an air of sophistication as he entered the room. He resembled his father's portrait with his white suit and red ascot, but this Cannon was thin, toned, and sophisticated in an old Hollywood way.

"Mr. Parker," he said as he took a seat behind the mahogany desk.

"Good afternoon, Mr. Cannon," Stephen returned the greeting.

Cannon swept his free hand toward a couple of chairs. "Please sit down."

We both took a seat in front of the desk.

"My butler said that you were from *USA Today* and were interested in my collection of cars?"

"Yes. That's correct," Stephen answered without taking his eyes off the old man. "We are particularly interested in the Austin Healy 100M."

"I see. I beg to differ with you on that point, Mr. Stephen Boudreaux."

Stephen sat back.

"Surprised? Your true identity was known as soon as you made the appointment with me." Cannon produced a smug smile. "I have many connections."

My hands started to perspire. Stephen looked calm, but my heart was beating like crazy.

Stephen put his notebook away. "You're good."

Cannon rubbed the palm of his hand against the gold eagle ornament atop his cane. "I have lived in Hollywood a long time. May I call you Stephen?"

My pretend partner nodded.

"You interested me, Stephen. I was curious to know why you wanted to see me."

I watched the two men in awe as they began to pit themselves against each other.

"I have many sources, Stephen, as I am sure you also have."

Stephen nodded again. This time he returned a sly grin.

"So, why are you really here?" Cannon focused on my cohort and ignored my presence.

I felt left out. My tenacity began to rise to the surface. I quickly interrupted, "I wanted..."

The old man gave me a furtive glance.

"I mean, WE wanted to know if Franklin Cannon was your father?" I looked over to the portrait. "Of course, while we were waiting, we discovered that fact by ourselves."

"And who might you be, young lady?" Gaylord Cannon turned his head to stare at me.

His look frightened me, but not enough to shut me up. "Nancy Caldwell. Does the name Gertie Foster sound familiar?"

Gaylord showed no expression, but I noticed his hand squeeze the top of the cane. "What was the name again?"

"Gertie Foster." I stared him right back. Out of the corner of my eye, I could see Stephen lean back and seemingly enjoy watching me in action.

"That name is not familiar. I'm an old man, Ms. Caldwell. My memory is not what it used to be."

He appeared to me to be cognizant of everything around him and, by the reaction of his hand on the cane, knew more than he was telling. "That's interesting, Mr. Cannon, because I have recently come across a 1947 L.A. Times news clipping of your father with his arms around a young woman. Her name was Gertie Foster."

Gaylord's hand grew tighter around the eagle's golden neck. I could see his knuckles turn pale. "My father was friendly with dozens of up-and-coming starlets and, let's say, a few ladies of the night. I was not privy to all of his doings."

I kept my stare on him. "Are you sure you've never heard that name before?"

"I'm positive. Now, if you'll excuse me, I need to attend to more serious matters." He stood and headed for the door. His cane swung ahead of him with jerky movements.

Even though we were strangers in his house, I was still stunned by his rudeness. Stephen and I stayed glued to our seats as he walked past us, then we swiveled around in our chairs in an attempt to follow him out the door.

Before he took his leave, he stopped, turned, and shook the tip of his cane at us. "If you two imposters are not off my property in five minutes, my butler has permission to call the police. I will not hesitate to press charges that both of you are trespassing and tricking an old man, with the intention of robbing him." With that he was gone.

Stephen stood up. "Well, that's that. Shall we leave?"

I stayed in my chair. "He's lying. He knows something."

"He may very well know the name, but at this moment, we need to go." Stephen held his hand out to me.

I refused his gesture and got up by myself. "Okay, I'm leaving, but I'm not through with him yet."

"Maybe so, but we have to get off his estate."

The butler was in the hallway, holding the front door wide open.

I walked up to him with a sheepish smile and asked if I could use the ladies' room. Pretending to look helpless worked, because he led me to a door under the stairway. Before I entered the small powder room, I caught a glimpse of the back of the house. The edge of a swimming pool was on my left and a golf flag from a putting green waved in the wind to my right. "I'll be right there, Stephen. You can pull the car around."

I closed the door behind me and then opened it a crack to watch the butler disappear up the stairs. It was my chance to do a little snooping.

The entranceway was decorated in simple furnishings, one painting and a few small palms. I took a closer look outside. There were three golf flags and the pool was bone dry. Scrub, bougainvillea, and large palm trees bordered the property. Nothing unusual for southern California. I turned to leave, but decided to peek behind two closed doors.

The first led to the kitchen; the second was locked. It was then I noticed a thin line a short distance from the locked door. It went from the top of detailed crown molding down to the floor. I recalled seeing this kind of secret door in an old mansion back in Ohio. Its edges did not interfere with the artful design of the walls any more than necessary. I placed my hand on one side of the line and then the other, gently pushing in a few times. My last push opened into a small room with very little light inside. I heard someone coming so I backed out of the room and away from the wall. It was the butler. With a smile, I blinked my eyes and in a sweet voice said, "Thank you so much. You're very kind."

"You're welcome, miss."

My heart was beating fast as I hurried outside and down the stone steps. Stephen was waiting inside his car in the cool early evening air. "Thanks for putting the top up. It's getting chilly." I slid onto the front seat. "God, that was so awesome."

"I thought you would appreciate it."

"Oh, my goodness, I felt like I was in a movie, with all the intrigue and pretending to be someone else." I leaned over to give Stephen a quick kiss on his cheek. I quickly sat back and stared at the floor of the car, surprised at my impulsiveness "Sorry. I guess I'm a little keyed up." I looked at him out of the corner of my eye.

He was grinning from ear to ear.

"What's so funny?" I asked.

"Nothing. It was fun for me, too." He started the car. "I did a little poking around and found some great looking cars in the garage. There was a beautiful mint-green convertible, from the '40s, parked right in front of the garage door window. Boy, it was sweet!"

I clipped my seat belt. "Well, I did some snooping too and found a secret door in the hallway. What do you suppose is behind it?"

"Could be a lot of things," Stephen said as he turned out of the driveway. "Maybe a wine cellar, an art collection, or something special that the owner wants protected from curious eyes."

"You mean like mine?"

"You guessed it." He turned on an Ella Fitzgerald radio station.

"Do you mind if we take a little detour before I drop you off at the hotel?"

"No problem. I'll probably be awake for most of the night anyway."

"Great. It's a favorite beach of mine." We headed for the coast.

18

Present Day – Tuesday
LOS ANGELES

THE MOON LIT up the whole sky above the coastal highway as Stephen pulled into a parking area close to the beach.

"Want to walk a little?" he asked in a gentle voice.

I couldn't resist and grabbed my scarf. "Absolutely."

We passed a few strollers along the sandy shoreline and then stopped to admire the glistening water. I turned around to see the twinkling lights from the mountains behind us. "I want to thank you, Stephen. I had a wonderful day. It was quite exciting."

We walked a little further on the beach until he stopped to point out an image that was halfway up the mountainside. I felt his arm around my waist. "See those three lights in a row and that green one next to them?"

"Uhhh. No." I squinted to see where he was pointing.

He leaned closer to my face. "Right below that big square picture window."

"Oh, I see it now. What is it?" His face was still near mine. I could smell his pleasant cologne.

"That house belongs to a very famous client of mine."

"Who?" I turned to look at him.

At that moment it seemed as if he wanted to kiss me. But he didn't. I wondered what I would have done if he did.

He laughed. "I can't tell you."

I lightly slapped him on his shoulder. "Oh, for heaven's sake. Who is it?"

"I don't know." He pulled me nearer to him. "I just wanted to get close to you. Nancy, I can't get you out of my head."

I didn't know what to say. "Stephen, we shouldn't be —"

And with that, he kissed me. I didn't stop him. His kiss was passionate, warm, and gentle. It made me feel like a teenager again. I didn't want him to stop. I put my arms around him and returned the kiss, almost hoping to encourage him. His kiss felt mysterious and inviting, making my whole body tremble. Suddenly I stopped short. My head filled with images of Paul and Stephen all at the same time. What the hell was I doing? I was a married woman with five children!

Stephen hugged me. "Nancy, I was hoping for this to happen."

I stared at the tiny lights reflecting across the mountain range and could feel my eyes start to tear up as he pulled me tighter to his chest. I didn't want to push away.

"I'm falling in love with you, Nancy."

I felt a tear roll down my cheek as my heart beat faster. "I can't do this," I whispered in his ear.

He leaned away from our hug. "What'd you say?"

"I can't do this, Stephen." I pulled back from him even further.

Our eyes met. I felt ashamed. We turned and walked along the edge of the water in silence.

On the drive back to my hotel, Jim texted me. *Natalie's mother sent email, I forwarded it to you.* I slowly put my phone away, unable to decide if I should let Stephen in on Jim's news. It was probably nothing. I decided to keep it to myself, considering what had just happened between us.

"I'll be leaving in a few days." I stared ahead on the road before us. "I want to thank you for making me realize, that as a woman, I'm still desirable. You've been such a gallant friend to me. I won't forget you."

"I'm going to miss you." Stephen kept glancing at me as we drove down the highway. "It's too bad we didn't meet under different circumstances, or in another time."

Any romantic notions about Stephen slowly simmered as strong feelings for Paul rose to the top. I knew in my heart, Paul was the only man in my life and would always be. "Stephen, I'm married to the most wonderful man there ever was." I looked over at him. "You know, I think he'd like you."

We pulled in front of the Georgian. As I got out, I said, "As far as this whole thing about the dead body and Cannon, maybe it's one mysterious occurrence I should just let the local police handle." I waved goodbye and then climbed the stone steps of the hotel.

Upstairs in my room, I couldn't stop thinking of what had happened on the beach. As I cleaned makeup off my face, I came to the conclusion that I shouldn't berate myself. After all, I'd never been with any other man besides Paul. I've always been faithful to him. One little kiss is not that terrible and I never went any further with Stephen, even though I was close to allowing it.

After undressing for bed, I opened the email that Jim had forwarded to me.

Hello, Nancy,

Natalie said you were interested in any information about her family, especially around the late forties. She explained to me that Jim had found a picture of two women next to the remains of a body (how terrible) and that Natalie resembled one of them. Well, I was curious also. There are several boxes from my mom, after she passed away last year, which I haven't gone through yet. Her name was Ethel Foster before she married my father. She was pretty quiet about her past after she relocated to New Hampshire from Cape Cod. It was only a short time after she moved here that she met my dad, married him, and then had me. Whenever I asked her questions about her past she would start to cry, so I stopped asking. I've attached two pictures for you that I discovered in a journal of hers. I don't recognize anyone, but one woman does look a little like my Natalie. Maybe you could send a copy of the picture Jim found so that I could compare the two? Hope this helps.

If I find anything else that is interesting, I'll email you. If you have any more questions, I'd be happy to answer them, if I'm able to.

Natalie's Mom...Marie

I opened the two attachments and couldn't believe what I was looking at. The first picture was almost an exact copy of the image that Jim had found in the old mesh purse, except for a slightly different pose by the two women, who were standing in front of Grauman's Chinese Theatre. The second photograph showed the same two girls and a short man with glasses. He was dwarfed between them, his arms around their waists. He wore a bellman's cap and a loose fitting uniform jacket. I looked closer. They were posing in front of the Georgian Hotel. I got up to get a drink of water and wanted to tell someone, anyone.

Jim was not answering his texts; he must be working, and I felt it was too late to call Stephen. Paul had gone to bed hours ago. Frustrated, I finally landed in bed sometime after midnight. My mind was racing a mile a minute, but I still fell asleep.

On Wednesday, the next morning, I woke with only a shred of regret. So what should I do now? I asked myself. Call Stephen? Show him the pictures? Stay another few days? Go back to the Cannon estate? Tell Paul about the kiss?

I got dressed and looked for coffee. Get yourself together, I told myself, as I walked across the street and stared out at the Pacific. Get back to what makes you tick. Solving mysteries.

The water was unusually calm and a mist was evaporating in the mid-morning sun. As I leaned against the rock wall that wound itself atop the Santa Monica cliffs, I went over what I already had discovered. So far I'd found a 1947 newspaper picture and the woman in it looked like the woman in the picture that Jim had dug up. The old news clipping labeled her as Gertie Foster.

Jim's friend, Natalie, resembled the woman and Natalie's mom had sent me pictures she'd found in her late mother's things. Her name before marrying was Ethel Foster. The email images from Natalie's mom, and the photo that was dug up, plus the newspaper all have the same woman in them. She had to be Gertie Foster and

Natalie was related to her. Gertie and Ethel have the same last name of Foster. But how does Gaylord Cannon fit in? He's the right age to be around in the forties, and his father was also in the old news clipping with Gertie.

I made the decision to go back to the Cannon estate and ask some more questions. I ordered another coffee to go and said I'd pick it up on my way out. As I passed the reception desk, I inquired with the concierge if he knew of any employees who might remember the hotel back in the forties or fifties.

"No, I don't. You're the first person to ever ask me about 'Old Hollywood'. Most hotel guests want to know about Hollywood today."

"Really? You'd think if they stayed at the Georgian, they would like the elegant feeling of old Hollywood and be curious about it." I turned to take the elevator. "Thanks anyway."

He called after me, "Come to think of it, there is someone you could talk to, but I'm not sure if he's here today. He was a janitor at the hotel for years, but he recently took a bad fall and now he's retiring."

"Do you have a way for me to contact him?"

"Let me see." The concierge went into another room, then re-emerged. "Sasha said his son is cleaning out his office, down in the basement. You could talk to him."

"Awesome. Thank you. How do I get there?"

"Just go down the hallway, through the door on the right, then follow the stairs to the basement."

The dented, gray metal door had CUSTODIAN written across it. It was dark on either side of me as I pushed it in slowly. A single lit bulb hung from a cord over a big workbench towards the rear of the room. A short man wearing jeans and a Hawaiian shirt had his back to me. I cautiously approached. "Hello there."

He turned around. "Can I help you?"

I walked closer. "I was wondering if I could ask you a few questions about your father? They said upstairs that you're cleaning out his things."

"Yes, I am. What's your question?" He opened a small drawer on the bench and sifted through its contents. I watched as he occasionally threw things into a big trash barrel and tossed other items into a cardboard box on the bench.

"How long did your father work for the Georgian?"

"I think he started in '47."

I kept glancing across the corkboard that was attached to the back of the workbench. It was filled with handwritten notes, letters, newspaper clippings, and pictures. The sheer volume of information kept pulling me nearer to read the words on the papers. I tried not to seem too nosey, but I couldn't help myself. "Will he be coming back here to the hotel?" I tilted my head to read some of the yellowed letters.

"Nope. He broke his ankle. He's not doing so good."

"Oh. Sorry to hear that." My eyes drifted back to the board. I spotted the corner of an old yellowed picture peeking out from under a business letter.

"Why do you want to talk with him?" he asked.

"It's kind of a long story, but I found a picture of some people back in 1947 standing in front of the Georgian." I pulled out my phone and showed him what Natalie's mother had sent me. "See the man wearing a bellman's uniform? Since your father worked here so long, I thought I could ask him a few questions and maybe he could identify who these people are."

He looked closer at the picture. "That's my dad in the uniform, but I don't recognize the others."

My heart skipped a beat. "Could I talk with your father? Does he live close?" I was finally getting somewhere.

"He lives in Venice Beach, but I'm not sure if it's such a good idea for you to see him. His head isn't so good these days."

I pointed to the corner of the picture that was peeking out from under the letter. "May I take a look at this?"

"Go ahead. I'm probably going to throw it out anyway." He threw some more papers into the trash and then swept his hand over the desk. "Be my guest. Maybe you'll find what you're looking for in all of this mess."

I lifted the corner of the faded letter and my eyes opened wide. The faces of two familiar women stared back at me, along with the young man who wore the bellman's cap, standing in front of the

Georgian Hotel. It was the same picture as on my phone. "This is your father again, isn't it?"

He stopped throwing things away and squinted at the picture. "Oh yeah. That's him too."

"What's his name?"

"Harry Gibson."

I moved to the other side of the corkboard and reached my hand up to an old news clipping. "You're okay with me snooping around a bit?" I was getting really excited and hoped I would find more clues to identify the second woman.

"No problem. Help yourself. It's all just a bunch of crap as far as I'm concerned." He returned to casually tossing rusty key chains, rubber bands, bottle openers, and scraps of yellow post-its into the trash.

The clipping showed his father holding the hotel door for Clark Gable with a date of 1950. At the top of the board, I spotted a lumpy white business envelope that was held up with a red pushpin. Before I examined its contents, I picked up one of the pens from the clutter, found a scrap of clean paper from the trash and wrote down Harry Gibson.

Inside the envelope were more faded photos of people in silly poses in front of an old classic convertible. My hand began to perspire as I realized that most of them looked familiar to me. At the bottom of one photo was scrawled the names Gertie, Maggie, Gaylord, and Blanche. Gaylord and Gertie popped right out at me. The man in the photo had to be Gaylord Cannon.

19

1947
HOLLYWOOD – LOS ANGELES

THE CLOSET WAS dark. A faint hint of mothballs hung in the stagnant air of the close quarters. Maggie, still crouched on the floor with her head resting atop her knees, had dozed off while waiting for Gertie's signal that it was okay for her to come out.

Her shoulders began to sway to one side as she slowly fell deeper into sleep, finally falling over with a smack into the wall; it woke her with a start. The beaded pouch slipped away from her lap and fell to the floor. She reached for it, then listened for any sign that someone was in the room. Everything seemed quiet. Maggie put the ring back into the pouch and stood up. With a soft push of the closet door, she cautiously stepped out into the small room. Gertie was gone. Now what? Both beds were made. There were a few wrinkles in the bedspread, but nothing more.

Where was her suitcase? Maggie looked around and found it under the bed. She kept her grip on the black pouch as she retrieved the case; her clothes were still neatly folded inside. It was 1:30 a.m. She quickly got dressed. The thought of leaving Gertie behind seemed unforgivable, but Maggie was desperate to get away from Hollywoodland. Gertie had, after all, promised she'd follow when she could.

Maggie looked in her purse for Harry's number. He would drive her to the train station. She hurried downstairs to call him. As she turned the corner, by the newel post, she saw Miss Sylvia reclining in her chair. Was her landlady drunk again? It didn't matter. Maggie had to head home for Cape Cod.

Harry's voice sounded sleepy. "Hullo?"

"Harry? It's Maggie."

Startled, he asked, "What's wrong?"

"I need you to take me to the train station. Now."

"I thought you said to come by around noon?"

"I know, but you need to come now."

"Everything all right, Maggie?" His voice became tense.

"Yes. Can you come now? Please, Harry. You must pick me up. I'll be waiting against the stairs in the bushes.

"In the bushes?"

"I'll explain when you get here. Please, hurry!"

Maggie hung up and crept over to the parlor's archway. Miss Sylvia's mouth was wide open and her eyes closed. "Miss Sylvia?"

No answer.

She spoke a little louder. "Miss Sylvia?"

Maggie glanced at the open door, expecting Big Paulie and Jeff to reappear at any moment. Should she call the police? No, she decided, Harry said it wouldn't do any good; besides she'd seen old Mr. Ellis back on Cape Cod drunk on his front porch many times. Miss Sylvia looked just like him. The frightened girl turned on her heels and bolted up the stairs to gather her things.

Grabbing her return train ticket from on top of the dresser, she stuffed it into her purse along with the jewelry pouch and scribbled a note to Gertie: *Please hurry home. Be safe. See you soon, Maggie.*

After placing the note in Gertie's undergarment drawer, Maggie fled with her suitcase down the stairs and out the front door.

Huddled in the dark, among the large shrubs that flanked the stone steps to the big rooming house, Maggie felt like it was an eternity before Harry pulled up in front. She didn't give him a chance to get out and open the door; she was by the curb in an instant and threw her suitcase into the back. She slid onto the seat next to Harry. "Oh, thank you. I was so frightened."

Harry, dressed in a thin jacket over his undershirt and trousers, had a glazed look on his face. "What's wrong?"

"Cannon's men came to see Gertie tonight and I think they took her away."

"What do you mean, took her away?"

"I'm not sure what happened. All I know is that I need to leave and Gertie said she would follow me." Maggie was afraid to tell Harry about the ring for fear he wouldn't take her to the station. He was still a friend of the Cannon family, so she stayed quiet about it.

"Tell me what went on?" Harry drove quickly down the deserted streets.

"I don't remember everything." Maggie didn't like to lie, but this was different.

"All I know is that Big Paulie hit Gertie. Hard!" Maggie's hand shook as she clutched her purse. "Before the men came in, Gertie said I should hide in the closet, and she would follow me home to Cape Cod when she could."

Harry cocked his head sideways. "I don't understand."

Maggie was beginning to have second thoughts about keeping the ring and pouch. Gertie must have stolen it. That's why the men came. If she returned it, maybe Gertie would be all right. She yelled out, "Harry! Take me back to the Cannon estate."

Harry pulled over to the curb. "What?"

"You must take me back there."

"Why? I thought you wanted to leave?"

"I do. But first I need to make things right. Please turn around."

Harry was willing to go along with whatever Maggie asked.

Maggie could see Jeff's car was parked in front of the main steps of the Cannon house. "Park back here, will you Harry?" She pointed to a short distance behind Jeff's car. Maggie got out, holding her purse that contained the pearl pouch and ring. "Don't worry. I'll be right back."

Maggie was still in his view as Harry lit a cigarette. He kept watch and was prepared to help her, if she needed him. He pulled out a small revolver from the glove compartment, just in case.

The Cannon estate was dark, save for one light above the outside door. Maggie crept alongside Jeff's car. There was enough light to reveal the cracked rear passenger window. She looked inside to see the darkened stains on the grey upholstery. Pulling back, Maggie said a silent prayer: *Please don't let this have anything to do with Gertie.* From somewhere inside the mansion, she heard dull popping sounds. Her intentions to return the ring quickly disappeared from her thoughts. She was more frightened than ever. Another round of the same sounds startled her again. She ran back to Harry.

At the sight of Maggie running towards him, Harry flicked his cigarette out the window and started the car. "What's goin' on?"

Maggie slid in as fast as she could. "Let's go, Harry. Take me to the train station. I'm finished here."

When the car pulled up to the station, Maggie looked over to her friend. "Harry, I just want to tell you that you've been absolutely wonderful. I mean, about not asking too many questions. I think something bad has happened to Gertie. I'll call you if she doesn't make it to Cape Cod. Maybe you'd be able to find her and let me know."

"Of course I will."

Maggie's hand shook as she grabbed her suitcase. "She'll probably follow me home soon. I know Gertie, she can take care of herself." She prayed again that Gertie was safe, wherever she was. She slammed the car door and leaned into the window. "You know where you can reach me. I need to go now."

Harry solemnly nodded his head.

Maggie turned back only once to watch Harry drive away and wondered what Harry was thinking about. Then she disappeared into the terminal.

* * *

Donny Jackson pulled his car into the back alley behind Miss Sylvia's. He had played only one set to the small crowd at the supper club. When he was finished, he'd joined some of his friends at the Café Trocadero until 3 a.m. His bed and a good night's sleep called to him as he lugged a large black leather case, containing his sax, up the back-porch steps. As he walked through the kitchen and down the hallway, he tried to avoid hitting the wall with the edge of the case. He rounded the corner of the stairway, noticed Miss Sylvia, and then the unlocked door. He dropped his sax and hurried over to his landlady's body. With his training as a medic during the war, he could tell right off that she was dead. Donny called the police and then sat on the stairs. It was 4 a.m. by the time they arrived.

* * *

Four hours later, Franklin Cannon enjoyed his breakfast out on the patio as usual.

Gaylord sheepishly came out to greet his father. "Good morning, Father." The young man looked terrible.

Franklin never broke away from his stare at the newspaper. "Son."

Gaylord stood against the stone wall and looked out at the lawn.

Franklin took a drink of his coffee. "Big Paulie and Jeff told me all about what you did."

Gaylord turned to face him. "They did?"

"Yes, before they turned in. I'm very proud of you. It seems that you finally became a man last night. Showed respect for me." Franklin slid his chair away from the table.

Gaylord ran his fingers through his hair in a gesture of relief that his father had not heard the gunshots.

Franklin slowly removed his linen jacket, placed it on the back of his chair; then he moved closer to his son. He placed his arm around his shoulders. "Yes, very proud."

Gaylord smiled. His mother would have been proud of him, too.

Franklin turned to face him. With his open hand, he hit Gaylord across the face with such force that his son fell backward against the other patio chairs. "But you're still an idiot," he yelled. "Now we'll never find my jewelry."

Gaylord lay on the ground. He wiped away blood from the corner of his mouth and tried to stand.

Franklin calmly put his jacket back on, took a deep breath and returned to his breakfast. Once he settled himself, he said, "That ring was a gift to your mother. God rest her soul. I gave it to her last year in Paris."

Gaylord tried to talk. "But I didn't do any—"

"Shut up! I'm not through with you." Franklin opened his paper to the funnies. "That ring meant a lot to your mother. She wore it all the way home across the ocean when we sailed from Europe. And the pouch, well, that was icing on the cake. That was my favorite."

"But I didn't kill the girl. Surely you'll believe your own son over two stooges?"

"The topic is closed. As for you, Gaylord, you need to find a way to get me my property back." Franklin took the last bite of a thick piece of bacon. "And until you find the ring and the pearl pouch, you're cut off from any money and from my source of those drugs you're addicted to."

"But Father, you can't do this to me. If mother was alive, she never would let you do this. I need—"

"Enough. Your mother was too soft on you. Your days as a momma's boy are over."

Gaylord seethed. He wanted to kill the old man.

"I have an early morning meeting with your friend, Blanche."

"Blanche?" Gaylord struggled to stand up straight.

"Yes, Blanche. I am in need of a leading lady. No thanks to you!" Franklin turned around as he left the patio. "Have you seen Big Paulie or Jeff this morning?"

"No, Father." Gaylord smoothed the sleeves of his sport coat. He wished he could see the look on his father's face when he found them dead. His mother would have been pleased; she'd also hated the two bodyguards. He missed her. She had always taken care of him and was there whenever he needed her. He should kill the old man right now, or maybe tonight in his bed.

Franklin headed inside the mansion. "Well, if you see either one of them, tell 'em to come to my office as soon as possible."

Gaylord's posture changed as his father went out of sight. His shoulders sagged as he thought about having no money. With a nervous twitch, he remembered he might still have some cocaine left in the bathhouse. It had been a long night, a very long and exhausting night. But he wasn't too tired to search for his magical white powder.

Gaylord reached between the mattresses in a spare bedroom of the pool house and pulled out a folded white pillowcase. Within it lay a small, flat, cotton pouch filled with cocaine. It wasn't much, but it was enough for him to feel like a hero once more. Before he indulged himself, he made sure his Colt .45 was wiped clean and hidden inside the rattan chest, under the bath towels.

Franklin found Juan in the kitchen cleaning up from breakfast. The house servant said he had not seen the two bodyguards. Curious, Franklin climbed to the top floor of his estate to search for Big Paulie and Jeff. It was unusual for them not to make an appearance by mid-morning.

He knocked on Big Paulie's door. "Hey, you in there? Big Paulie!" He banged on the door again and then entered the bedroom. Big Paulie lay in bed, surrounded by a pool of blood and pillow feathers. Franklin's hand covered his mouth as he cringed at the gruesome sight. He immediately left for Jeff's bedroom.

Flinging open Jeff's door, Franklin found the same horrendous scene. "Awww, Jeff." He fell against the dead body and began to wail. "Who did this to you?" He reached for Jeff's pale hand as tears wet his cheeks. "You were like a son to me." After several minutes of weeping, Franklin stood up to cover the bloodied head of the man he'd taken under his wing when no one else would, twenty years ago. His grief slowly twisted into rage.

On his way to find Gaylord, Franklin stormed past the kitchen and told Juan to go home for the day. "I'll call you when I need you!" he barked.

The door to the pool house was ajar. Franklin rushed inside only to find his son sprawled across the couch in a daze. Franklin grabbed him by the shirt and pulled him to a standing position. "Get up! I need your help!"

"What? What's going on? You're hurting me."

Franklin let go. "Big Paulie and Jeff are dead." He quickly turned around and yelled, "Follow me!"

Gaylord swallowed hard. He shook his head, trying to clear the effects of the drug. He needed his father to think he was there for him, under any circumstances.

The two men hurried up the stairs to the crime scenes. First they rushed into Big Paulie's room. Gaylord scowled. "Don't worry, father, I'll find out who did this." He put his arm around the large man's shoulders to comfort him.

Franklin twisted away. "Leave me alone." He left for Jeff's bedroom.

Gaylord followed, reminding himself to be smart and strong. Things would be different now.

He knew Jeff was a favorite of the old man. A troubled teenager from Texas, with no family, Jeff was feisty and could fight his way out of any problem. Franklin had admired that and hired him on. Jeff had followed him to Hollywood, along with Big Paulie, where they'd both become the old man's right and left hand men. "Poor Jeff." Gaylord leaned in over the body and lifted the sheet. "He was a good guy."

Franklin sat down on one of the upholstered chairs. He took a cigar from an inside pocket and lit up. He stared at the floor in silence.

Gaylord stood by the bed and waited to see what his father's reaction would be.

Finally Franklin spoke, "We have to clean this mess up. No police." He looked over to his son. "You understand?"

"Of course."

"Good. The first thing you need to do is get out back and start digging."

Gaylord's eyes opened wide. "Me? By myself?"

"Yes. I'll stay here and try to figure out who might have done this."

"But Father—"

"No buts! Got any ideas about who might have something against these two?"

"I've heard that Jeff and Big Paulie were selling drugs on the side with your connection in Chinatown, that Cheung guy."

"Maybe so," Franklin said as he blew a long stream of smoke into the air. "I'll do some checking on it myself. Maybe call in a few markers for information." He stood up to leave. "I told Juan to go home." As he stepped into the hallway, he turned around. "Burn anything that looks like it might be evidence. Make me proud of you, son. I don't want any police or reporters coming around here. Got it?"

"Yes, Father. I'll take care of things from now on." Gaylord smiled at the mention of the word *son* from his father's lips, but his hatred for the two men still lingered. Maybe now his father would think differently of him and reinstate his allowance.

After stealing Big Paulie's switchblade and wrapping his body in the blankets, Gaylord left for Jeff's room. He gingerly flipped the sheet away to reveal another semi-nude body and sickening bloodied head. He took Jeff's pocket watch from the bed table and slid it into his pants pocket next to the other grizzly memento of a satisfying night's work. He wrapped Jeff's corpse in a coverlet, carried it down the stairs, and dumped it into a wheelbarrow. Then he went back upstairs to get Big Paulie's body. He transported both of them to the back of the house, where he began digging two graves. Jeff's hole, he laughed to himself, will be much smaller than Big Paulie's. The idea didn't escape him that he was becoming quite an expert on the disposal of dead bodies.

20

1947

HOLLYWOOD HILLS – LOS ANGELES

IT WAS DUSK by the time Gaylord finished his gruesome job of burying Big Paulie and Jeff. He found his father in the office talking on the phone to Blanche. Gaylord stood by the door to listen.

Franklin was breathing heavily into the phone. "I know, I know you were supposed to be picked up this morning, but a few things came up. I'll send a car for you tomorrow. I have important business to tend to first." He hung up.

Gaylord entered; his clothes dirty and hands smudged with dirt. "Everything's taken care of, Father." He took a seat in front of the desk.

"That's good, son." Franklin reached for his glass of Johnny Walker Black and waved Gaylord away.

The tired young man stood to leave. "I'll be in my room."

"I suggest you clean yourself up, boy. We'll talk tomorrow." Gaylord was almost to the doorway before his father added, "I need you to pick up Blanche in the morning and bring her here."

"Yes, Father. Whatever you say."

As Gaylord climbed the stairs to his bedroom, he reassured himself that his life was going to be better. His father was finally delegating some business responsibilities to his only son, as it should be. Of course, if approval and respect didn't come soon enough, he could wait. The old man wouldn't be around much longer.

The following morning, Juan was back in the kitchen making breakfast. Gaylord felt on top of the world as he pulled his mint-green convertible out of the garage and headed for Blanche's apartment. His father was finally paying attention to him and he was picking up the love of his life. Gaylord knew that Blanche would be very grateful for the offer of a leading lady role. Very grateful, he thought, and grinned all the way across town.

By mid-morning, Franklin was still on the patio enjoying a leisurely breakfast of a quarter-pound of bacon and four eggs. He scanned the edges of the grass in front of him and thought his boy did a good job. No trace of any disturbance upstairs or outside. He took the final sip of his coffee as Blanche and Gaylord joined him.

Blanche wiggled her way across the patio stones to give the producer of her newest film a kiss. "Good morning, Franklin dear."

Gaylord stood back and wondered why she needed to do that.

Franklin never looked away from the *L.A. Times* sports page as Blanche took a seat opposite him. "I'll be with you in a minute."

Blanche fidgeted with her skirt.

Gaylord moved behind his girlfriend and placed his hands on her shoulders. "Father, I wish you'd stop reading your paper. Blanche is waiting."

Franklin looked over at the two of them, then focused back on his paper, slowly and methodically turning to the last page before he stood up. "I'm through here now. Come, my dear Blanche. Shall we go to my office?" He held his hand toward Blanche, then glanced at Gaylord. "We don't need you. And we don't want to be disturbed."

Gaylord pursed his lips as he watched them exit the patio and disappear into the main house. He took a deep breath to calm himself. All in good time, he thought.

The office door remained closed for most of the afternoon. By 2 p.m., Gaylord was impatient. He quietly turned the door handle and peeked in to see his father lying on a settee in his underwear, socks, garters, and shoes. He then saw Blanche, over by the window, straightening her nylons. All she had on was her slip. Gaylord's body stiffened with rage. He closed the door, leaned back against the wall and clenched his hands into fists. He then ran outside to the pool house and slammed the door behind him. Pillows and bedcovers flew into the air as he upturned the mattress to claim his cocaine; his reward for not killing anyone. But his rage could not be calmed. He paced. He lay on the bed trying to quiet his fury. He paced again, only to find himself looking for Blanche.

He remembered his first kill as he walked alongside the edge of the illuminated pool. Gaylord pictured the woman's body in his head. Was it the drugs or his anger that had pushed him beyond his limits that night? He was never sure, but she shouldn't have made fun of him. He whispered to himself, "The bitch shouldn't have called me a momma's boy."

He reached for the door of the main house. Every son loves his mother, he thought. Besides, that whore was like all the rest of those kind of women, always bringing trouble. And now his Blanche had become one of them.

A gust of wind chilled the air and blew leaves onto the marble floor as the door opened. A similar wind had blown cold across the empty lot back in January. He unconsciously rubbed the palm of a hand on his pants. He would need to wipe the blood from his hands tonight, once more. He and his friend had used gasoline-soaked rags to clean up the last time. Then they had shoved everything into a duffle bag along with the victim's purse.

He shook his head. What a shame he had had to burn everything including his clothes: $100 wing-tip shoes, a $200 Dior jacket and trousers, shorts, undershirt, all were thrown into the mansion's burner. He called to mind standing naked, watching the rush of flames burst against the glass window of the metal door until everything burned to ashes in the fiery hot belly of the iron oven.

Tonight his father was out, as usual, playing poker until early morning. He would be alone with Blanche. As he climbed the curved stairway to the second floor searching for her, Gaylord could hear the groaning of the furnace pushing heat through the pipes and vents of the manor house.

* * *

Harry Gibson took a ride to the Cannon estate after working his shift at the Georgian, with hopes of getting some answers from his friend about Gertie. His car pulled onto the estate at around 9 p.m. When he didn't see Mr. Cannon's car, Harry assumed the old man must be gone for the night.

He knocked on the door. No one answered. He knocked again. Nothing. Maybe Gaylord was in the pool house.

Harry walked around to the back of the house and found the French doors ajar, couch cushions on the floor, towels strewn across chairs, wine glasses shattered, and nylon stockings hung on a small palm plant by the window. The disarray suggested to Harry that either some good sex had been enjoyed, or someone was very angry. He headed out to the pool where he noticed a flicker of light in the darkness, coming from the edge of the woods by the golfing greens. Harry then heard the distinct sound of shoveling.

As he followed the digging noises, Harry called out, "Gaylord? Is that you?" The noise stopped. "Gaylord? It's me, Harry." Creeping closer to the light, Harry paused when he recognized his friend who was throwing dirt into a hole. "What're you doing?"

"None of your business."

Harry leaned into the black opening to see the outline of a woman with blonde hair half covered with dirt. "Oh God, Gaylord. That's not Blanche, is it?"

Gaylord resumed shoveling dirt over the woman's body. "So what if it is?"

"You'll never get away with it."

"I had to do it, Harry. I thought she loved me. But she was just like that other one." Gaylord jammed his foot against the shovel and picked up a huge mound of dirt. He threw it at the head of his beloved Blanche. "I'm almost done here. Get a shovel from the shed and help me finish."

"No, Gaylord, I don't want to get involved in this." Harry began backing away.

"You don't have a choice." Gaylord never looked up at Harry as he continued to load his shovel with more dirt and throw it across the body's impression. "Don't you remember, Harry? This past January? You were right alongside me when we both, may I remind you, we BOTH did something we shouldn't have done." Gaylord was breathing heavy now. "Go and get a shovel!"

Harry helped Gaylord smooth the loose soil and hide the fresh crumbly surface with leaves and old palm fronds. The last thing he said to Gaylord as he left was, "I'll keep quiet about all of this. But if I'm taken down, you'll come with me. I want nothing more to do with the Cannon family. Understand?" Harry then backed away from his childhood friend and said his final words to him. "I never want to see you or your father again."

As he drove home, Harry couldn't stop thinking of poor Gertie. Could Gaylord have killed the girl? God only knows what he was capable of, especially after Gaylord told him that Big Paulie and Jeff were also dead. Maybe he'd even killed them. Look what he did to Blanche. Harry hated to think about it.

* * *

The next morning, Franklin Cannon finished his breakfast and retired to his office. Gaylord slept late.

By one o'clock, Franklin was tired of calling Blanche's apartment with no answer. He went upstairs and pounded on Gaylord's door. "Gaylord! Get up!" He grew impatient and burst into the bedroom and dragged the covers off his sleeping son. "Gaylord! Get out of bed. Go over to Blanche's place and see why she's not answering my calls."

Gaylord rolled over. "Not now, Father." His words were slow and mumbled.

Franklin grabbed Gaylord's leg and pulled him onto the floor. "Get over to Blanche's. Now!" He stormed out of the room, only to meet Juan in the hall.

"Excuse me, Mr. Cannon. Richard Thompson from the studio is on the phone and he doesn't seem very pleased."

"I'll take it downstairs."

Franklin's face was beet red as he flung his portly body into his desk chair. "This is Cannon. What do you want? I know shooting starts in two weeks. My leading lady seems to have disappeared again." He tapped his fingers on the glossy oak desktop, as he listened impatiently to the irritated voice on the other end. "I'll let you know tomorrow."

He slammed the phone receiver down onto its cradle just as a pain shot through his chest. He couldn't breathe. Pushing himself up out of the chair, he leaned against the wall for support as he struggled over to the bar. After pouring a glass of Johnny Walker, he gulped half of it down, then reached for the armrest of his fireside chair.

Gaylord sauntered into the office.

Franklin leaned back in his chair and rubbed his heart. "It's about time you showed up." His face was pale. "Why the hell haven't you left for Blanche?" His breath became labored. "And, God damn it, I want my jewelry back." He winced as he continued to rub his chest and sip his whiskey.

Gaylord poured himself a drink and sat by the fireplace, opposite his father. "What's so important about that stupid ring?"

"It's not stupid. You're the one who's idiotic." Franklin hung his head low, his eyes closed.

"Well, I don't know where the ring is and I don't intend to go out of my way to find it for you." Gaylord finished his drink in one gulp. He didn't want to listen to anyone, anymore, especially his lecherous old father. He was his own man.

Franklin found enough strength to pound his fist against the armrest. "Listen, you sniveling brat, I don't care about the ring. I want the beaded pouch." He felt another sharp pain. It doubled him over and he rolled onto the floor. Lifting his body up on one side, he reached out his hand to his son, "Gaylord! Get my pills."

Gaylord quietly watched his father stretched out on the floor in front of him.

"Gaylord! Please! My pills." In a final effort, Franklin lifted his head and pleaded, "Gaylord, please..."

Gaylord got up and slowly poured himself another drink. As he returned to his chair, he picked up an orange bottle of pills and placed them in front of his father, but not close enough for Franklin to reach his life-saving medicine. "Old man, you should've treated my mother with more respect, and you shouldn't have soiled

Blanche for me. Now you must pay for your sins." He leaned back on the cushioned headrest to watch his father squirm and twist for each painful breath.

After his father lay still for several minutes, Gaylord stood up and felt for a pulse. Leaving the office, he quietly closed the door behind him. He waited for a few seconds, re-opened the door and yelled, "Juan! Come quickly! It's Father! I think he's had a heart attack!"

21

Present Day
HOLLYWOOD HILLS – LOS ANGELES

I HAD NO idea how I was going to get inside the Cannon estate, but I would figure it out on my way there in the taxi. Settling myself in for the ride, I reached into my backpack for my phone, only to discover I'd left it back at the hotel room. I remembered putting it on the bed right before I went to the bathroom. The excitement and anticipation of confronting Cannon again must have distracted me. I checked my purse once more. I had my wallet, sunglasses, the white envelope holding the photos I'd found on Harry Gibson's workbench, and my room keycard. I secretly wished I had my pepper spray. Gaylord Cannon may be elderly, but he still made me nervous.

Approaching the hills of Hollywood, I criticized myself after every mile for forgetting my phone, instead of thinking about what my excuse was for returning. After the taxi pulled up to Cannon's gate, I got out and stood by the intercom, counted to three and then pushed the button.

"May I help you?" a voice answered.

"Uhh...you may remember me from yesterday. I'm Nancy Caldwell."

"Yes. I remember. Mr. Cannon is not available to you."

"I realize that, but I...I think I may have lost one of my earrings. I used the powder room and that's probably where it fell out."

"Please stay by the gate. I'll take a look."

I quickly yelled into the speaker. "Could I come in?" The wait for an answer seemed like an eternity. I gave the taxi driver a smile. He didn't seem to care about my niceties because the meter was running.

A voice came back. "I'm sorry, miss, but I could not find anything."

"Please. Those earrings belonged to my grandmother and I'm just devastated to think I've lost one of them. They mean so much to me. Please let me in? I won't be long."

A few more seconds passed before the gates began to open. I jumped back into the car and we drove down the long driveway. At the entrance to the mansion, I asked the driver if he would wait for me. He nodded.

I could see the door was open as I ran up the steps. The butler stood aside as I passed him. "Thank you. You're so kind. What's your name?"

"Donald."

"Well, Donald, I'll just be a minute." I pointed to the powder room under the stairway and hastily headed towards the small door. I closed it behind me and then opened it a crack to see if he was watching. I heard him going up the stairs and took my chance to see what was behind the secret door. If I couldn't talk to Cannon himself, at least I could find out what he was hiding.

I pushed the wall in at a few places. After only seconds, I was inside the room. The two night-lights near my feet gave off a small glow. I patted the wall for a light switch and found it. Surrounding me, on three sides, were shelves holding fifteen to twenty shoeboxes on each wall. The front of every box had a numbered year and one or two letters written with a black marker. To my left, and on the top shelf, was a box labeled 1947/ PK+JS, another box read 1947/ BJ and then it went to 1948. I glanced to my right and saw 1951, 1952, and so on, with only a few gaps in the years. Out of the corner of my eye, I spotted a box on the bottom shelf with the date 1980. The last box was dated 1992. As I was about to look inside one of the shoeboxes, I heard the phone ring in the hallway. I quickly flipped the light switch off and pulled on a small handle to open the door.

The hidden door silently sealed itself closed behind me. I stood in the hallway for a few seconds and took a deep breath. As I passed the office door, Cannon appeared and stood between the front door and me; blocking my escape.

"Mr. Cannon! I know I shouldn't be here, but Donald was kind enough to let me in to look for my lost earring. I'll be leaving right away."

"Donald!" He yelled up to the balcony.

"Yes, sir." The butler came running down the steps.

"I gave you specific instructions to NOT let these people in."

"I'm sorry, sir. The lady had lost an heirloom from her dear grandmother."

"Grandmother? A likely story. Correct me if I'm wrong, Ms. Caldwell, there is no lost earring, is there?"

All I could come up with was, "What do you mean?"

"You did not have earrings on when you last visited me."

"But I—"

"You forget, Ms. Caldwell, this is Hollywood and fashion is everything. Just because I'm an old man doesn't mean I don't notice what people are wearing."

"Forgive me, Mr. Cannon. I really need to talk with you one more time before I leave Los Angeles." I pulled out a tissue and whimpered a few fake sniffles. "I'm very sorry. It's just that it would mean so much to me if I could only find some answers."

"Oh, for God's sake, woman! Come into my office...and stop that sniveling."

Cannon took his seat behind the desk and I sat on a mahogany armchair in front of him.

He rubbed the top of his cane. "I'll give you five minutes."

I pulled out the envelope I'd found back at the hotel, and spread the pictures out so that Cannon could look at them.

He leaned in closer over the desk.

"I happened to come across these old photos from a man named Harry. He worked at the Georgian Hotel in Santa Monica. Do you recognize anyone?"

Cannon looked at each one slowly, taking his time, but also wasting away my five minutes.

"Take a look at this photo of four people." I pointed to the names written at the bottom. "One person is identified as Gaylord. Is that you?"

"Well, it seems that my memory is not what it used to be, but I actually do remember that day." He leaned back in his chair. "It was sometime in the late forties. Yes, that's me. It says Harry under the other man, but I can't for the life of me recall his last name."

"Would it be Gibson?"

"Maybe it was, but I'm afraid I don't know anything about the two women." He leaned in again and put a well-manicured finger on the picture to study it. "Gertie and Maggie?" He sat back. "I vaguely remember those names. I believe they were friends of this man, Harry Gibson. That's probably why I didn't recognize the name of the woman you asked about during our last meeting." He leaned over the desk to take another look at the photos. "What was the name again?"

"Gertie Foster."

He stared at me. "Why are you so interested in these people, Ms. Caldwell?"

"My son, who recently moved to L.A., was digging a patio next to his apartment, in Venice Beach, when he found some remains and this photograph." I pointed to the copy of the photograph showing the sterling mesh purse and Gertie and Maggie standing in front of Grauman's Chinese Theatre. "Two different pictures, but the same two women."

Cannon took out a linen handkerchief and swiped at his nose. His hand was shaking. "Do you practice law, or are you in the police business, Ms. Caldwell?"

"No."

"Then I believe you should let the local police handle this matter."

"Yes, I suppose so."

Cannon crossed his leg, leaned an arm over the armrest and placed a hand under his chin, as if he was bored.

"There's something else." I looked directly at him. "These two women appear in several other pictures that I've found. One of them just happens to resemble a girl my son knows, right here in Hollywood."

He cocked his head slightly.

"She called her mother, back east, to ask about distant relatives and whether the name Gertie Foster was familiar to her. So far, there's really no concrete connection between any of these people and my son's friend except…maybe you, Mr. Cannon. You're in the photos with these women."

His knuckles turned white as he gripped the top of his cane. "You say your son found the bones of one of these women?"

"Well, I'm not certain who it is, but I believe the police are testing them to make sure they're human bones."

"I hope you're not insinuating that I had anything to do with her murder?" His face grew more intense as his eyebrows furrowed.

"Mr. Cannon, I never said the woman was murdered."

He stared at me. In a terse voice he announced, "Ms. Caldwell, your five minutes are up, and I need to rest." He stood up aided by the shiny black cane. "Where did you say you lived?"

I never mentioned where I lived and kept my answer vague. "New England."

"Then I suggest you get going, because you have a long trip home ahead of you. Donald will see you out."

I waited for him to leave the room before I stood up. I was disappointed in Cannon's lack of cooperation. Maybe I could go back to the Georgian and see if Harry Gibson's son would allow me to visit his father. I may even have to stay a few more days in L.A.

Donald held the door open once more for me to exit. I flashed a quick smile goodbye. "Thanks, Donald. Here's my card. Just in case you happen to find that earring or anything else you might think would be important that I should know about."

22

Present Day
HOLLYWOOD HILLS, LOS ANGELES

GAYLORD CANNON spent most of the afternoon in his office. The last thing he did was make a phone call to a long-time business contact, Margaret Cheung.

"Lotus Blossom Antiques, may I help you?"

"It's Gaylord."

"Yes?"

The old man's voice sounded strong. "I need a favor."

"Is there a problem? Your delivery should be arriving after five today."

"Yes, I'm aware of that. I have something else I need you to do for me."

Margaret waited in silence.

"There is an elderly man called Harry Gibson. According to my sources, he is located on Venice Beach and has lived there for most of his life. Pull from your special sources for this one. I want no connection to be found with me after it's done. Understand?"

"Certainly. Give me the details."

Margaret Cheung pulled out a black journal, placed it on top of a glass-enclosed counter that was filled with ivory trinkets and oriental jewelry. She wrote down Gaylord's instructions.

This was a fairly simple request from a business associate who'd supported her mother and her family for years with generous amounts of cash. As always, she was happy to help him.

23

Present Day
LOS ANGELES

BACK AT THE hotel, I was so happy to see my phone on top of the bed covers. It was like I'd found a long-lost friend. I had two voice mails and ten text messages, mostly from Jim and Paul, one from Stephen, and one from his secretary. She said Stephen was going to be out of town for a few days, but I could try his cell. Paul sounded eager to talk with me and had some news. Jim texted he was anxious to meet with me before I left California.

I called home first. "Hi, Paul, sorry I didn't get back to you. I'd left my cell up in the room. I'd gone to visit with—"

Paul interrupted me. "I've got some exciting news." He sounded like a little kid with a big secret.

"What is it?"

"Brian called this morning."

"And?" Now I was anxious.

"He's getting married."

"What?" I sat on the edge of the bed.

"Yes, he and Patty want to get married at our house, in two months."

"I can't believe it. Why so soon?" It doesn't matter; Patty's such a nice girl. I began to think about becoming a mother-in-law, what it meant for them to use our house, and whether the house would even be ready in time to host a large group of people.

"They got jobs as traveling nurses in Alaska. They want to go as a married couple."

"Oh, my God, Alaska?"

"Yup. We've got a lot of work to do when you get home."

"I'm meeting Jim in an hour, to say goodbye. He'll be surprised to hear about his brother getting married. I'll call you tomorrow."

Time was of the essence. I wanted to speak with Stephen before I left L.A., but right now Jim was the most important person I needed to be with. I knew I might not see him again for a while; except maybe for his brother's wedding. We'd probably have to fly him home. Jim couldn't afford anything extra; he was barely making it with all of his part-time jobs as it is. I called and told Jim to meet me at my hotel at 6:30 p.m. and that if he would find a good restaurant, I'd treat for dinner. He said no problem.

As I packed for my flight, which was leaving the next day, I half expected a call from Stephen. Even as I got dressed to meet Jim, I kept checking my messages. He must be making up for lost time in his PI business, I thought. Spending a few days with me on a whim and a wild goose chase had been generous of him. Of course, I now realize why he really stuck around. Maybe he's no longer interested in me since I said no to him. I wondered if I'd ever see him again. I felt torn between his helping me to solve a mystery and how I was going to act in front of him after that stupid kiss.

* * *

Jim's choice of a wonderful taco restaurant with seating right on the boulevard was delightful. I was introduced to fish tacos, not wrapped in a taco, but in lettuce. Outstanding! We laughed as Jim ordered himself a beer. It was the first time he'd ever ordered a beer in front of me.

The noise from all the other patrons created a din that made it difficult for us to talk. Jim wasn't that surprised to hear about Brian and Patty. He thought they were a good match. Of course, I tried to tell him about my last two days with Stephen, Cannon, and Harry Gibson's son, but it was only on the walk back to the hotel that I was able to explain all of the things in detail that convinced me that Natalie's family and Gertie were connected and that Gaylord Cannon was the link within the mystery.

"Mom, you're something else," Jim said with a smile.

"What do you mean?" I knew what he meant; I just wanted to hear it.

"Well...you're so curious and determined." He put his arm around my shoulders. "That's a good thing."

I laughed.

"I hope that when I reach your age—"

"What do you mean, my age?" I was still laughing.

"I mean, when I get to be your age, I want to be interested in life just like you are, and still be challenging myself."

"You're a good son, Jim. I don't think you'll have a problem with those goals."

As we reached the hotel, I became melancholy about saying goodbye to my oldest child.

Jim gave me a big hug. "Don't look so sad. If you're paying, I'll be at Brian's wedding. You can count on it."

He disappeared out the front door and back into his L.A. world filled with fun, opportunity, and plenty of work. The next morning, I was headed home to Cape Cod and also a lot of work. We're having a wedding!

* * *

I arrived at LAX a few hours ahead of my flight, checked my baggage, and looked for a cup of coffee. Clouds were rolling in, but no rain was forecast. Once at the gate, I took a seat to read the latest *L.A. Times* that someone had left on the bench. Nothing unusual, the same tired words from politicians and which movie stars were caught doing something they shouldn't be doing. In the criminal activity log, which I find interesting to read, was a small listing about a local Venice Beach character whose home had been robbed, resulting in his death. The man's son had found him on the kitchen floor. According to the police, the home was broken into through a locked window, but what may have been stolen was not disclosed. I almost choked on my coffee when I read that the victim's name was Harry Gibson.

I quickly called the one person who might understand the importance of this information. "Stephen, I finally got a hold of you."

"Sorry. I've been a little busy with some cases that have been on my desk for too long." He sounded reserved and business-like.

"I'm leaving L.A. today, but I couldn't let some news slip off my radar."

"What's going on?" He asked in a more animated voice.

After an explanation of how I got pictures from Natalie's mom, met Harry Gibson's son, paid a visit to Cannon by myself, and the coincidental death (at least I thought it was) of Harry Gibson, I waited for Stephen to answer. I hoped he'd be on the same page as I was.

"What exactly do you want me to do?"

"Go back and question Cannon again, or go to your police connections and run the whole scenario by them. Ask them what they think." I quickly added, "It's too coincidental for Harry Gibson to be killed the day after I mentioned his name to Cannon. I feel almost responsible for his death. After all, I told Cannon about him."

"Nancy, you can't possibly blame yourself for this guy's death. You'd also better be careful; you can't go around accusing people of murder."

He sounded like he was scolding me, but Stephen was right. "I still think that old man in Hollywood Hills is hiding something. I just know it."

"Nancy, I'm only a few minutes away from the airport. Maybe we could meet for coffee?"

"No. I don't have much time before I board." I secretly thought phone conversations would be best right now.

"Okay then, let me make a few calls to the police to see if they've found anything new about the remains Jim found. Then I'll go from there."

"Thanks, Stephen. I really appreciate it."

"No problem. Anything else?"

"Don't you think the hidden room I found was weird?"

It was good to hear him laugh. "I guess so. But we don't know what's in those shoeboxes. People collect strange things all the time."

"My flight is starting to board. I'd better go. Oh, can Jim call you if he has any questions about this?"

"Sure."

"Say, if you go back to the Cannon estate, make sure you say hi to Donald, the butler, from me. He was very nice."

"IF I go back." Stephen laughed again.

"Well, I'm off to become a wedding planner. Wish me luck."

"Good luck, Nancy."

It was nice to end on pleasant words.

24

Present day
HOLLYWOOD – LOS ANGELES

CLOUDS CONTINUED to blanket Los Angeles as Stephen hung up
the phone. He held it for a few extra seconds. A smile slowly grew
across his face just as his assistant entered his office.

"Someone special?" she asked.

"Could be, but probably not. Patricia, would you please get me
Jimmy Fredericks on the phone over at Pacific Division and find me
Gaylord Cannon's number?"

* * *

Gaylord Cannon got settled in his office and waited for his breakfast.
The patio was always his first choice, but not today; the forecast was
for grey skies and maybe a small chance of rain. It hadn't rained for
over a month and most people in L.A. wanted rain. Cannon stayed
inside; he did not like to get wet.

After serving Mr. Cannon his standard fare of one egg, two
pieces of bacon and rye toast with jam, Donald returned to the
kitchen. He had found employment at the Cannon estate after his
wife died a year earlier. Childless, and widowed at fifty, he
appreciated the good salary and large bonuses that Gaylord Cannon
provided. These generous payments were intended for Donald to

look the other way in regards to all of Cannon's activities. The butler was happy to oblige and stayed passive with all of Cannon's requests, even accepting the scheduled weekly deliveries of cocaine and the Tuesday night visits with young women. None of this bothered Donald, who thought it must be the drugs that kept the old man going. His employer was in great shape for an eighty-year-old man, and Donald was confident he would last into his nineties. The longer Cannon lived, the more money he would make for his retirement plans on a Caribbean island.

Donald poured himself a coffee and sat by the granite counter, waiting for the hour to pass so that he could clean up after breakfast. Maybe he'd take a look inside that secret room. The Caldwell woman hadn't noticed him up on the balcony, watching her exit the room during her last visit. He'd been aware of the room since he'd moved in last fall, but after nine months, his curiosity had reached a point of no return. Now he wanted to see for himself what was in there. He quietly left the kitchen, listened for any movement from Cannon's office, and then pushed in on the secret door.

* * *

Cannon stirred his coffee, opened the *L.A. Times* and checked the police log; a favorite ritual to start his day. Years ago, the results of his disturbing activities had been listed regularly, but there was never a mention of his name as the perpetrator. He always relished reading: *Investigations continue as to who may have been involved in these strange disappearances. Foul play is suspected.*

This morning, Cannon felt a spark of excitement to read that Harry Gibson had been found murdered in his home. It was invigorating to know he still had power over someone else's life. Hungry for another piece of bacon, he took a sip of his coffee, then called out, "Donald!" Impatient, Cannon stood to grab his cane. He really didn't need the extra support, but he enjoyed the pompous swagger that the black stick gave him. "Donald!"

The cloudy skies had made the house darker than usual. He headed towards the kitchen, but stopped short when he saw a faint light coming from under the secret door. Without hesitation, he entered his private room.

Donald spun around; in his hands was an open shoebox. He turned ashen gray.

Cannon stood quietly and stared at the intruder to his inner sanctorum. "Donald, what are you doing in here?"

"I'm sorry, Mr. Cannon." Donald quickly closed the box and replaced it on a shelf.

"I thought I told you to never enter this room."

"I realize that, sir. I don't know what all of this is and I certainly won't tell anyone about it."

"No, I don't think you will."

Donald relaxed a little. "You have my word, sir."

"That's good to hear." Cannon stood a little taller. "Donald, would you be so kind as to hand me the box marked 1968, behind you, towards the bottom?"

"Yes, sir." Donald turned and bent over to reach for the shoebox.

Cannon lifted his heavy cane and whacked Donald across his back. The butler fell to the floor. The old man reached down and rolled Donald over onto his back. With a twist of the gold eagle on top of the cane, a six-inch blade appeared at its tip.

Donald's eyes slowly opened to see the end of a knife enter his heart with such force that he never had time to scream out.

Cannon stood over the butler, his heart pounding. He pulled out his handkerchief and wiped the tip of the blade clean. Twisting the eagle, the deadly weapon disappeared back into its secret hiding place. Before he exited the room, Cannon emptied Donald's pockets. He only found a brown leather wallet, a tissue, and Nancy Caldwell's business card. After stuffing them into his jacket pocket, he headed towards his office.

He stopped by the sidebar for a snifter of brandy before he picked up the phone to dial for help.

A voice came through the earpiece. "Lotus Blossom Antiques."

"Margaret?"

"Yes?"

"Cannon here. Find me two able-bodied men who know how to hold their tongues." He casually opened Donald's wallet and examined the driver's license, social security card, some charge cards, and a few twenty-dollar bills. "They must be willing to do whatever is asked of them. I pay very well, as you know. Tell them to bring their suitcases. I may need them for a longer time than usual."

Nancy Caldwell's business card stood out on the desk. Cannon placed his finger on it to examine the words more closely. He then picked up the card and brought it nearer to his face as he kept talking. "I trust that you will find what I request as soon as possible? I have a little matter that needs to be cleaned up here at the estate."

Margaret spoke calmly. "Of course, I'll get right on it, Mr. Cannon. I'm thinking of two men, right now, who will be suitable for the job. It will be my pleasure to accommodate you."

Cannon dropped the card on his oak desk. "Margaret, you remind me so much of your mother, God rest her soul."

"You are so kind to think of her."

"That little matter of Harry Gibson was nicely taken care of. Thank you." He hung up, snatched Caldwell's business card off the desk and leaned back in his chair.

25

1947
CAPE COD

MAGGIE FOSTER left her seat on the train only a few times each day during her week of traveling from California to New England. Franklin Cannon's ring and pouch were in her purse, which she never let out of her sight. Mulling over the events of the last few days, Maggie concluded that she should have never left Gertie.

With just enough money for one meal a day and a single phone call to Peter, on Cape Cod, she waited until mid-week to ask the porter which stop would be the longest. He replied that she would have plenty of time to make a phone call when the train stopped in New York.

They reached the New York station by mid-morning on Sunday. Maggie hurried onto the platform for the nearest pay phone and quickly deposited the exact coinage requested by the operator. She hoped Peter would pick up.

"Peter?"

"Maggie?"

Maggie's voice trembled. "I'm coming home early. Can you pick me up in Hyannis tomorrow night?"

"Sure. Is everything okay?" Peter inhaled a deep breath.

"I'm fine. Please don't tell anyone you're picking me up."

"Why not?"

She hesitated. "I want to surprise my parents."

"Okay, when does the bus get in?"

"It'll be late...around 10 p.m."

"Is Gertie with you?"

Maggie chewed at her nails. "Uhhh...no. I'll explain when I see you."

"Stay safe. See you soon."

Nighttime in the village of Hyannis was usually quiet after 10 p.m. Peter arrived early; he didn't want Maggie waiting alone at night. He pulled his truck opposite the depot and watched several busses dispatch passengers.

Taking a sip of coffee from his thermos, Peter noticed two men leaning against the ticket office wall. When he saw the approaching headlights of Maggie's bus, he threw his remaining coffee out the window, got out of the truck and stood outside with his arms crossed in front of him.

The driver unloaded suitcases as passengers disembarked. The two men never moved to greet anyone as Peter walked closer. He gave them a quick glance and recognized one of them as Sam Donavan. They had gone to high school together. Sam never had a kind word for Indians, especially Peter. He didn't know the other man.

Maggie was the last to leave the bus. She ran to Peter and wrapped her arms around her friend. "I'm so happy to see you!"

Straight-faced, Peter pulled her arms away, grabbed her suitcase and whispered, "Keep close to me until we get to my truck."

"What's wrong?"

Peter held her elbow and ushered her past the two men who were now approaching them from behind. "Just keep walking." He opened the passenger door for Maggie and tossed her suitcase into the back of the truck. He handed her his keys. "Roll up the windows, lock the doors, and keep the engine running."

Maggie followed his instructions, getting more frightened by the minute.

Sam and his buddy got closer. "Hey! Soaring Eagle. What the hell are you doing with her?"

As Peter positioned himself a safe distance from the truck, he noticed Sam was holding something in his hand.

"What do you want, Sam?" He stood with his legs apart, fists clenched, ready to defend himself. He had no weapons but his sheer strength and a keen sense for defense. He had beaten Sam in fights in high school and felt he could do it again, if necessary, even if it was two against one.

Sam carried a wooden club and planted himself a few feet away from the truck while his friend stayed to the side.

Peter swiveled his eyes back and forth between them.

Maggie cowered in the front seat.

"I asked you what you're doing with a white girl?" Sam tapped the wooden club on his open hand.

Peter held back his urge to throw the first punch. "I don't want any trouble from you."

Sam signaled to his friend, then they both stepped closer.

"Take it easy," Peter warned.

Sam swung his club. It was a miss, and it threw him off balance. He fell to his knees.

The other guy rushed from behind Peter and managed to hit him with both fists across his back, knocking Peter to the ground.

Sam regained his balance enough to stand up; then, he kicked Peter in the stomach. "When I ask you a question, I expect an answer." Sam threw another violent kick at Peter's mid-section.

Peter didn't move as he lay in the dirt, but he wasn't completely out. From the corner of his eye, he saw Sam heading for Maggie in the truck. He couldn't breathe and his gut hurt, but he stumbled to his feet. Sam's buddy was hovering close to the driver's side, trying to get in. Peter knew Maggie was trapped. He zeroed in on Sam first, grabbed him by the shoulders, spun him around and landed a hard right to his jaw. The bully went down.

His buddy rounded the truck's hood, rushing to Sam's aid. The frightened look on Maggie's face kept Peter fighting. He threw another hard right and the second man went down.

Maggie quickly unlocked the passenger door. Peter collapsed on the seat. Within seconds, she gunned the gas and the truck took off, almost hitting Sam's shoes as he lay in the dirt.

Adrenalin raced through her whole body. Just missing a trash barrel on the side of the road, she managed to set the wheels straight on the tarred road ahead, anxious to get as far away as possible from the depot in case Sam and his accomplice followed them.

Glancing over to her dear friend, she couldn't tell if Peter was breathing. She wanted to pull over. But where? Then she remembered Peter had told her about the desolate woods, near the depot, where he would sometimes run. When she saw the entrance to the woods, off Mary Dunn Road, she pulled in and drove the truck down the rutted, dirt road until she felt they were safe enough to park. "Peter? Are you okay?"

Peter's face winced from pain. "Maggie, are you hurt?"

"Of course not. You're the one who got beat up." She turned towards him.

Peter managed a smile. "I've been through much worse. I'll be fine." He sat up straighter and looked over to her. A full moon filtered through the trees and lit up his face, revealing a small drop of blood that dripped from the corner of his mouth. "I'm so sorry you got involved in this...all because of me."

Maggie cried out, "You're bleeding. Oh, Peter." She used her handkerchief to wipe the blood away.

He took hold of her wrist and pulled her close to him. "When I saw those two thugs going after you, I wanted to kill them. Maggie, I..."

Their eyes met. Peter slowly caressed her hair, then his lips touched hers in a soft kiss.

Maggie pulled back, but not for long. She quickly felt a spark of desire. It ignited a passion she had never felt before. Her heart exploded with a longing for Peter. She leaned closer and then moved her body across his lap to face him.

Peter sat back against the seat and began to unbutton her blouse, losing himself in her beauty.

Maggie knew it was wrong, but she didn't stop his hands. Her thoughts repeated that they could never be and that she should stop him, but she ignored the sensible Maggie and let Peter's fingers move under her skirt and between her legs. Her whole body said yes, pushing her excitement further and further.

Maggie's anticipation of what was about to happen blinded her from everything around them. She could only see Peter's handsome face as she kissed him over and over. Peter was slow and gentle, accepting everything she offered to him. Maggie found herself in a dizzying sexual frenzy. She felt as if she was falling into a deep hole filled with pure pleasure, and she didn't care about anything else.

Peter never stopped himself from discovering Maggie's innocent body. He had waited for this moment for so long. He never wanted it to end.

The two lovers finally became one. The consequences of their actions were buried deep beneath their longing for each other.

It was 1 a.m. before Maggie opened her eyes. Satisfied but sleepy, she found herself leaning against Peter's shoulder. She sat up and looked over to him. Why hadn't she ever noticed how attractive he was, with his dark hair and strong features? Why hadn't she ever thought about the two of them...together? She gently shook him. "Peter. Wake up. You need to get me home."

Peter opened his eyes and smiled at his Maggie. For the first time, he felt happy that she now knew how much he loved her. "I love you," he whispered. "I've loved you since we were kids."

Maggie held his hand, but fear quickly took over her thoughts. What had she done? "I need to go home."

Peter sat up and wondered if maybe she didn't love him after all.

Maggie sat motionless, almost ignoring him. She repeated, "I need to go home."

Peter got out of the truck, felt a twinge of pain through his middle section and hoped he hadn't broken a rib. He could hardly move his arms. As his attention slowly focused away from Maggie, and onto his duty to take her home, his bruised body became wracked with strong waves of pain. Once he was behind the wheel, no words were spoken between the two young lovers as they drove away.

Maggie was in her own bed before 3 a.m. She had sneaked in the back door with the aid of a hidden key used only in emergencies. She lay awake, tossing and turning, with too many unanswered questions circling around her head. Where was Gertie? What would she tell Aunt Ethel? What should she do with the ring and pearl pouch? Would anyone from Los Angeles come after her? She shouldn't have made love with Peter.

Maggie finally woke after only a few hours of sleep to the smell of bacon. She ran into the bathroom to wash her face and saw that her eyes were puffy and crusted over from crying. Quietly, she got dressed. When she felt ready to face her parents, she slipped down the stairs and into the kitchen.

26

1947
CAPE COD

MAGGIE COULD SEE her mother rinsing dishes at the sink. "Hello, Mamma."

Alice Foster turned around and nearly dropped a cup on the floor. "Maggie!"

The young girl walked over to hug her mother. "I snuck in last night. Didn't want to wake everyone up."

"Oh, my goodness, you silly girl. I'm so happy to see you, all safe and sound." She hugged her daughter as she called out over her shoulder, "John, look who's home."

John Foster walked out of his workroom carrying a radio that he had fixed for one of Fletcher's customers. Within seconds, he wrapped his arms around his wife and only daughter. "Maggie, we missed you."

Maggie grabbed a glass for milk and a piece of toast from the kitchen counter. "It's good to be home." She sat down.

Alice poured some milk into Maggie's glass. "Did Gertie come home with you?"

"No." She took a tiny bite of the bread.

John sat across from his daughter with a cup of coffee. "Did she find a job in the movies?" He kept staring at Maggie. He thought about how grown up she looked...his little girl.

Suddenly Maggie stood up and ran back upstairs in tears.

Alice stared at John.

John stared back and then looked at the kitchen clock. It was almost 8 a.m. He had to leave for work. "I'm going to be late."

"I'll go talk with her." Alice headed for the stairs.

"We'll discuss it tonight at dinner," John said. On his way out, he stopped at the bottom of the steps and called up, "Bye, Maggie. I love you."

Alice found Maggie crying, face down on her bed. She sat next to her, lightly patted her daughter's back and whispered, "What's wrong, honey?"

"I'm so frightened, Mamma." Her tears flowed down her cheeks.

Alice wiped her daughter's face with the edge of her apron. "You're safe now that you're home; don't cry."

Maggie sat up and swiped at her nose with her handkerchief. "It's Gertie."

Alice held her hands in her lap and shook her head in disapproval. "That Gertie, what did she get herself into now? I knew that Hollywoodland was dangerous."

"I don't know where she is."

"What do you mean you don't know where she is?" Alice looked stunned.

"The night before I was going to leave for Cape Cod, Gertie came back to the rooming house, woke me up, and told me to hide in the closet. Then two men came into our room. I was frightened, but I stayed hidden behind the door. Then she left with them." Maggie started to sniffle. "I don't know why they came or where they went." Maggie knew the men probably wanted the ring, but she was afraid to tell her mother about it after promising Gertie she'd keep quiet. The least Maggie could do now was to follow Gertie's instructions to not tell anyone about the jewelry.

She fell back onto the bed and buried her face into the covers.

"Did you call the police?"

Through muffled tears, Maggie sputtered, "The police are bad there, Mama. I never called them."

It pained Alice to watch her daughter suffer, but she knew she had to do something. Always the disciplinarian in the family, Alice sternly said, "Now listen, my girl. Sit up. Dry your eyes. Meet me downstairs and let's get to the bottom of this."

As she descended the stairs, Alice's fears grew stronger with each step. She prayed for strength and grace. At the bottom of the stairway, she held onto the post for a few seconds, looked up to where Maggie was still sobbing, bowed her head and thanked God that it was *her* daughter who'd returned home safely.

A few minutes later, Maggie sat opposite her mother in the kitchen and recounted everything that had happened in Hollywoodland, except for telling her about the ring. She closed her eyes and shook her head as she tried to erase the image of Big Paulie hitting Gertie.

Alice was careful not to ask too many questions for fear she'd interrupt and not be privy to all the details. When Maggie stopped talking, Alice said, "Maggie, we need to tell your Aunt Ethel."

"I know, Mamma." Maggie twisted her handkerchief between her fingers.

"She has a right to know everything about what may, or may not, have happened to her daughter. She's not going to take it very well. First, her husband…and now this."

"I don't think I can face her yet."

"Don't worry," Alice said as she looked up at the white-faced clock on the wall. "She only has one shift at the theatre today, so she'll be at home now." Alice got up, took her apron off, found the smelling salts, and grabbed her handbag. "I'll go over and talk with her. You stay here; unpack your clothes and rest. I'll be home in a few hours."

"Yes, Momma."

*　*　*

Ethel's eyes were wide and her body shook as Alice repeated what Maggie had said. She swooned and then collapsed across the living room's settee at hearing that Gertie was still missing.

Alice used the salts to revive her sister-in-law.

Ethel moaned, "How much can a woman take in her lifetime?" Her face grew more desperate than ever. She cried out, "Why is God so cruel to me?" Her tears flowed freely as curses spilled out of her mouth from deep inside of her.

Alice was speechless as she held Ethel in her arms. The two friends swayed together on the settee in a slow rhythm.

Ethel scanned the living room. Her eyes flitted between green plants, framed photos of her loved ones, the old upright piano, and all her favorite memories that decorated the room. Then her emotions exploded once more into a piercing wail. She rocked back and forth, beating at her heart.

Alice wondered why, indeed, so much misfortune had visited Ethel. It didn't seem fair. After several hours, she finally asked, "Do you think you'll be all right?" Alice was willing to wait with Ethel until she felt it was safe to leave her alone. She held her hand. "I need to go home soon."

Ethel's eyes were red, her nose blocked. She struggled with each breath. "I don't know what to do." She looked to Alice for answers.

"I'll call John at work and ask him to pick you up on his way home." She stood to leave, grabbed her purse and said, "Maybe if we all put our heads together, we can figure out what to do next to bring your Gertie home safe." She left Ethel lying on the settee with a cold rag across her swollen eyes.

Just after 6 p.m., John walked into the kitchen supporting his late brother's widow on his arm. He'd heard only bits and pieces of the tragic event, on the way from Ethel's house, and from his wife's earlier phone call. He had so many questions.

Alice met them at the bottom of the stairway. She glanced a wary eye to her husband before she took charge by grabbing Ethel's hand and leading her into the living room. "Here. Sit and rest. Supper's almost ready."

Back in the kitchen, out of sight, she fell into John's arms. "Oh John, it could have been our Maggie. We're so lucky."

He rubbed his wife's back and held her close. "Where's Maggie now?"

"Upstairs in her room."

He continued to hold her. "Tell me what you know."

They sat at the table and whispered back and forth. John tried to absorb all of the terrible details.

Maggie came down the stairs.

Aunt Ethel looked up at her niece and screamed, "Where's my Gertie?" She jumped off the couch and yelled, "Where's my Gertie?"

Maggie stopped on the last step, frightened by her aunt's outburst.

Alice came between them. "Calm down, Ethel. Maggie's just as upset as you are."

Ethel knew that Maggie was probably the last person who saw Gertie. She tried to calm herself and stepped back. "Maggie," she whimpered and started to cry all over again. "What happened?"

The young girl threw her arms around her aunt. "I'm so sorry." She began to cry also. "I didn't know what to do. I'm sorry I left her there. I thought she would be all right. I was so scared. I just wanted to come home."

John walked in.

Maggie flew into her father's arms. He held her tight as tears welled in his eyes.

Alice spoke up as she headed for the kitchen. "We all need to eat something, even if it's just a little." Everyone was crying, and then she felt herself almost losing control. Quickly, the stern rule-maker surfaced. She turned around. "Come! Our dinner's getting cold." Once in the kitchen, she called out, "John, get in here and tell us what you think we should do to find Gertie."

It was the quietest dinner Maggie had ever experienced in her young life. Even the cleanup was stoic and sad. After a while, her father went into the hallway to make a phone call to a friend in California while the three women washed and dried the dishes.

By the time he'd finished talking on the phone, Alice had the coffee ready. "Were you talking to Jack?" Alice asked her husband as she put a plate of cookies on the kitchen table.

"Yeah." John looked over to Maggie and Ethel. "Jack Talbot was an MP in the army, then a policeman after the war, but he quit to become a private detective. He liked working on his own better than under the thumb of some other guy."

Ethel wiped her eyes and looked intently at John for anything positive.

"The information that Maggie has already told us can go a few ways. According to Jack, the first thing we should do is call the police, in Los Angeles, to report Gertie missing."

"Will Mr. Talbot help us?" Ethel wiped her eyes.

"He says we could hire him right away, but it costs money." John folded his hands together on top of the table. "Like he says, we need to call the police first."

"But Papa, the police are crooked there." Maggie blew her nose.

"He said there are still some good men on the force." John patted Maggie's hands. "We'll get to the bottom of this."

Ethel looked apprehensive. "Would you make the call for me? I don't think I could get through it without crying."

John held her hand. "Certainly." He went into the hallway and picked up the black phone once again.

On the ride home to Ethel's house, John tried to reassure his sister-in-law. "Don't worry, Ethel, we'll find her. If the police don't find anything, Jack is a good and thorough guy."

"I'm praying so." She blew her nose, said goodbye and then entered the dark house. Too numb to feel afraid, she felt there wasn't anything else that could frighten her after what had already happened.

*   *   *

Sergeant Walker hung up the Los Angeles police's phone. He scratched his head, wondering what he should do with the missing person call he'd just received. "Hey, Reynolds. Come here, will ya?"

Officer Reynolds sauntered over to the call desk. "What's up?"

"I got a call from someone back East who wants to report a missing person. Says it's his niece. Says she moved to Hollywood to be a movie star, but she hasn't been heard from in over a week."

"So, what of it?"

"Her name is Gertie Foster. He mentioned someone she was acquainted with."

Reynolds looked over his sergeant's shoulder to read the name. Reynolds went stiff as he read out loud, "Franklin Cannon?"

Sergeant Walker noticed his reaction. "You thinking the same thing I'm thinking?"

"Yeah. Throw it out."

"Will do. The Captain said to play dumb with anything connected with the Cannons. I'm only following his orders." Sergeant Walker threw the paper into the wastebasket and went back to reading his newspaper.

27

1947
BREWSTER – CAPE COD

SLEEP WAS STINGY to Maggie. She had tossed and turned through the night. It was 9 a.m. and she still had no answers. Sitting on the edge of the bed, the palms of her hands covering her face, she wondered where poor Gertie was. The slatted floorboards felt cold to her bare feet.

The phone rang and her mother's voice trailed up the stairs. "Hello?"

Maggie lifted her head to listen.

"Hi, Peter." There was a pause. "She's sleeping right now." Another pause. "I'll tell her. Noon? She should be awake by then."

Maggie stood in the hallway, out of sight from her mother. Embarrassed and frightened of what had happened between her and Peter, she quickly got dressed. What had she done? She couldn't face him. Within minutes, she flew down the steps and out the front door. "Momma, I'll be home later. Gonna' see about a job at the inn."

Alice came around the corner of the living room and called after her daughter, "Okay, dear. Peter Marsh is coming by to see you around noon."

Maggie walked down the side of the road. She never turned around, only waved her hand to acknowledge that she'd heard her momma's words. As her shoes kicked up the summer dust, she questioned who she really loved, Peter or Eddie? It was too hard to think about it now. She was so confused. The best thing would be for her to never see Peter again. She couldn't be with someone like him. He was just too different. Their relationship had to stop, for the safety of both of them.

As she approached the familiar sight of the Crosby Inn's stables, Maggie saw a sign out front: *For Sale – Inquire Within*. She ran to the back of the inn and burst into the kitchen. "Mrs. Crosby? Where are you?" She pushed on the swinging door that led to the hallway, walked into the office, and found the elderly woman. "Mrs. Crosby!"

The innkeeper wore a flowered apron against her cotton dress. She swiveled around from her desk to greet the young girl. "Maggie. When did you get back?"

"Yesterday. Are you selling the inn?"

"Yes, I'm afraid so. It's getting to be too much work for me." Mrs. Crosby pulled her wire-rimmed glasses down onto the brim of her nose so she could look at Maggie. "I'm not getting any younger, my dear. It's the best thing for me." A sad expression surfaced across her ruddy-complexioned face.

Maggie plunked herself into a tufted fireside chair. "I was hoping to get my old job back."

"Now, Maggie, I haven't had any offers yet. I will certainly need your help to make a good impression for any potential buyers."

"That'd be swell. When should I come back to work?"

"How about tomorrow?" Mrs. Crosby pushed her glasses back up her nose and returned to paying all the bills that had accumulated over the last month.

The kitchen door swung closed behind Maggie as she left for her favorite spot by the bay…the inn's gazebo. Peter had built it a few years ago for Mrs. Crosby. Maggie cherished his gift of the secret compartment in the hollow post just for her. The last time she'd visited, it was a few days before she'd left for California, and Eddie had been by her side. Maggie wished she had never agreed to go with Gertie as she leaned back against the entry post.

*   *   *

Peter Marsh pulled up to the Foster house. He could hardly wait to see Maggie.

Alice met him by the door. "So sorry, Peter. Maggie's not here, she was up early and raced out the door to look for a job."

His shoulders sunk. "Oh, thanks anyway, Mrs. Foster." He turned to get back into his truck. "Tell her I stopped by."

Alice watched him drive away and wondered what was wrong with him. He always had such a nice smile on his face. Today, he looked as if something terrible had happened.

As Peter drove down Route 6, he tried to figure out where Maggie could have gone. He'd feel better once he found her. If she was looking for a job, he guessed she'd stop by the Crosby Inn.

He pulled into the driveway of the inn, got out and saw Maggie sitting in the back by the bay. "Maggie!" He ran towards her.

She looked up, her heart racing. There was no place to hide. She inhaled a good breath of salty air, stood up, and waited to face him.

Peter looked so happy to see her. "Maggie, I went by your house, but your mother said you were out looking for a job." He stopped directly in front of her. "I knew I'd find you here." He held her shoulders and tried to kiss her on the cheek.

She turned away from him.

"What's wrong?"

Maggie couldn't face him; she stared at the ground. "I can't see you anymore."

Peter was stunned. "What do you mean?" He dropped his hands away from her.

She glanced up and caught his eyes. "I mean, we can't be together, Peter."

"Maggie, you're not serious. You know I love you. I always have." He moved in front of her.

She didn't want to hurt him, he meant so much to her, but she had to tell him. "You and I can never be together like we were last night." Tears started to wet her cheeks.

They stood apart in silence. In the distance, the ocean continued its tidal surge against the beach. It had always been soothing to Maggie, but today she couldn't stand to hear it. She wanted to go home and started to leave. "I'm sorry, Peter." She took off in a run, sobbing all the way.

Peter stood there and watched the only girl he had ever loved turn away from him. He hadn't cried since he was little, and yet, he couldn't stop the salty drops from covering his face as Maggie disappeared from his sight. Now he needed to do what he always did whenever he needed answers…he ran. He sprinted to the bay, stripped off his shirt and shoes, then rolled his pant legs up over his calves before he took off down the beach.

It didn't take long for Maggie to reach her house. She ran in the front door, up the stairs, and into her room, where she threw herself onto the bed and burst into tears.

Her mother called up to her, "Maggie! Get down here this instant." Alice Foster wanted to get to the bottom of her daughter's sadness. She called again, "Maggie!"

Her daughter obeyed the anger in her mother's words and sulked into the kitchen.

"Sit down."

"Yes, Mother."

"Now tell me everything. Does that Peter Marsh have something to do with how you feel?"

Maggie nodded her head.

Alice pulled up a chair and waited for her daughter to explain.

* * *

Eddie Clark was on his lunch break at the drugstore in Orleans. He needed ointment for his hands and overheard some men talking at the counter. Now that he was working on the line for Mr. Gordan, his hands got cut up handling the big wires that connected the transmission poles.

One man asked the other, "Did you hear about Sam? He got beat up pretty bad the other night, in Hyannis."

"No kidding. Who did it?"

"They think it was the Marsh kid, but no one's talking."

"Wouldn't be surprised. They hate each other."

"Well, I guess the Foster girl was in on it. She was coming in from some kind of a trip out west."

Eddie didn't wait for his change. He hurried out of the store, jumped in his car and drove over to Maggie's house.

In the short drive between towns, Eddie tried to figure out if he was happy to know Maggie was home or mad to know she had been with Peter. The street was quiet and the Foster's front door was open. As he was about to knock on the door, he overheard Maggie and her mother talking. He listened.

Maggie sniffled. "Peter met me at the inn this morning."

"I guess he wanted to talk to you pretty bad."

"Peter kissed me, Momma."

Maggie's words hit Eddie like a rock.

"Do you love him?" Alice tried to understand her daughter's predicament.

Maggie started to cry harder. "I'm not sure."

At hearing Maggie's indecision, Eddie left in a rage. He repeated in his head as he drove to find Peter: *If I catch that damn Indian, I'm going to beat the shit out of him.*

When he pulled into the driveway of the inn he saw Peter's truck. Eddie ripped off his leather jacket and headed to the backyard. He knocked on the kitchen door. No answer. He looked around the outside of the inn; his anger pushing him to look further, no matter what interfered.

He headed to the beach where he found Peter's clothes in a pile on the sand. Eddie could see Peter running along the edge of the incoming tide, barreling towards him. The Indian's stride looked relentless. Eddie hesitated for only a moment before he took off to meet his rival head on.

They met by a rocky outcrop on the Brewster flats.

Eddie shouted, "You son of a bitch," and threw the first punch. It caught Peter off guard, but missed him.

Peter quickly returned a hard right and knocked Eddie to the sand. He stood over Eddie, waiting to hit him again. As he watched Eddie struggle to get to his feet, he suddenly dropped his fists. Peter wanted to be punished for loving Maggie, so he stood with his arms down at his side and waited to be beaten.

When Eddie regained his balance, he yelled, "Maggie's mine." He then put all his weight into a hit that he hoped would lay Peter flat. It did. Eddie was surprised at his own strength as he stood over Peter.

The tide splashed against the Indian's body. His arms and legs moved back and forth in the water.

Eddie pulled Peter's body higher onto the beach and against one of the bigger rocks. He thought of himself as not totally heartless. He didn't want Peter to drown; he just wanted to teach him a lesson so he would leave Maggie alone.

28

1947
BREWSTER – CAPE COD

MAGGIE HAD A plan and hurried out the door early the next morning. In her bag she carried her operator's license, a few dollars, and the pearl pouch containing the diamond ring that she'd wrapped in a piece of leather from her dad's workroom. Before she checked in with Mrs. Crosby, she slipped around to the back of the inn. Once under the roof of the gazebo, she knelt down to open the wooden square cut into the side of the post. Then she quickly hid the pearl pouch inside the secret compartment. After a furtive glance to see if anyone saw her, she felt confident to report to work.

Maggie's workday went fast, and the clock struck four before she knew it.

To her surprise, Eddie was waiting for her outside of the inn. She was pleased to see him and ran over to his car. "Eddie!"

He looked as handsome as ever. His blond hair shone in the sunlight against his fair, freckled face and created a slight glow around him. Maggie felt herself drawn to him as never before. She leaned into the driver's side to kiss him.

He got out of the car and lifted her up in his arms. "Now that's the way I'd pictured you greeting me after you've been away in California." He returned a passionate kiss.

Eddie's kiss was nice, but it wasn't as exciting as Peter's. Maggie pushed the memory out of her head as she climbed into the passenger side and snuggled close to Eddie. "It feels good to be next to you."

Halfway home, Eddie asked, "Can we talk?"

"Sure." Maggie began to think of their last conversation, at the gazebo, before she left for California. She felt nauseous.

He pulled into Nickerson State Park and parked at the first trailhead. "Maggie, remember what we talked about last time we were together?"

"I remember." Maggie prayed that he didn't want to do it now.

"I think we should get married before we, you know, do it."

She took a deep breath. "Eddie Grant! Are you asking me to marry you?"

"I guess so. I'm not much of a romantic guy. All I know is that I want to be with you and make love to you forever." He fumbled in his pocket and pulled out a small velvet box.

"Eddie!" Maggie squealed and then covered her mouth.

He opened it to reveal a lovely ring. "It's not very big. While you were gone, I worked a lot of hours on the line in Orleans and...well...here it is." He placed the ring on her finger. "Whaddaya say, Maggie?"

She flung her arms around his neck. "Yes!" Then Maggie threw up over his back with a projectile that just missed the inside of the door and splashed out the window.

* * *

Frank Sinatra crooned on the radio while Alice Foster sat in the living room, sewing up a hole in one of John's socks. The summer breezes refreshed her and cooled the house. When she heard someone pull into the driveway, she got up, and saw that it was Eddie Grant.

"Momma!" Maggie ran through the open screen door. She held her hand in the air so her mother could see the engagement ring. "Look what Eddie gave me."

Alice dropped the sock she was mending into her basket and met Maggie halfway across the room. "Let me see." As soon as she came close to her daughter, Alice could smell the vomit. "Maggie! Are you all right?"

"Yes, Momma. I got a little excited and lost my lunch. I feel much better now."

Eddie strode in wearing a big smile.

Alice looked at him. "Well, you look pleased."

"I love your daughter." He went into the kitchen to wash his hands.

Maggie kept looking at her engagement ring as she ran upstairs to change her clothes. All thoughts of Peter and Gertie were hidden behind her fairy-tale vision of getting married that she'd dreamed of since childhood. Within minutes, she came bounding back down. "What do you think, Momma?"

Alice sat down. "Well, it's all very sudden."

Maggie knelt in front of her. "I'm so excited. Isn't it beautiful?"

Alice took hold of Maggie's hand to examine the ring. "Very nice." She looked over to Eddie. "Are you going to speak with Mr. Foster?"

"Yes, ma'am." He stood over to the side. "As soon as he gets home from work, ma'am."

"Yes, that's a very good idea, young man."

Maggie stood up and hugged Eddie. "It's all so romantic."

"Supper will be ready in a little while. Eddie, would you like to stay?" Alice went into the kitchen.

"Yes, ma'am."

John was as surprised as Alice about Eddie's marriage proposal, but he knew that his little girl was eventually going to get married. During dinner, he watched her giggle and fawn over her ring and her intended husband. "Young man, tell me about your job. I heard it pays well."

"Yes, sir. I like it a whole lot and Mr. Gordan says electricity is in the future for the Cape. Big things are going to be happening." He reached for some mashed potatoes.

John put his fork down and leaned back. "Have you set a date?"

Eddie looked over to Maggie.

Her ring sparkled as she moved her hand back and forth, cutting a piece of meat.

"Mr. Foster, I was thinking we could marry as soon as possible. There's nothing to wait for—"

Alice interrupted. "We need to announce the banns, as is custom."

Eddie smiled. "I'm aware of that, but it could be the following weekend?" The sooner he married Maggie, the quicker he could get her into bed. His heart raced at the thought.

Alice stood up. "I'll call the rectory tomorrow and arrange everything. Are your parents all right with this?"

"Yes. They're very happy for us."

"I'll get the coffee and cookies." Alice turned towards the sink. Her thoughts reluctantly returned to Gertie's mother. Her hand trembled at how she was going to tell poor Ethel that her own daughter was not only safe, but she was about to marry a nice boy like Eddie Grant.

* * *

Peter Marsh kept to himself for over a week after his encounter with Eddie on the beach. He couldn't face anyone connected with Maggie on that end of the Cape. He could hardly say her name without becoming melancholy.

Mr. Phillips, over at the Sky Meadow Airport in Eastham, was waiting for a cabinet that Peter had custom built to store small repair parts for the airplanes. Peter couldn't wait much longer to make the delivery. By chance, if the owner was there, he thought he might ask if he could take flying lessons in trade for his carpentry. Peter decided there was nothing more on the Cape for him. He had saved his money and was ready to make it on his own. He'd finally do something he'd always dreamed of...he would fly.

It was a small airport. Peter pulled the truck next to the hangar to unload the cabinet. "Mr. Phillips?" His voice echoed through the cavernous building.

"Peter. I've been waiting for you." Mr. Phillips's reddish complexion reflected his ruggedness.

After taking care of the paperwork, Peter said, "I wanted to ask you something."

"Sure, what is it?"

"Will you teach me to fly?"

Phillips liked the idea that the young man was interested in learning. "I could use some help around here," he said, tapping his pipe on the corner of his shoe. "In fact, you see that little baby over there?" He pointed outside and to the left of the hangar toward a small plane in the distance. "That's an old workhorse from the war, a Piper L-4. I got it for a steal and I'll let you have it for what I paid…$250."

Peter looked out to the open field. His voice wavered. "But…I don't know how to fly yet."

"Listen, boy. All you'll need is a couple of lessons and you'll be on your way."

"You think so?"

"Absolutely! You're a smart one and you'll catch on real quick."

Peter smiled and stood taller. "I've got some money saved. I can give you half now and the rest later."

Phillips put his arm around the young man's shoulder. "You know, I heard they're looking for crop dusters out West." He slowly steered him out onto the grass, next to the runway, to inspect the little Piper. "Listen son, you can rig this beauty up in no time. All you gotta do is put a tank in the backseat, hang a spray boom under the wing, and install a propeller-driven pump to supply the pressure. Why, you'll be dusting those crops in no time."

He opened the cockpit door for Peter to climb inside.

Phillips swept his arm across the horizon and from the corner of his mouth, he said, "Can't ya' picture yourself buzzin' the farms, going real close to the ground, and then back up into the sky? You'll love it. I guarantee it."

29

1947
CAPE COD

MAGGIE HADN'T HAD a solid night's sleep in the two weeks since she came home. One morning she woke with a start and was sick to her stomach. The window was open, the curtains were gently blowing in the breeze, but her room was still stuffy. Her skin felt damp to the touch. She wondered what was wrong with her. Maybe she should stay home and just sleep. Stretching her arms above her head, she noticed her engagement ring was sparkling in the morning light. Her stomach rumbled. She flew out of bed and into the bathroom to throw up.

She literally crawled back into bed, hoping to sleep, but then thought that perhaps some fresh air would make her feel better. Maggie forced herself back out of bed to sit by the open window. She watched a few cars drive by and noticed the grass surrounding the five-step granite stairway, on the edge of their property by the road; looked like it needed a trim. She smiled as she remembered her best friend, Mary Kate Simpson, who had lived across the street. How many times had they waited together on those steps for the school bus to take them to the new high school in Orleans? They'd always giggled about the boys in their classes. Mary Kate had gone out with Jerome Madison. He was older than she and already working, but Mary Kate didn't care. She told Maggie that she loved him.

Maggie's stomach churned again and her face turned serious as she recalled when everything had changed with her friend. It had been a Friday and Mary Kate had looked pale and was crying. She wouldn't tell Maggie what was wrong, except that she was going away and would never come back. The next day, she was gone. The Simpsons sold their house and they moved shortly after. Jerome Madison also left town. Momma told Maggie that Mr. Simpson had got a better job, but gossip had spread all over the school that Mary Kate was pregnant, and that's why they'd moved away. Maggie had never believed it, but now she wondered if the rumors were true after all.

What if I'm pregnant? She cringed at the thought. She couldn't be. Could she?

Maggie stayed in bed for most of the day. Her mother only came up once, to see how she was doing, and agreed that her daughter should stay home. There had been a lot of excitement swirling around the household, and Maggie probably needed more sleep.

By late afternoon, Eddie pulled into the driveway and knocked on the screen door. "Is Maggie around?"

Alice came to the kitchen doorway and yelled to Eddie, "She's upstairs. Come on in."

Eddie sat down on the couch. "I went by the inn to pick Maggie up, but she wasn't there."

Alice wiped her hands on her apron. "She's feeling a little under the weather. Let me go and get her." She hurried up the stairs and knocked on her daughter's door. "Maggie?" She knocked again. "Maggie, your Eddie is here."

The door slowly opened. Maggie looked a little pale, but was already dressed. "Thanks, Momma. I'll be right down."

As the two young people left the house, Maggie turned around to tell her mother that they would not be eating dinner at home. With a slight smile, she added, "Eddie has a surprise for me."

Maggie was surprised to see a new Ford in the yard. "You got a new car?"

"Nope. My Dad let me borrow his. She sure is spiffy."

The newly engaged couple began to drive west down the Old King's Highway. By the time they passed the Crosby Inn stables,

Eddie had his hand on Maggie's upper thigh. She didn't mind. She laid her hand with the engagement ring on her lap, letting her other hand dangle out the passenger side window, gently resting on the metal trim of the door. The air felt refreshing. Within ten minutes, the winding curves of the old road began to make her nauseous again.

"You feeling okay?" Eddie kept driving.

Maggie was determined to fight her uneasy stomach, remain positive, and dismiss any thoughts of being pregnant. "I'm fine," she said.

Eddie had packed a few sandwiches and a thermos of lemonade in a basket. Maggie saw it on the backseat and thought it was so sweet of him. He was going to be a wonderful husband.

They stopped to eat their picnic supper near Barnstable. Just as the sun was setting, they drove further to Sandwich. Eddie pulled into a desolate spot on the bay side.

Maggie was not familiar with it. "Where are we, Eddie?"

"Don't worry. No one comes here."

She didn't like to be surrounded by such darkness. "Maybe we should get back?" She inched towards him, grabbing onto his arm for protection.

"Not yet," Eddie whispered. "Maggie, you know I love you?"

"Of course, Eddie."

"And you love me?"

She nodded her head.

He opened the door, took off his jacket, and held his hand out to her. Maggie halfheartedly reached out to take his hand.

Eddie helped her out of the car and gently kissed her. Then he opened the rear door and waved his free hand, gesturing for Maggie to climb into the back. "Let's have some fun tonight, since we're getting married so soon."

"Oh, I don't think we should, Eddie." Maggie started to pull away.

Eddie drew her tighter. He held her arm behind her back and brought her closer to his chest. "Come on, Maggie. You promised me, back in June, and I can't wait any longer." He backed her nearer the open doors. "I asked you to marry me, just like you wanted."

She didn't want this now. It was not right.

He let go of her to unbuckle his pants. She fell backwards. Within seconds, he was on top of her, kissing her on every exposed part of her body. He started to unbutton her blouse for more.

Maggie's breath came quickly, not out of passion or love, but out of fear. This was not how it was supposed to be. She tried to enjoy what Eddie was doing to her, but Peter kept appearing in her thoughts. She pleaded, "Please stop, Eddie!" He was stronger than she and unrelenting. There was nothing she could do except quietly whimper, as Eddie buried his face against her bare breasts. She kept her eyes closed and couldn't stop thinking of Peter.

Eddie softly moaned, "Oh, Maggie, your body is so exciting." His hands were now between her legs.

She opened her eyes and tried one more time to push on his shoulders so he would get away from her. "Please, Eddie, we shouldn't be doing this." There was a wild look on his face, one she had never seen before. It frightened her.

He leaned back and stared at her, panting like an animal. "I'm not stopping now. I want you and I'm going to have you, whether you like it or not." He lifted up her skirt and pulled off her white panties. "You're mine. No one else will ever have you."

Maggie turned her head to the side until her gaze finally settled on the moonlit stars in the dark sky through the rear window. She lay passive, allowing Eddie to enter her. Tears gently wet her cheeks as she reluctantly accepted him.

30

1947
BREWSTER – CAPE COD

ALICE WAS SITTING alone at the kitchen table, finishing her breakfast of pancakes when the phone rang twice, signaling the Foster's party line. "Hello?"

"Sorry to bother you, Alice. Has John heard anything from the police?" Ethel Foster's voice sounded anxious.

"Nothing yet, dear. John thought we should give it a few more weeks before we called again."

"I hate this waiting."

"John's handling it."

There were several seconds of silence. "I just can't believe that my Gertie is dead."

Alice tried to be positive. "You need to be patient. I'm sure we'll hear something soon."

"Alice? I've been thinking. If my Gertie is truly gone, I'm going to move away from Brewster and start fresh."

Alice heard Ethel sniffle through the receiver. "Where would you go? And what about the house?"

"I have a cousin up in New Hampshire. She said I could stay with her for a while."

"Now let's not talk crazy. We don't know what has happened to Gertie and—"

Ethel hung up.

News that her sister-in-law might leave Brewster worried Alice. She knew that frightened and vulnerable people sometimes make rash decisions. Maybe a long walk would give her a chance to think about what she should encourage the poor woman to do.

Alice made a list of a few things she needed at the grocery store and headed for the A&P, a little over a mile away, in Orleans. The air was warm and she enjoyed her time outside. After shopping, she stopped to see John and asked him if he could take the groceries home with him in the car. He told her he'd be happy to bring them.

A quick stop at the drug store was all Alice needed before going back to Brewster. The store was empty for a weekday afternoon. She moved over to the cosmetic counter. "Hello, Lucille, how are you today?"

Alice loved how Lucille knew everything about making a woman beautiful and admired how she applied her makeup; it always looked professional. Lucille was so friendly to all the ladies and young girls who needed advice and gave wonderful recommendations for their individual purchases. There was a lot to choose from. Alice looked confused as she scanned the enclosed glass counter.

Lucille placed her manicured hands on the glass. "What can I help you with today, Alice?"

She laughed. "Oh, it's not for me."

Peter Marsh walked into the store and overheard Maggie's mother talking. He lingered near the light bulb display, a short distance from the two women.

"Our Maggie is getting married and I was wondering if you could help her choose the right colors of makeup for her special day?"

Lucille beamed. "Who's the lucky young man?"

"Eddie Grant."

Peter felt weak in the knees at the news that Maggie would marry Eddie. His hand accidently knocked a bulb to the floor and it smashed to pieces.

Both women looked toward the crash.

"Sorry, ma'am. I'll pay for it." Peter bent over to pick up the broken glass.

Lucille raised her voice in annoyance, "Well, you'd better, young man. Leave that alone. Go over to the register before you break anything else. Make sure you take care of that."

Alice was shocked at Lucille's behavior. "My goodness, it was an accident."

"It doesn't matter. I don't like those people coming in here." Lucille reached under the counter and showed Alice a new foundation powder that recently came in.

"What do you mean those people?"

Lucille leaned in, held her shiny painted nails to her lips and whispered, "Indians."

Peter overheard the prejudice in her words and almost regretted his love for Maggie. He didn't want to hurt her.

"Excuse me," Alice said as she turned to catch Peter before he left. "We'll talk later, Lucille."

Peter saw her coming and kept his head down. "Hello, Mrs. Foster."

Alice walked right up to him. "Peter. I want to apologize for Lucille. Her rudeness was unacceptable."

"It's all right." He took his change and started for the door.

Alice followed him into the parking lot. "Peter," she called out.

He stopped at his truck and waited for her.

"How've you been?"

"Fine." He reached for the door handle.

"How's your family?"

"They're all doing well. Thank you." He hopped into his truck.

"Maggie said Mrs. Crosby is selling the inn. I hope your family finds enough work."

"They'll be fine."

"What about you? Where are you working?"

"I'm learning to fly with Mr. Phillips, over at the airport." As soon as he said those words, Peter realized that he needed to follow his dream now and forget all about Maggie. She didn't want him.

"Peter, that's great news. I can hardly wait to tell Maggie."

"Yes, it is good news." He started the engine.

Alice backed away and watched him drive out onto the street. It was better that Maggie told him herself that she was getting married to Eddie. If there were something between the two of them, it was not up to her to say anything. She'd be sure to tell Maggie that she saw Peter and share the news about his new job.

*   *   *

The weekend had been busy for Maggie at the inn. She was happy it was Sunday, but still upset with Eddie for forcing himself on her. She hurt all over her body, even more so in her heart. With the news that Peter was learning to fly, she was sure he'd leave the Cape the first chance he had. It was probably for the best, she decided. They could never be together; people wouldn't accept them and would treat them differently. It just wouldn't work. The threat of being pregnant kept surfacing in her mind and, after a while, finalized her decision that Eddie would have to be her husband, even if he wasn't the father of the child she might be carrying. On the walk home, she told herself she'd find solace in her child.

That evening, when Eddie showed up at the Foster's door, Alice invited him in for dinner.

Maggie arrived in time to sit down at the table right before they began to eat. She was surprised to see Eddie. He hadn't come around since their mid-week ride to Sandwich.

John greeted his daughter. "Almost gave up on you. Pretty busy at the inn?" He pulled a chair out for her next to Eddie.

"Hi, sweetheart." Eddie flashed a wide grin.

Maggie returned a reluctant smile and pecked him on the cheek.

Eddie settled in his chair and concentrated on Alice's delicious food. He always enjoyed a nice roast with mashed potatoes and gravy.

Dinner was quiet. Alice eventually spoke up and asked Eddie, "Did Maggie tell you that Peter Marsh is learning to be a pilot?" She glanced over to Maggie. "Sounds exciting, doesn't it?"

Eddie looked surprised. "You mean that Indian?"

Maggie dropped her fork on the plate.

Eddie ignored Maggie's reaction and answered for Maggie with a slight irritation in his tone. "No, she didn't mention it to me. Why would she?"

Before Alice could chastise Eddie for his rudeness and prejudice, John interrupted, sensing his daughter was uncomfortable. "Well, Maggie and Peter have been friends since they were little."

Eddie reached for some bread. "I guess flying would be exciting. But believe me, Mr. Foster, my job laying wires will make a lot more money than he ever will."

Maggie finished her dinner and tried to think of an excuse to go to her room. She wasn't ready to even look at Eddie. His comment about Peter bothered her even more. Before dessert was served, she asked to be excused. "I'll walk you to the door, Eddie," Maggie said with another false smile.

Eddie abruptly got up and followed her. They stood on the porch to say goodbye.

He sensed Maggie was upset and gently pulled on her shoulders so he could look directly at her. "I'm sorry for the other night, Maggie. I didn't mean to hurt you."

He sounded sincere, but she still twisted away from him and showed her back.

He held her again and whispered in her ear from behind, "I just love you so much. You drive me crazy whenever I see you."

She turned to face him. He wasn't Peter, she thought, but he was all she had now.

He stole a kiss.

She went to wipe it off, but stopped herself. It wouldn't do her any good to be angry. He softly stroked her cheek and his gentleness felt nice. Maybe Eddie wasn't all that bad.

"I gotta go now," he whispered. "I know you're friends with Peter, but you're marrying me. I know what's best for you. I want to protect you." He kissed her again.

She stiffened, but kept herself in control.

"Cutting ties with that Indian will be the right thing for our future. Trust me on that. I love you, Maggie." He jumped down the steps and hustled over to his car. He gave a parting wave and drove off whistling.

Maggie ran upstairs crying.

Alice hurried to the bottom of the stairway. "Maggie!" She heard the bedroom door slam. "I guess she'll figure it out. She's a smart girl."

John stopped washing a large kettle. "Let me go talk to her." He double-stepped up the stairs and knocked on Maggie's door. "Maggie? Can I come in?"

"Of course, Papa."

He found her lying across the bedspread. "I know you're upset. You want to tell me what's bothering you?"

Maggie remained quiet.

John placed his arm around her and gently lifted her to a sitting position next to him on the bed. "Is it Eddie?"

"He's just a part of it. I'm not sure if I really love him, and I feel so guilty about leaving Gertie in California. Everything seems so unsettled."

John sighed. "I can't tell you what to do about Eddie, but as far as Gertie is concerned, it's a waiting game."

Maggie blew her nose, took a breath, and said, "Papa, I think I know why the men were after Gertie."

John sat up taller, eager to listen. The phone rang downstairs.

She started to explain as she sniffled. "I think she stole some jewelry and that's why—"

Alice interrupted with a shout up the stairs, "John... Stella Talbot from California is on the phone. She says it's urgent."

"Be right down." He leaned over and gave Maggie a kiss on her head. "See, I bet Mr. Talbot has some news for us about Gertie."

John quietly listened to what Stella was telling him. Her husband, Jack Talbot, had been found two nights ago in one of the old tunnels in Santa Monica – murdered. He cautiously hung up the phone.

Alice came over next to him. "What's wrong? Did they find Gertie?"

"No."

"Why did Stella call and not Jack?"

"I think it would be best if we stop looking for Gertie."

"Why, John?" Alice looked worried.

"Jack was killed, murdered." He sat down at the kitchen table. "When Stella was cleaning out his office, she found my name on a notepad along with the name of a big Hollywood producer, Franklin Cannon and his son, Gaylord. She said these men were trouble and that I should stay put and not come to Hollywood. She also told me to forget about ever trying to find our niece."

Alice sat down. She began to rub her hands together.

Maggie walked in; her parents were staring, in silence, at each other. "Momma, Poppa, I've decided to go back to California and try to find Gertie. I owe her that much."

Her father lowered his head and muttered, "You can't go back there."

Maggie stood defiant. "I won't rest until I do something more than just wait."

He slapped his hand on the table. "You're not going anywhere!"

John's raised voice startled Alice and Maggie. "You have no money and I'm not giving you any. You're staying right here so you can marry Eddie." He stood up. "Talbot is dead, Maggie. Maybe by the same people who took Gertie. There's nothing more we can do." He headed for his workroom off the kitchen. He stopped in the doorway. "There's no news about Gertie. Case is closed." Before he shut the door, he said, "And Aunt Ethel never needs to know about Talbot. Let her have some hope in her dreary life."

Alice had never seen her husband react like he did. Maggie looked stunned. Her father rarely raised his voice to her. She returned to her bedroom in a state of disbelief and confusion.

She had another restless night. As the clock struck midnight, her thoughts returned to Peter. She realized that she did love him, more than ever. She had to do something about it and quick. Peter would probably be at the airport in the morning. She had the day off so she'd find a way to get there and tell Peter she wanted to be with him and not Eddie.

The morning sun shone into Maggie's bedroom and cast shadows across the floorboards. Her clock read 7:30 a.m. After dressing, she ran downstairs and met her father in the kitchen. "Daddy? I need to use the car." She crossed her fingers behind her back.

"Slow down, honey." He poured himself another coffee. "What're you all fired up about?" He sat down with his newspaper.

"I can't explain now. Just trust me. You know I'm a safe driver. Please?"

John realized he wouldn't have many chances left to make his daughter happy after she was married. He also regretted yelling at her last night. He reached into his pocket and slid the keys across the table. "You be careful and have the car back in an hour."

Maggie hugged and kissed her father. "Thank you, Daddy." She ran out the back door. "I love you." If she couldn't bring back Gertie, at least she would save herself from a life with the wrong man.

The drive to Sky Meadow Airport was only a couple of miles. Maggie drove carefully, even though she wanted to speed all the way. She kept her eyes on the road ahead and tried to think of what she was going to tell Peter. She loved him; this she knew. That's all she really needed to say to him. She smiled as she passed through Orleans and headed towards the airport.

She pulled up as close as she could to the hangar. Maggie saw someone inside towards the back. She jumped out of the car and yelled, "Peter!"

The figure turned around.

Maggie stopped in her tracks. It was Mr. Phillips. "Morning, Mr. Phillips, I'm looking for Peter Marsh."

Mr. Phillips grabbed a rag and wiped his hands on it. "He's not here."

"Will he be back soon?" Maggie looked hastily around, only to see a plane's engine in pieces and tools lying around. She was impatient as she watched the older man move closer to her.

Mr. Phillips walked right past her and onto the sandy runway. He signaled for her to follow him out.

Maggie ran over to him.

The sound of a plane got louder and louder above their heads. Maggie looked up to the sky, but didn't see anything. All of sudden, a small, dark, olive-green plane buzzed the ground in front of the hangar, almost blowing Maggie off balance. The pilot had his head positioned straight ahead; he never glanced to the side.

"That was Peter." Phillips began laughing as he placed a pipe between his teeth. "That boy is the best gosh-darned pilot I've ever seen in my life."

Maggie's eyes followed the plane as it flew up, turned, and buzzed the ground once more. Then it seemed to fly straight up and into the sky. It quickly disappeared across the horizon on a course heading west.

Phillips smiled and waved goodbye to Peter as he watched the plane fly away. "Yes sirree! That Peter Marsh is a fast learner. He's going to go far...real far. I suspect that's the last time we'll ever see him again on old Cape Cod. He'll make a fine crop duster out in California."

The swirling dust blew into Maggie's eyes. It mixed with her salty tears, making long streaks of black that streamed down her cheeks.

Mr. Phillips noticed. "You alright, honey?"

"Yes. I'll be fine."

Maggie walked to the car. All the way home, she cried over her future and what awaited her. The idea that she would be married in less than two weeks frightened her. As she pulled into the driveway in Brewster, she came to the conclusion that now that Peter was gone, she had no other choice but to marry Eddie Grant. He would have to be her savior and protect her from the cruel eyes of the community, if she was, indeed, pregnant with Peter's child.

31

1947
BREWSTER – CAPE COD

PREPARATIONS WERE underway at the Foster household for Maggie and Eddie's wedding. A full week of evening meetings between all the parents and the engaged couple were exhausting for Maggie as they discussed the event. Each day the bride-to-be felt more frustrated. Not only did she think she might be pregnant, but the news about Mr. Talbot frightened her even more. Her emotions flipped from joy to despair to guilt and back again with the slightest word or comment from those around the kitchen table. Everyone had an opinion on what the young couple should do.

Her mother suggested that Maggie wear her wedding dress. Twenty years ago, she was a little heavier than Maggie. Alice thought she could take it in.

When Maggie tried it on she was relieved to find that it did fit and needed no altering. She was thankful no one had noticed her mid-section had grown a little thicker and her skirts were just a touch tighter than usual. She stood in front of the mirror and felt a twinge of excitement as she modeled the dress that made her look like a princess.

A marriage ceremony at the local church and a simple reception at the Foster's house were on the agenda for the coming Saturday. Thirty people, combined friends and relatives, were invited. Roast chicken, mashed potatoes, and assorted vegetables were on the menu. Alice's best friend, Marian Nickerson, would supply a very nice sheet cake. The Grants would provide the alcohol, Coke, and lemonade.

John Foster worked hard on sprucing up the backyard and built a pretty wooden arbor for the newlyweds to sit under as they ate their wedding supper.

Maggie pushed her guilt over what happened to Gertie aside and allowed herself to enjoy all the attention. She felt like royalty on her wedding day. After all, this was her day, and she knew that Gertie would have done the same thing if the situation had been reversed. When Aunt Ethel joined the party, everyone crowded around her to offer ideas and hopeful optimism about Gertie's return. The young bride did her best to sound hopeful too.

When the wedding festivities were over, Maggie and Eddie Grant spent their one night honeymoon at the Crosby Inn, a wedding gift, courtesy of Mrs. Crosby.

Over the following week, the young couple moved into a small brown bungalow down the street from the Foster home, in Brewster. Eddie's father worked in real estate and had quite a few houses in his portfolio that had been foreclosed on since the war ended. Eddie took over the mortgage payments with his lineman salary. When he told his new wife that he didn't want her to work, Maggie agreed it was a good idea. If she were pregnant, it would be better for her to remain at home.

Maggie began to consider herself lucky to already have a house they could call their home and she was pleased that she was slowly beginning to warm up to Eddie again. He had been very sweet and gentle since the wedding.

By August, Mrs. Eddie Grant was comfortable in her new role as housewife. Her time of the month had come and passed twice, which signaled that she was pregnant. She took a walk to visit her mother. The air was hot so Maggie walked slower than usual.

Alice was sewing on the front porch next to a small fan. "Maggie, my dear." She got up from the swing to greet her daughter.

Maggie hugged her mother. "Hello, Momma." She sat down and held the swing so it wouldn't sway. "I need to tell you something."

Alice sat next to her. "Yes, honey. What is it?"

"I think I'm pregnant."

Alice threw her arms around Maggie.

The young girl felt relieved.

"Did you miss this past month?"

She nodded.

"You need to call Dr. Mason, in Orleans, right away and set up an appointment."

"Okay. I will."

"I'm so happy for you and Eddie." Alice started for the door. "Let's have some lemonade to celebrate."

As they sat in the kitchen, Maggie asked, "How's Aunt Ethel?"

"We haven't heard much from her since the wedding. Your father's hoping that time will heal Ethel's sadness. It still bothers me to keep the news about Talbot from her. Your father says it's the right thing to do."

"I'm sorry, Momma. I feel so terrible."

"It's hard to believe that someone can just disappear. I wish we lived closer to California, but then again maybe not; it sounds too dangerous to me."

"Sometimes I wished I'd never gone to Hollywood. Most of all, I'm sorry I wasn't strong enough to stay and help Gertie. I should never have left her behind." Maggie blew her nose.

"You can't blame yourself for whatever happened to her. Gertie was a handful." Alice took Maggie into her arms once more.

"I'll be all right, Momma." She moved towards the back screen door. "I think I'll stop by Doane's and pick up the mail."

"Good. Let me know what the doctor says."

Maggie could feel a slight breeze as she walked to the center of Brewster. She stayed under the huge trees that cast a refreshing shade along the road. It was almost lunchtime when she arrived at the General Store. She reached for a cold Coke from the rear of the store and then went over to the window where the mail was sorted into small cubbyholes with numbers written on each one.

"Hello, Maggie," said Mr. Doane. "How's married life treating you?"

"I'm just fine, thank you for asking."

"Picking up your mom and dad's mail today?"

"Yes. Thank you."

She went outside and sat on one of the long benches that fronted the street. An awful odor filtered close to her nose. From the corner of her eye, she could see the 'goat lady' climbing the store's front steps. The well-known Brewster character wore a long woolen coat and a towel wrapped around her head, like a turban. It made her hair stick out and hid her face. The temperature was almost eighty degrees. Maggie felt sorry for her. Word around town was that her husband was a jealous man, so to control his temper, she always covered herself up.

Maggie returned to the mail. Nothing for her parents, but she noticed a postcard among her letters that pictured an orange grove in California, and it was addressed only to her.

> Hi Maggie. Sorry I missed saying goodbye to you. I'm flying! Mr. Phillips had a lead for a job here in Southern California for crop dusting. I had to leave quickly. I'll keep you posted on my adventures. Hope you and Eddie are happy.
>
> Forever, Peter

Maggie was shocked that Peter would send her anything. She held onto the postcard, but decided Eddie shouldn't see it. Her stomach went into a cramp. It began to subside, but not before the awful smell reappeared in Maggie's nose. She looked up to see the goat lady leaving the store with Mr. Doane spraying cologne at her back.

"Sorry, Maggie. That woman drives me crazy. It's a good thing she didn't bring her goats with her today. What a mess!" He stood with hands on his hips and watched the woman walk away from his store, headed for Run Hill Road, by the town dump.

The smell continued to make Maggie queasy. She bundled the mail into her shopping bag and started the long walk home. As soon as she got back, she would call Dr. Mason, but first she needed to find a hiding place for any more mail that Peter might send her. The last thing she needed was for Eddie to get jealous – she didn't want to end up like the goat lady.

* * *

Dr. Mason's office was on the second floor, above the stores, on Main Street in Orleans. The doctor had agreed to see Maggie before his regular hours so that Eddie could drop her off on his way to work. She would walk home after her appointment. Eddie knew she hadn't felt well lately and didn't question her visit to the doctor. Maggie kept the real reason to herself.

The wooden floorboards squeaked as she walked down the door-lined hallway toward Dr. Mason's office at the end. The door opened into a spacious room. A small green lamp cast a soft glow across a large dark wooden desk. Over to the side was a black leather exam table, a long piece of white cloth draped down its length. To the rear were two closed doors. Books surrounded the room in dark cabinets.

"Hello?" Maggie called out.

Dr. Mason entered from behind one of the closed doors. "Good morning, Maggie. Take a seat." He motioned to a chair in front of his desk. "Now, what seems to be your problem?"

Maggie looked down at her folded hands. "I think I'm pregnant."

"That's wonderful, my girl." He grabbed a pen and some paper. "Tell me why you think you're pregnant."

"I've been feeling uneasy in my stomach in the mornings. I'm very tired and my clothes are tighter than usual. I also missed my time of the month."

"Those are all good symptoms. Now go into the bathroom and give me a sample." He laughed as he handed her a small cup. "Let's see if the rabbit dies."

"Oh, my goodness," Maggie said.

Dr. Mason gently looked at Maggie. "I'm afraid the only way to test for pregnancy is to inject your urine into the ovaries of a rabbit. If there's a change in the rabbit's ovaries, it means you're pregnant."

Maggie got up to leave for the small bathroom.

As she passed the doctor's desk, he added, "They have to kill the rabbit to examine the rabbit's ovaries."

When she finished, Maggie returned the sample to him.

"I don't need to examine you just yet. Let's see what develops first." He closed Maggie's file and stood up. "Say hello to your parents for me. Now, if you'll excuse me, my next patient will be here in a few minutes."

On the walk home to Brewster, Maggie couldn't stop thinking about the poor rabbit that had to die in order for her to know if she was going to have a baby. Maybe her child would grow up to be a scientist and find another way to test for pregnancy.

The Foster house came up quickly as she crossed over into Brewster. She noticed the Marsh truck parked out front and wondered if Peter was back in town.

Maggie entered from the front porch and walked into the living room. Peter's parents were talking with her mother. A big wrapped box sat on the floor.

"Maggie, I was telling Mr. and Mrs. Marsh that you might stop in after your trip to Orleans." Alice beamed at the thought that she might be a grandmother, but kept her hopes inside.

Maggie hugged the two visitors. Their two families were such good friends. "It's so nice to see you. I was disappointed you couldn't come to my wedding."

Mr. Marsh quietly said, "Pay no mind to it, Maggie. You know how some people react down here to people like us. We wanted you to have a perfect wedding, with no problems."

Maggie shook her head in frustration about how prejudice was still prevalent in their community.

"That's just the way it is." Mr. Marsh handed her the box.

"For me?" Maggie opened it. Inside was a beautiful handmade wooden box. On the golden-hued lid were carved a sun, moon, stars, and water waves. A small key was set in a brass lock on the front. "It's beautiful."

"It is, isn't it?" Mrs. Marsh smiled. "Peter made it. He wanted to give it you himself, but he left so quickly that he didn't have a chance to deliver it. We hope you like it."

Maggie followed the delicate carvings with her finger and felt the smooth surface of the honey maple. "I love it." She hugged Peter's parents again.

Mr. Marsh turned to Alice. "We must be going now. We have to deliver our last piece of furniture to the Crosby Inn."

Mrs. Marsh wiped her nose with her kerchief. Maggie gave her another hug and whispered to her, "Eddie's really nice to me."

Peter's parents walked towards the door. "All the best, Maggie dear. Give our regards to your husband."

After lunch with her mother, Maggie carried her gift home. She thought it would be the perfect place to hide Peter's letters or postcards. There was no reason why she couldn't have this little secret. Besides, Eddie would be so pleased he's going to be a father that he won't even care about her new box.

32

1948
BREWSTER – CAPE COD

March 10, 1948

My little Alicia was born two weeks early on March 8, at 8lbs, 3oz. and 20 inches long. Thank you, God. It's good to be home in my own bed. My baby's hair is dark and so is her skin, but the Doctor said not to worry, it's just a little jaundice. Weather's been cold and damp. I can feel spring in the air. Yesterday I saw yellow aconite peeking out in the snow by the front steps. Feeling much better, my milk has finally come in. I was worried I couldn't make any. Eddie is working hard on the lines; they're in Eastham now. Momma came to visit yesterday and brought more mail for me. Harry Gibson sent the pictures we took in front of the Georgian Hotel, and there was another postcard from Peter in California. I hope they're both happy.

* * *

By the first of April, Maggie could hardly wait to go for a walk outside with her little one. Her parents appeared one Saturday morning with a new buggy and a nice casserole that would stretch for a couple of suppers.

"Thank you," Maggie said, as she hugged them with one arm and cradled the baby with the other. "Little Alicia and I will make good use of such a nice pram."

"Where's Eddie this morning?" Alice asked.

"He had to go into Orleans to get a part for the truck. It hasn't been starting in the mornings."

Alice grabbed her purse, and from inside, she pulled out a postcard. "Here's another one from Peter." She took her granddaughter in her arms. "Honey, has Eddie seen these postcards?" The baby started to fuss and Alice heard a little rumbling from the baby's bottom. "Uh oh. Do you want me to change her?"

Maggie reached for her child. "No, Momma. She's been having some pretty messy diapers lately. The doctor said that's good, though, the more she eats and poops, the better her skin color gets. I'll do it." She put the postcard on the kitchen table next to some papers and yesterday's mail. The Fosters left soon after.

Eddie arrived home around noon. As he came through the back door, he yelled out, "Maggie!" His keys flew across the counter and he threw his leather jacket onto a wooden peg and grabbed a cold beer. "Maggie, what's for lunch?"

Upstairs, Maggie quietly closed the door to Alicia's nursery. She hurried down the stairs and into the kitchen. Eddie, already seated at the table, was reading something.

"Hello, Eddie, I can make you a nice ham sandwich. Would you like that?" She stood in front of the open door of the Frigidaire and pulled out the ham and mustard.

He threw a postcard on the table.

Maggie put her hand on his shoulder. "What's wrong?"

"Explain this?" His voice sounded threatening.

Maggie's heart flip-flopped as she grabbed Peter's card. "My mom brought it over this morning. I don't know why he's sending me mail. It was a surprise to me when I saw it."

She tossed the card back on the table, as if she didn't care, then went back to prepare Eddie's sandwich. She tried to be calm, even though Eddie's tone had frightened her. It was careless of her to leave it on the table.

Eddie stood up, grabbed the card, ripped it up and scattered the pieces on the floor. He reached for his jacket and headed for the door. "I'm not hungry. Tell your mother to throw anything that Indian sends to you in the trash."

"Where are you going?" Maggie bit her lip to prevent herself from crying. "Please don't drink." She called after him.

He slammed the door.

She knew where he was going. He was drinking more since Mr. Gordan had said they were almost finished with laying the poles and the wires in the area. This meant Eddie's job might be in jeopardy come the first of the year.

April 15, 1948

Eddie twisted my wrist. Momma came over to help me with Alicia, or Ally, as we have now nicknamed her. It hurt to hold her. I've got to be more careful. If any more mail comes from Peter, I better throw it out.

Maggie closed her journal and locked it in the maple box next to Harry's pictures and Peter's postcards. She hid it under a quilt in the bedroom closet.

As the summer months flew by and fall approached, Maggie's days were filled with the work of washing diapers, canning produce for winter, cleaning, and trying not to give Eddie any reason to be angry. He'd developed a terrible temper when things didn't go his way. Maggie assumed that the thought of being unemployed made him depressed and maybe even a little scared. He came home drunk at least once a week.

* * *

One cold day in early December, when the sky was pitch black, Maggie had supper ready, and Ally was in a small playpen in the living room with an animal mobile slowly turning above her head. Maggie was in her rocking chair beside the open fireplace, darning Eddie's socks.

Eddie was late.

When she finally heard his truck pull into the driveway she got up to greet him by the back door. She fixed her hair as she passed the dining room mirror and straightened her dress.

The door flew open and banged against the counter as Eddie staggered in.

Maggie stiffened. "Eddie, are you okay?" She drew back and away from him.

"Why do you ask me that every time I come home?" He wiped his mouth with the back of his hand. "Nothing's wrong." He took off his jacket, but missed the hook so it fell to the floor.

Maggie went to pick it up.

Eddie grabbed her by the arm and pulled her close to him. "Come on, Maggie. Let's go upstairs." He tried to kiss her.

She turned away from the strong smell of alcohol on his breath and clothes. "Eddie, please. You need to eat something. Don't yell. You'll scare the baby."

He let go of her; then he slapped the white porcelain table with his hand. "I want you, Maggie." The force of his hand rattled the dishes and silverware. The noise startled Ally and made her cry. Eddie repeated louder, "Come on, Maggie. Upstairs. Now!" He tried to grab her again.

The baby's cries got louder.

"Shut that kid up," he shouted as he reached for a bottle of whiskey from on top of a high shelf. He mumbled under his breath, "The kid's probably not mine, anyway."

Maggie heard him and screamed at him in horror. "How can you say that, Eddie? Of course, she's yours." She ran to pick up Ally.

Eddie sat down by the table and deliberately swept his arm across it, sending the dishes smashing to the floor. "No one in my family has dark hair. We're all blond and fair-skinned." He poured himself a drink and then scowled at his wife. "What else should I think?"

Maggie pulled the baby close. Her hand held the back of little Ally's head. "Shhh," she cooed and swayed back and forth. The baby's cries slowly turned to whimpers and then she was quiet. "I'm going to put the baby to bed and then we'll talk." She headed towards the stairway. "Ally is yours, Eddie." Maggie pursed her lips together; she hated to lie.

Later, Maggie found Eddie in the kitchen sweeping up the broken dishes. She abruptly turned the oven off, wrapped the casserole in wax paper, and placed it in the refrigerator.

Eddie threw the shards into the garbage and gently took Maggie's hand as she stood at the sink. "I'm sorry."

She turned to look him in the eyes. He looked desperate for her forgiveness. "I know you're sorry, but you frighten me when you drink so much."

He slumped into the chair and buried his face into his folded arms. "I love you, Maggie, and I love our child." He looked up at her with tears in his eyes. "I don't like myself either...when I drink."

Maggie knew he was worried about his job. She also realized that, as a man, he needed to work and provide, and if he couldn't, Eddie would probably feel worthless. She leaned down to hold his face. "I know you're hurting, but you can't keep drinking. I don't trust you with the baby anymore."

He whispered, "I'm sorry I frightened you. I really do love you."

She remembered the day he'd asked her to marry him and how happy she had been to become his wife. Things were so different now. She'd even stopped saying the words 'I love you' to him.

Eddie sat up a little straighter. "I promise to stop drinking."

December 24, Christmas Eve, 1948

The presents are wrapped, Ally is asleep. Eddie has kept his promise; he has not taken a drink. My milk stopped a few weeks ago. Doctor said not to worry. Eddie got the news that he will be laid off in January. I pray we'll be okay.

January 10, 1949

The snow hasn't stopped for a week. Roads are closed. My canning is keeping us well-fed and Eddie's woodpile has kept us warm. Eddie still has not taken a drink. Thank God, we saved our money.

The month of March was filled with rain, ice, and sleet. Eddie drove Maggie and Ally over to her mother's house on his way to a job interview.

"Bye, Eddie. Good luck. I hope you get the job." Maggie scrambled out of the truck with Ally. She scurried into the Fosters' home as Eddie tooted the horn goodbye and then disappeared around a curve in the road.

Grandma Alice appeared at the door. "Quick. Maggie. Come in where it's nice and warm." Alice reached for the baby and began singing to her. "Hello, my sweet baby Ally. Grandma loves you. Hello, my sweet baby Ally. Grandma loves you."

As Maggie removed her coat she stood to watch her mother fawn over her beautiful granddaughter. Ally was quite a gift for the Foster family and Maggie was proud that she could share her joy with her parents.

Grandma Alice took the baby out of her snowsuit and cuddled her in her arms. "Maggie. You got some more mail over the past few weeks. It's over on the kitchen table." Alice sat on the settee with the baby. "Go get yourself a cup of coffee and a cookie. See what that Peter's been up to." Alice started to make motorboat noises to Ally and hoped the baby would mimic the sound. "Little Ally and I will be just fine."

When Eddie had promised her that he would never drink again, Maggie had taken everything of Peter's out of their house and given it to her mother, who was happy to let her leave the maple box upstairs in her old bedroom. She still kept her journal hidden in the bottom drawer of her dresser at home.

Maggie sat down and began to look at Peter's postcards. This time, he'd sent pictures of Hollywood. One was of Grauman's Chinese Theatre and the other was the Ferris Wheel at Venice Beach Pier. She didn't bother looking at the familiar images; she wanted to see what Peter had written. He was doing fine and still flying, but his last sentence took her by surprise; he had met someone. Maggie reread Peter's words telling her that another person was in his life. She wanted to be happy for him, but found it hard to accept that now he'd never be hers. She took the postcards upstairs. From her closet, she lifted out the honey maple box that held all the cards from

Peter, and Harry Gibson's photos. The phone rang two times. "I'll get it, Momma."

Maggie hurried downstairs. "Hello?"

"Is that you, Maggie? This is your Aunt Ethel."

"Why, hello, Aunt Ethel. Do you want to talk with Momma?"

"Yes, dear."

"Momma, it's for you." Maggie was happy not to talk with her aunt.

The disappearance of Gertie was still a sore spot in the family, even after a year. With no clear answers and no money to pursue the case further, Aunt Ethel had finally given up hope. Harry Gibson had collected Gertie's things and shipped them home to Brewster. The whole California trip always brought up feelings of guilt and regret for Maggie, so she tried not to think about it.

Maggie pointed to the phone and whispered, "It's Aunt Ethel."

Alice picked up the receiver. "Hello, Ethel." She listened intently for a minute. "Are you sure?"

Silence.

"Well, if you think that's what you want to do. I'll let John know when he comes home from work."

Maggie held Ally. "Anything wrong?"

"Not really. Aunt Ethel is putting her house up for sale next month."

"Is she going to relocate to New Hampshire, like she said she would?"

"I guess so. I suppose it's for the best." Alice poured herself a coffee.

"Momma? Do you think I should give Aunt Ethel some of those pictures of Gertie and me in Hollywood, from that fella' I met there? Do you think it's okay to talk about it with her?"

"I think that's a good idea."

Maggie felt relieved, in a small way, as she went to retrieve the pictures. Her guilt for abandoning Gertie seemed to lessen with the finality of Aunt Ethel moving away. She thought back to that night, when Gertie had told her to take the ring and leave for Cape Cod, and remembered Gertie's words: "I've decided to go home. I'll follow you as soon as I can. Don't worry." Maggie had finally accepted that there was nothing she could have done to change anything.

As the afternoon wore on, Eddie returned to the Fosters' house.

"So what happened? Did you get the job?" Maggie hoped he got the job. Maybe Eddie would not be so angry all the time.

Eddie took off his coat and grabbed a cookie. "You're looking at the new representative for Allied Insurance Company. One of the largest companies on the East Coast."

Grandma Alice took the baby from Maggie as Eddie reached for his wife and then swung her around in a joyful embrace.

"Congratulations!" Maggie smiled at him. "Tell us all about it."

"I start next week. There will be a lot of driving, but with the commission I get, we'll be able to buy another car."

"Really?"

"No more trudging around the roads for you, lugging groceries. You'll have my truck to use instead. And you'll be able to go anywhere you want in a flash."

Maggie thought that maybe her life was making a turn for the better.

September 25, 1949

Eddie adores Ally. He never talks about whether she is his child anymore. He's doing well with the insurance business. When he leaves to make his rounds and collect the payments, he carries a briefcase and a big leather-bound ledger book. He's been sober for over a year. I know it's hard for him and worry his terrible temper will come back. I feel afraid more often than not. Grandpa Foster had a small stroke last month, but he's better now. Doctor said he has to watch his diet and eat healthier.

33

August –1950
BREWSTER – CAPE COD

MAGGIE HUNG the wash on the line as Ally tried to pull herself up in the playpen. "You're getting to be such a big girl." She smiled at her first-born.

Summer was almost over and the weather had been hot and dry. Eddie still had not taken a drink and was doing well collecting insurance payments from families throughout New England. He told her he'd be home on Friday. She'd planned a nice picnic for Saturday, with potato salad and hamburgers. Eddie was eager to try out his new Brazier Grill. He told her over the phone that he'd thought of a way to keep the meat from burning.

By late afternoon, clouds gathered across the northern skies of the Cape. Maggie scurried to bring the dry clothes inside and then dragged the playpen across the grass and onto the back porch. As the screen door closed, big drops of rain turned into a downpour. She hoped that Eddie would make it home soon. The Cape hadn't had rain for several weeks and the roads, now soaked, were slippery. Maggie occupied her time washing floors to keep her mind off the storm.

After the baby fell asleep for the night, Maggie settled in front of their Philco-49 television set. Grandpa Foster had gotten it for a good price from Fletcher's TV and Radio in Orleans. Now that Eddie was on the road more, he thought it would be nice company for Maggie. She tuned into her favorite show, *The Goldbergs*.

She could still hear the rain against the house, even though the windows were all shut. A loud thunderclap frightened her as she sat with her cup of tea. The hot liquid spilled to the floor. As she ran to get a dishtowel, the phone rang three times; the Grants' party line signal.

"Hello?" Maggie answered. A few seconds passed. "Hello?"

"I'm looking for Mrs. Eddie Grant." The voice on the other end sounded official.

"That's me," she replied.

"Mrs. Grant, this is Officer James, from the Sheriff's Department. I'm afraid there's been an accident."

Maggie's heart skipped a beat. She couldn't breathe as she slumped into a chair at the kitchen table.

"Mrs. Grant? Are you still there?"

"Yes. I'm here."

"It's your husband…"

Maggie could barely speak and felt tears pooling. "Yes?" She tried to understand the officer's words.

Eddie was dead.

"No. Dear God. No!" she screamed.

* * *

A week after the tragic news of Eddie's death, Maggie struggled through the funeral preparations, her parents by her side. On the final day of the ordeal, Maggie sat in the living room, dressed in mourning clothes. She never liked the color black and thought it was ironic that when a distant relative had died last month, her mother had convinced her to buy a simple black dress, saying, "You never know when you might need one."

Grandma Alice sat close to her daughter. Grandpa John kept an eye on his wife and Maggie while he played with Ally. The two kept a vigil over Maggie as she became enveloped in such an unexpected turn of events.

"So sorry to hear of your loss."

"If there's anything we can do for you, dear, just let us know."

"What are you going to do now?"

Eddie's parents sat across from Maggie. They held hands while mourners paraded in front of them and whispered their pity on losing their son.

Peter's parents arrived to pay their respects and walked right over to Maggie. Mrs. Marsh took hold of Maggie's hands. "So sorry, my dear."

Elwood Marsh hung back behind his wife and then chose to sit by his old friend, John Foster. "Ally is such a pretty little girl. I remember when Peter and his sister were small. Our Sarah had dark hair just like Ally's."

John stood up to get Ally a cookie from the kitchen. "Alice's side of the family had a lot of dark hair. They're from Austria-Hungary. Some were mixed with the Romas; part gypsy, you know."

Elwood followed his friend. "I didn't mean nothing by it, John. I just thought that maybe now that Eddie's gone, me and the wife could come by and visit with Maggie and Ally sometimes."

John looked him straight in the eye. "Brewster is a small town, Elwood. It's best if you keep your distance. My Maggie has gone through enough already."

Elwood understood. It was the way it'd always been. The Marshes left quietly out the back door. On their way out, Mrs. Marsh leaned over and gave Ally a gentle kiss on the cheek.

After the last visitor left, Maggie just wanted to lie down and cry by herself. Relief that Eddie was finally out of her life and the fear of what lay ahead in her future whirled in her head like a wobbly spinning top. She was exhausted. She asked her parents to take Ally overnight and assured them she would be fine on her own.

Alice asked Maggie, "Are you positive you'll be all right?"

"Yes, Momma. I have plenty of food. I just need to be alone tonight." She kissed the baby. "Don't forget Ally's little teddy bear. She won't sleep without him."

Maggie watched them drive away from the house and into the darkness, knowing that Ally would be safe and loved. The house was eerily quiet when she locked the front door behind them. She turned off the lights and calmly walked up the stairs to her bedroom, closed the blinds, changed into her nightgown, and flung herself across the bed. Tears ran down her cheeks and her head ached with the reality that she was now a single parent and had no hope of a future with Peter. She was alone. Maggie could hear fireworks in the distance. They had been cancelled because of a rained-out Fourth of July and re-scheduled for the end of summer. Her body shook with each reverberating explosion, when the finale ended, her cries continued into the lonely night.

September 18, 1950

Eddie is gone over a month now. I need to be strong for my Ally. The bank called today asking how I was. I pretended the baby was crying so I could hang up.

As Maggie balanced the checkbook at a small desk in the dining room, she thanked the Lord no big bills were due for another month. The bank had frozen the couple's money because they needed a death certificate. Eddie had neglected to change the word 'and' to 'or' between their names on the account. This meant that Maggie had to wait for the lawyer to read the will and disperse the funds to her as the beneficiary. She felt fortunate that she had become the budgeter in the household and she was good at it. She calculated that she'd be able to stay current at least until Thanksgiving.

She closed the drawer that held the banking materials. Eddie's favorite pen stuck out of a ceramic cup. She threw it into the garbage. Maggie recalled Eddie had faithfully handed his paycheck over to her each month. He'd had his faults and there were many; at least, he was good about the money. She heard Ally babbling after her nap and went upstairs. She wondered who was going to hand over the paycheck now.

One morning in mid-November, Maggie sat up in bed and remembered the ring. It was as if a light bulb went on in her brain. She whispered to herself, "Why didn't I think of this before?" She could sell it! Gertie would want her to have it. After all, she had kept her cousin's secret. No one knew about it and no one had come looking for it.

Within the hour, Maggie had packed up the baby and dropped her off with Grandma Alice. "I'll be back in a little while, Momma. Just a few errands."

She kissed Ally goodbye and drove to the recently sold Crosby Inn. It was going to become a school for girls who needed special guidance with their diets and was scheduled to open next fall. She had to retrieve the ring before it was too late. The new owners might remove the gazebo.

The inn was boarded up and no one was around as Maggie pulled Eddie's truck onto the weedy driveway. As she walked behind the building to the gazebo, she thought of Peter and then berated herself for even thinking about him. He had stopped sending her postcards over a year ago. The last thing she heard was that he'd finally married someone out west. Concentrate, she reminded herself. Just get the ring. She was doing this for her little family.

It wasn't hard to find the secret compartment in the wooden post. When she pushed in on the square it swung right open. Maggie reached in and pulled out the piece of leather that was wrapped around the pearl pouch. It felt good in her hands, like an amulet of good fortune. When she unfolded the leather, she saw the pearls were still pretty on the black velvet pouch. Inside, the ring sparkled, as beautiful as ever.

Maggie went home to change into her black dress. She would play the widow's role for her meeting at the Radcliff Auction House, in Dennis. It was known for being discreet and she wanted to impress upon Mr. Radcliff that no one must know she was the seller of the ring. It was a small town and gossip could spread quickly. The last thing Maggie needed was someone to connect her with Gertie's disappearance, other than her being the girl who'd accompanied her cousin to Hollywood. No one had to know the real reason why Gertie went missing. Besides, Maggie didn't want people wondering where she'd suddenly gotten so much money.

As she waited in Mr. Radcliff's office, Maggie questioned why Eddie had neglected to finalize an insurance policy for them. She guessed he was just too busy. Gazing out the window, she wondered about the policy, which was probably even discounted for the company's employees.

Maggie pushed her emotions aside and returned to addressing her financial situation. She took out her handkerchief to dab at her nose, hoping her somber appearance would generate compassion from Mr. Radcliff for her situation.

Mr. Radcliff strode into his office and greeted the lady in black, "Good afternoon, Mrs. Grant. So sorry to hear about your husband." He extended his hand. "How may I help you today?"

After a quick explanation of why she was there, Maggie presented the yellow diamond ring to Mr. Radcliff for his inspection.

He took out a small magnifying glass from his breast pocket. "This is very beautiful, Mrs. Grant."

"Yes, it is." Maggie twisted her handkerchief in her hands.

"I'm certain we can make an arrangement here that would generate a spectacular profit for you."

"That's very good news. I trust no one will know my identity?"

"Absolutely not."

For the first time in a long time, Maggie felt in control of her life.

Before Maggie returned to her mother's house to pick up her daughter, she took out the empty pearl pouch from her purse. It felt heavy in her hand. Maggie didn't want her mother to see it and decided to store the pouch in the maple box away from curious eyes.

She burst into the house and ran up the stairs. "Momma, I have to use the bathroom. I'll be right down." It was a good excuse to cover up her swiftness and secrecy.

Once upstairs, she retrieved the maple box from the closet and stuffed the receipt for the sale of the ring inside the pouch and hid it under Peter's postcards. With a quick turn of the little key she locked it. Then she sensed a real urgency to use the bathroom. She tossed the key onto the bed next to the box. As she ran from the room, Maggie didn't notice the key bounce off the bed and slip between the cracks of the wooden floorboards.

While she was washing her hands, little Ally began to cry. Maggie hurried downstairs to comfort her child and forgot about the box.

A few days later, Alice Foster called her daughter. "Maggie, honey, do you want me to put away the maple box that Peter made for you? You left it on the bed. Or do you want to take it home when you come over next time?"

"Sorry, Momma, I forgot about it. Just leave it there. I'll get it later."

Thanksgiving 1950

I have a lot to be thankful for today. Gertie's ring was sold to a wealthy buyer for $50,000. I created a trust fund for Ally and put aside $20,000 for myself. I told no one about my fortune. It's hard to keep it secret from my parents, but it's for the best. Mr. Radcliffe introduced me to a good lawyer in Boston who swore his silence. Thank you, Gertie. In the spring I will find a job. Ally is growing so fast.

34

Summer – 1961
CAPE COD

ALLY WAS ALMOST a teenager. As a single mother, it had been difficult for Maggie, but she had kept it all together. Eddie's parents had felt bad that their son hadn't taken out an insurance policy for his family, so they had given Maggie $5,000 soon after his death. At first, Maggie had refused it, because of the secret fortune she'd already received from the sale of the ring.

With the help of Grandma Alice and Grandpa John to watch Ally, Maggie had been able to find work at a restaurant near the Cape Playhouse, in Dennis. Eddie's parents had also paid for Ally to attend the Sea Camps, in Brewster, where she was taking sailing lessons on the bay and enjoying a wonderful summer camp experience. Maggie's first shift at the restaurant began at 9 a.m. so she had time to drop Ally off at camp on her way into work. She parked her Corvair Monza in front of the big white house and waited for her daughter to gather her things.

She loved Ally's dark hair, which was tied in a neat ponytail. "Have a nice day, honey."

Ally took her time to leave. "Okay, Momma."

Maggie knew Ally liked the Sea Camps, but also was aware she would have preferred to stay home and read Nancy Drew mysteries all summer.

She waited until Ally disappeared behind the big house to meet up with her friends.

A tall handsome man got out of his car, next to Maggie's, to walk his daughter to the back of the house. He sported a deep rich tan; his hair was dark and thick.

Thoughts of Peter Marsh filled Maggie's mind once again. She had tried to erase him from her heart after he'd stopped sending her postcards, but her sweet Ally reminded her of Peter daily.

The only news of Peter had come from her father back in 1953. He'd seen Elwood Marsh at the hardware store. Peter was still flying, happily married, and was chauffeuring the rich and famous across the country.

Maggie smiled; she was happy, too. Her daughter filled her with enough love to last a lifetime. She reassured herself, as she had many times before, that not telling Peter about Ally had been difficult, but necessary. Telling him might have ruined his marriage and she didn't want to hurt him. Maybe someday she would tell Ally who her real father was.

The Beach Dune Inn was a popular place for the stars to stay when they were performing in productions at the Cape Playhouse. Maggie enjoyed her interaction with the royalty of Hollywood at the inn's restaurant. Compared to her California experience, back in 1947, she was far more comfortable with all the glitz and oddities of the rich and famous in her own little home on Cape Cod.

She tied on her apron and checked to see that the coffee urn was filled. After pouring herself a mug of coffee, she waited to greet the breakfast customers. As she took her first sip, she was relieved that Shelley Winters was not at the Playhouse this summer. Ms. Winters had a penchant for consuming too much alcohol. Often times, the actress would come down to breakfast wearing only her nightgown and a thin robe, laughing and joking with the other patrons in the dining room, disrupting the quiet of the morning. It seemed she always managed to find her favorite drink as soon as she woke up. It was unsettling to Maggie at the very least, but nothing bad had ever happened, just a few awkward moments.

The dining room started to fill with hungry customers who were eager for a good cup of coffee. Maggie retreated into the kitchen to place her orders and help with the plating of the breakfast foods. It looked like it was going to be a busy day. After she served the first order, she noticed a man sitting by the window with his back to her. He had been seated while she was in the kitchen. She headed towards him. "Good morning."

He looked up from the menu and stared at her.

"What can I get for...?!" Maggie's eyes opened wide in surprise.

"Maggie Foster?" Peter was as stunned as Maggie was. He got out of his seat and gave her a hug. "I can't believe it's really you, I mean Maggie Grant."

His hug had sent a spark through her body; she quickly put the hot coffee pot on the table. "It's so good to see you, Peter."

His eyes met Maggie's. "I was going to stop by to see your parents while I was here."

"So you weren't going to come and see me?" She laughed. "Here, let me pour you some coffee."

Peter sat back down, but kept staring at her. She had maintained her youthful figure and still looked beautiful to him. "I was going to ask your parents how you were doing, you know, since Eddie passed."

Maggie took a seat across from him at the table. "It's been hard, but I manage okay." She held onto the pot's black handle and kept her eyes down for a few seconds. "Ally keeps me busy."

Peter reached across the table and touched her free hand. "Maggie. I'm so happy to hear that."

His touch was familiar and comforting. "Ally is twelve. I know I'll have some bigger problems when she gets to her full-blown teen years." She smiled at her old friend who kept his hand on top of hers.

A customer caught Maggie's attention for more coffee. She pulled away from Peter and returned a nod to the patron that signaled she would be right there.

"It was great seeing you, Peter, but I need to get back to work."

"Can we meet after you're done here? We have a lot of catching up."

"I work until 3 p.m. and then I have to pick up Ally from camp at 5 p.m. You could meet me a little after 3 here at the inn. The place will be empty so we can talk."

"Okay." Peter took a sip of coffee. "Maggie? Do you think you can bring me a couple of eggs, over easy?"

She laughed. With her free hand, she touched his shoulder. "Coming right up."

After Maggie finished her shift, she brushed her hair and refreshed her makeup in the employee's bathroom. She examined her face; not too many wrinkles. She smoothed out her light blue shirtwaist dress, adjusted the matching belt, and perked her collar up around her neck. How strange that Peter had reappeared in her life. Over the years, after she lost Eddie, she had been on a few dates, but they had always turned out to be nothing substantial. After a while, she had resigned herself to never being involved with another man again. It wasn't worth the heartache. Besides, she was happy now, and Peter was married. She studied herself in the mirror once more and said, "Don't get yourself all excited, Maggie. It's been a long time since you've even spoken to Peter Marsh, and he loves someone else."

Peter was over an hour late. "Sorry, Maggie. Business."

"That's all right, Peter." She was just pleased that he even showed up.

They hugged each other and then sat on the open front porch in cushioned rattan chairs.

"Are you still flying?" she asked and thought how ruggedly handsome Peter still looked.

"Of course. That's why I'm here. I fly a lot for Cliff Robertson. He's partnering with Dina Merrill in *Voice of the Turtle* at the Playhouse." Peter couldn't help but notice how attractive Maggie was after so many years.

"I've heard good things about the play," she said as she turned towards him. She rested her arm on the side of the chair and pressed her chin into the palm of her hand.

Peter leaned in closer to her.

Maggie noticed he wasn't wearing a wedding ring.

Their faces were about a foot apart. Short on time, they only managed to talk about the early years that had fallen silent between them. But both also grew more and more at ease with each other.

Maggie checked the time. It was almost 4:45 p.m. "Gosh, it's late. I need to pick up my daughter."

Peter quickly asked, "Would you like to have dinner with me tomorrow night?"

Maggie hesitated for only a few seconds. The next day was her day off and she'd been feeling tired lately, but with a smile she said, "I think that would be fun."

"Can I pick you up at your house around 6 p.m.?"

"Sure. It's a brown bungalow on Main Street, near my parents' place…9567."

Peter stood to hug her once more and then watched her get in the little blue Monza and drive away.

Maggie couldn't sleep that night. She was excited to see her friend and her first lover again, but she felt nervous about what may come of their meeting after all these years. She wondered if he was still married. They hadn't really talked very long at the inn. But if he wasn't, she would have to tell him about Ally.

The next morning, Ally was slow to get moving. "Hurry up," Maggie called upstairs. "We're going to be late." She hurried down the stairs into the kitchen.

Ally burst in slamming her backpack onto the porcelain table. "Will Grandpa John pick me up tonight from camp?"

"Why would he do that?" Maggie looked around the kitchen for her purse and car keys.

"I'm supposed to stay the night with them. Remember? They were going to take me to see *Parent Trap* in Hyannis."

"I guess I forgot. I'll give them a call to confirm."

Ally picked her pack up and stuffed several books inside. "Well, I'm ready for anything."

"Okay. Let's go." Maggie waited for her to leave so she could lock the door.

By mid-morning, Maggie had called and made sure her mom and dad would indeed pick Ally up after camp and keep her for the night. Then she was off to do all the errands that never seem to get done. It was 5 p.m. by the time Maggie got home. She unpacked the groceries and then collapsed in a chair by the kitchen table. She really didn't want any company, but it was important she see Peter again. Too bad it was such a short visit. She went upstairs to freshen up.

Within minutes, Maggie heard Peter's car pull into her driveway. She peeked out the window and watched him step up onto the porch. Fixing her hair in the hallway mirror, she took a deep breath and opened the door. "Hi, Peter."

A broad smile grew across his face as he stepped over the little bungalow's threshold. He looked her up and down. "You look wonderful," he said, and then glanced around the tidy, comfortable-looking house. "Will I meet Ally tonight?"

"Not today, maybe next time. My mom and dad are taking her to a movie. She's staying the night with them. Say, have you made reservations somewhere?"

"No. Why do you ask?"

"I'm exhausted. I brought some of the inn's famous chowder home and their wonderful homemade bread. I can make a quick salad."

"That sounds great, Maggie." Peter took off his jacket.

"Thanks for agreeing to stay in tonight." As she walked over to the sink, she added, "We can relax on the back porch and just talk."

Peter followed her, taking in all of the decorative accents that surrounded him. He stopped in the dining room to admire a few framed photos on top of a small hutch. "Is this Ally?" He pointed to a portrait taken when she was a baby. Peter looked again and for a second, he thought he was looking at his little sister, Sarah.

"Yes, that was actually right before I lost Eddie."

"I'm sorry, Maggie. You seem to be coping okay, though."

"I am, but it took a while."

"I'm happy for you," he said, and reached to carry a tray of glasses and a bottle of wine to the wicker table outside.

Maggie sliced a tomato. "Sometimes I just want to eat at home. I'm always so busy at the restaurant."

"What else can I do?" Peter came up next to her and leaned against the counter.

Maggie felt so comfortable with him. "Grab some plates from the cabinet over there."

Peter did as he was asked and set the dishes on the table outside.

"I heard by the grapevine that you're married. I'm happy for you." Maggie tossed the salad.

Peter folded his arms. "I was. I lost Elizabeth about three years ago...to cancer."

Maggie put the salad fork down and turned to him. "Peter, I'm so sorry to hear that."

He stayed quiet for a few seconds. "We had a wonderful five years together. She was kind and so beautiful." He reached for the salad bowl to carry it out to the porch.

"Any children?" Maggie asked.

"No. We tried, but with no luck. I guess I was gone more than I was home."

Maggie watched him carry the chowder bowls to the table. Did she have enough courage to tell Peter about Ally? Would he be angry with her for keeping it a secret from him for such a long time?

As the evening wore on, the sun's soft yellow glow filtered through the trees in the backyard.

Maggie leaned back and said, "How about we catch a sunset?"

"That's a good idea."

Peter stood and reached for one of the empty soup bowls just as Maggie reached for it too. Their fingers met.

It nearly took her breath away. They had hugged before, but this felt different to her. It seemed that the years that had separated them had now magically disappeared and it was 1947 again. She quickly withdrew her hand, as if a spark of electricity had touched her fingertips.

Peter noticed Maggie's reaction. "Everything all right?"

"Of course. We'd better get moving or we'll miss the green flash."

Peter laughed. "Remember when we were small and our dads took us to the beach? It was always around sunset."

"Oh, that was fun."

Peter wistfully looked over to the yellow sky. "They made us sit real still on the rocks so we could see the setting sun as it hit the horizon. It did make a green flash, didn't it? Always hoped I could teach my own child that magic."

Maggie felt herself growing more attracted to Peter, just like on the night she came home from Hollywood, when they had made love. She had to tell him about Ally.

There were only a few spaces left to park at Crosby Landing.

Peter pulled his rental car right in. "Today's our lucky day." He got out to open Maggie's door.

"You are such a gentleman." She took hold of his hand to get out of the car. The same spark that she'd felt before happened again. This time she didn't pull back. She held tight to his hand and enjoyed every sensation that rippled through her body. It had been so long since the presence of a man had excited her.

They stopped at the entrance to the beach path. She leaned on him to remove her shoes. Peter let go of her hand to take his shoes off. Then he reached out to her and she eagerly accepted. They watched the beautiful sunset with close to fifty other people, but the lack of privacy didn't bother either of them. They waited for the green flash on the horizon and laughed when the green dot stayed in their eyes as they left the beach.

Once in the car, Peter softly spoke. "Maggie, I know you probably won't understand this, but I've never stopped loving you."

Maggie's heart skipped a beat.

"After Elizabeth died, I grieved for a long time and then buried myself in flying. It always amazed me during those sad years, when I couldn't sleep, that it was your face that calmed me."

Maggie turned towards him, but said nothing.

Peter stared ahead. "I've tried to make myself fall in love again, but it never works. I guess I've always wanted you."

Maggie remembered the day she drove to Sky Meadow Airport to find him. "Why did you leave Cape Cod so suddenly?"

"I felt there was no hope for us to be together, and I couldn't bear the thought of you marrying Eddie. I had to leave."

She took hold of his hand.

He looked over to her. "I'm sorry I wasn't strong enough to win you."

Darkness quickly covered the parking lot.

Maggie leaned towards Peter, held his cheek and brought his face closer to hers. She kissed him. "Peter, I have something to tell you." She took a deep breath. "I want you to listen first to everything I tell you, and please, don't judge me."

"Of course, Maggie."

"Remember the night I came home from Hollywood?"

"How could I ever forget it?"

"The next morning, I was afraid of what people would think of us...together. I was so stupid and weak."

"Maggie you're not—"

"Let me finish. Over the next several weeks, I didn't feel very well. At first, I thought it was because of all the travelling, Gertie's disappearance, and just lack of sleep. I was so young. Then Eddy asked me to marry him. A few days later, I still felt sick and started thinking of Mary Kate Simpson and Jerome. Remember how she left and never came back to the Cape?"

Peter lowered his chin.

"Everyone said she was pregnant. I thought I was, too."

"Why didn't you tell me?"

"I was scared, but that's not all. Before we got married," Maggie whispered, "Eddie raped me."

Peter clenched his fists. "That son of a bitch!"

"That's when I realized that I loved you. You would never have done that to me."

He put his arms around her.

Through her tears, Maggie trembled. "I went to Sky Meadow on the day you left, but I was too late. I didn't know what else to do. If I was pregnant, I knew I had to marry Eddie."

Peter stroked Maggie's hair. "I'm so sorry I left."

They held each other in silence.

Peter eventually leaned away, "Is Ally my...?"

Maggie was so happy to finally say, "Yes, Peter, she's your daughter."

When Maggie opened her eyes the next morning, she saw daylight peeking through the blinds. Peter lay sleeping peacefully beside her. She rose to find her robe and then sat opposite the bed, near the window. She watched her love sleep while waiting for him to wake up.

After a while, Peter stirred, rolled over, and stretched his arm across her pillow. Finding the bed empty, he woke with a start and cried out, "Maggie!" Peter leaned on his elbow to search the room for her.

"Here I am, Peter," she whispered.

When he saw her, Peter relaxed.

Maggie took off her robe and crawled back into bed with him. "I love you, Peter."

They made love again. By mid-morning, neither one could sleep any more. The possibility that they could be together was too exciting.

Maggie stroked Peter's dark hair. "Ally won't be home until after camp and I have another day off from the restaurant."

"Maggie, I'm nervous about meeting Ally. Maybe she won't like me."

"Don't worry. She'll love you just like her mom does. We don't have to tell her right away that you're her father. We can wait a little while, so you two can get to know each other."

"I think you're right." He pulled her close to him. "We have a whole lifetime to decide."

Maggie kissed him once more. "Meet you downstairs."

As Peter came down the stairs, it felt comforting to Maggie to hear the presence of a man in the house; especially a man like Peter.

He grabbed a coffee cup. "Can we talk, Maggie?"

She poured. "I'm listening," she said with anticipation and hope that he felt the same way she was feeling.

"You know, I can still be a private pilot and use Sky Meadow as my home base."

"What are you saying?" Maggie stood closer to him. He smelled so good.

"Maggie Foster Grant, I'm asking you to marry me." He took her in his arms and waited for her answer.

Without hesitation, she said, "I would love to marry you, Peter Marsh...finally."

35

Present Day
CAPE COD

MY FLIGHT HOME landed around 9 p.m. in Boston, after which I finally fell asleep on the two-hour bus ride to the Cape. We arrived at the Hyannis bus depot at 11:30 p.m. It was raining and dark, but I could see Paul was waiting for me.

He greeted me with, "I missed you, honey," as he lifted my suitcase into the car. He took me in his arms for a big hug.

"I missed you, too." It felt good to see his familiar face and he made me feel safe.

Even though I was tired, I found the energy to talk non-stop about everything I'd uncovered, and how I had met Stephen.

I kept rambling on until Paul finally interrupted me. "Don't you want to know about Brian and Patty?"

"Oh, my goodness. I forgot about the wedding." I looked over to him and laughed. "Don't tell the kids I said that."

By the time we reached Brewster, Paul had filled me in with whatever he knew about the pending nuptials, which wasn't much.

"It seems there are still a lot of unanswered questions," I said with some anxiety.

"Yes. But it'll all work out." Paul held my hand. "We're a good team. Don't worry."

Yes, we are, I thought. And that's what I love about Paul. He's always there for me. He may not agree with everything I do or say, but he remains my soul mate in love and life. Seeing his handsome face and strong presence next to me rekindled my feelings for him. I decided he didn't have to know any more about Stephen than was necessary.

My own bed felt so comfortable that I slept through the night and into mid-morning. Once in the shower, my mind started to mull over the facts I'd learned in L.A., the evasive Gaylord Cannon, and, of course, the mysterious but still unidentified remains from Venice Beach. I felt sure the bones had to belong to Gertie Foster. There was a connection, according to the photo from the buried purse, the matching pictures from Natalie's mother, and Harry Gibson's photos. Of course, getting people to believe me was another matter. Maybe I'd call Stephen in a few days to see if he'd found any new facts to back up my theories.

As I put my makeup on, I looked in the mirror and reminded myself to concentrate on being the best mother of the groom and friend to my future daughter-in-law. I was determined to be there for my children. As I went downstairs and into the kitchen, I promised to file away my inquisitiveness under unsolved mysteries. After the wedding, I'd have plenty of time to consider the facts with a clear head.

"Good morning everyone," I said and went over to kiss Danny and Molly. "I missed you guys." I looked out the window and could see Paul outside in the van. "You better get going. Dad's waiting."

The kids left for their day at camp without a hitch. As I finished my morning coffee, I wondered when the wedding problems would begin, and, with that, the phone rang.

Martha answered and handed it right over to me. "It's Brian."

When Paul returned, I met him at the door. "Let's go for a walk. I just got off the phone with Brian about the wedding plans."

Paul kissed me on the cheek. "No problem, we have plenty of time before I open the gallery."

"I'll tell Martha we're heading out and meet you by the car in five minutes." I ran to change into sneakers.

At 10:30 a.m. almost all of the parking spaces at Crosby Landing were filled. We parked near the dog path; a favorite walk for both of us. We'd walk parallel with the bayside of the ocean for about a half-mile, across an open field of grass and marshes, then walk back along the beach to return to our car. It gave us the best of two worlds; the beach and the dunes.

Paul stopped walking after about fifteen feet and put his arms around me to give me a kiss. "I just want to say that I missed you."

The spontaneity of his kiss sent a ripple through me. "I love you too." Feeling a spark between us was encouraging. That's probably all I needed, I thought, to convince me never to look elsewhere again.

We held hands until the path narrowed and then we separated for another thirty feet. Paul came up alongside me again. "So what did Brian tell you?"

"Well, the key word was 'simple.' Not a lot of fuss. Those were his exact words."

"Go on." The path narrowed again so Paul slipped behind me.

I spoke a little louder over my shoulder. "Brian said that Patty has already found her dress in a consignment shop. He's going to wear a navy-blue sport coat and khaki pants. They intend to only have a maid of honor and a best man."

Paul came up next to me. "How many people?"

I stopped to admire a pretty *Rosa Rugosa* bush and take in its heavenly scent. "About fifty."

As we climbed a dune along the curved path, the shoreline appeared before us. Paul asked, "Should we have a tent?"

"I guess we could." I took off my shoes to go barefoot in the tidal rush. "I'll call when we get home to see if anything's even available to rent." The blue-green water shimmered in the sunlight as we made our way back to the car.

As soon as we arrived home, Martha said Brian had called again and that he and Patty would come down to the Cape on Friday for a few days, to talk about the wedding. We hadn't seen Brian for almost three months and had only met Patty once before, last year, at our house for Thanksgiving.

I rinsed my sandy feet on the deck. "I'm glad they're coming," I told Paul. "Maybe now we can figure out what we'll actually need."

The happy couple arrived on Friday, around noon. I watched from the deck as Patty, a slim, blonde, beautiful young woman, stood next to the car and stretched her hands up to the blue summer sky. Brian came around the car and took her in his arms for a kiss. They looked so much in love. It made my heart sing and I thought of Paul and myself when we'd gotten engaged.

Dinner was loud and talkative, just the way I like it.

Martha stayed longer and served us dessert and then she joined us at the table. "So, it seems from all the conversation that you two want a simple, country, but elegant affair?"

Brian smiled. "That's right."

Patty added, "I know it's short notice, but your home is so New England. It would be perfect for our wedding."

Paul leaned back. "We're honored that you thought of our home."

"I think the tent will be a nice addition," I said. "We could have the food in there, like a buffet."

Patty beamed. "Sounds wonderful. Maybe we could set the tables with colorful flowers and baby's breath, candles, antique teapots, little white lights around a chandelier and across the tent in the corners and —"

"Whoa. Where are we going to find these antiques?"

Brian smiled. "Mom, you love to go to estate sales. We could go to some tomorrow. We're not leaving until Tuesday morning."

"What if we found different flowered plates for everyone to eat off of?" Patty was bright-eyed. "We wouldn't have to rent any then."

Brian looked at the dining room clock. "Everything sounds great, but we'd better get going. We're supposed to meet some friends at the Salty Dog in about an hour."

I got up to join Martha for the clean-up, pleased that the first official meeting of the wedding planning committee was over. We had made progress and there were no arguments…so far.

Later that evening, Brian and Patty were still out, the kids were in bed and Paul was dozing next to me in front of the TV on the couch. My cell rang. It was Jim.

"Sorry, Mom. I forgot how late it was."

"That's okay, honey. What's up?" I put the TV on mute.

"The police finally got back to me about the bones."

I sat up. "And??"

"They *are* human bones...female. She would have been in her late teens or early twenties."

"That would put them in the right timeframe, based on the year of the picture."

"Yeah. They also said that their files for missing persons were not great from that time period. There was a lot of corruption and hush money floating around. Things didn't get reported."

"Do you think Natalie would be willing to have a DNA test done to compare with the DNA of the found bones?"

"I'll ask her. The police told me they'd file everything in their cold case department."

"Would you mind emailing Stephen Boudreaux the police report? He said he would like to be kept in touch with anything new."

"Sure, Mom. Say, how are the wedding plans coming along?"

"Pretty good. I'll email you what we're thinking. It'll be nice to see you in September."

"Thanks for the plane ticket. Love you."

* * *

Most everyone was up early for breakfast on the back porch. Paul had finished with the paper. I grabbed it to scan the garage/estate sales. As he left for his studio, Brian and Patty appeared in the doorway.

"Good morning. I was just telling your father that I'm going to check up in the hayloft for items you might want to use. Then maybe we could take in a few sales nearby."

Patty poured a coffee for herself and Brian. "Sounds exciting. I'm ready to go."

Up above the barn, I could see some boxes that we'd never unpacked when we moved out of Ohio, almost eight years before. I began my search and quickly found an open box of old plates. I'd collected them to use under some of my potted houseplants. There were about a dozen and they had no chips in them. I pushed the box closer to the stairway to take it downstairs. Then I found two old flowered teapots and a silver-plated one. They went next to the box of plates. Not bad for less than an hour, I thought. Let's see what Patty thinks.

I waited for the young couple in my office. Before I sat down to answer some emails, I went over to the bookshelf that held a very special blue-flowered teapot. I carefully removed its lid to see the 18th century gold coins hidden inside; the remnants of my last adventure. I thought about what greed and the desire for power can do to ordinary people, when dangled in front of them. The coins sparkled at the bottom. When I picked one up, the sun caught it at the right angle, creating a shimmering dot against the opposite wall.

Patty knocked on the office door. "I'm ready to go."

I quickly replaced the coin and fit the lid back onto the teapot. As I reached up to put it back on the shelf, I heard Patty ask, "Oh, that's a pretty one. Could we use that?"

"Not this one. It has too many memories for me," I said and turned to grab my purse from the desk. "Let's find Brian and go scavenging, I mean, antique hunting."

We didn't have to drive very far before Brian called out, "Hey Mom, look! There's an estate sale at that little brown bungalow you were always curious about."

I only managed to get in a quick look to my left before I drove past the house. "I didn't see it listed in the paper. Maybe we can stop on our way home."

I continued driving to the end of Brewster, almost into Dennis, for our first sale. We got lucky and left with several flowered dinner plates and a teapot.

Patty counted them. "With the plates you found in the hayloft, these get us up to thirty plates. Isn't that great?"

I closed the trunk on our treasures. "I can go to a few of the swap shops around the Cape next week to fill in what we need."

Brian checked his phone as we headed back to East Brewster. "What do you say we call it a day? I think we'll have enough for the wedding. I'd like to go into Hyannis this afternoon and do some shopping for a new sport coat."

"I don't mind." Patty turned to the back seat and blew Brian a kiss.

"Sounds fine to me," I said. "Let's make one more stop to check out that sale at the bungalow."

I'd always admired the craftsmanship of the old brown bungalow. Every time I passed it, I wondered who lived there. It reminded me of our first house, back in Ohio. Paul and I had been married for only a few years. Jim had just started walking and Brian was still a baby. I pulled in and parked to the side of the driveway. Tools were displayed outside of the garage. Porch furniture and gardening pots were set up across the lawn. The front door was propped open onto the large porch where big round posts flanked the stone steps. Inside, the walls were covered with floral wallpaper and trimmed in dark wood. I felt like I was stepping back into the '40s.

We walked through a small foyer to face a dark chunky wooden stairway that led upstairs. To my right was the living room and to the left was the dining room. I began my hunt in the kitchen, at the rear of the house. Brian disappeared into the basement and Patty wandered upstairs. After finding nothing that interested me in the kitchen, I also headed down to the basement, where the bargains could usually be found at this kind of sale.

Patty joined Brian and me downstairs. She picked up an old birdcage that had been retrofitted with a metal spiral for tea light holders. "I like this." The price was marked $10.

Brian found some old real estate signs that he could use for announcing where the beach ceremony was being held.

I whispered to both of them, "Let's see if we can find the owner and ask for lower prices. Doesn't hurt to try."

After a few minutes, I spotted a middle-aged woman in the dining room who was wearing a nametag that read *Ally*. She had a pleasant smile and her dark hair was cropped at the shoulder in a nice modern style. She wore a zippered sweatshirt and jeans.

I asked, "Hello. Can you help us?"

She turned to face me. "Yes, I can."

Brian and Patty held up their choices for her to inspect.

"What's the price on them now?" Ally asked.

Patty answered, "Ten for the birdcage, but we couldn't find a price on the signs."

Ally studied them for only a few seconds. "How about $10 for everything?"

"We'll take them," I said and handed over the money.

Brian spoke up, "Mom, let me get this."

"Shhh. My treat. It's not often that a son chooses to get married at his parents' house."

Ally looked over to me. "Isn't that nice. Do you live on the Cape?"

"Yes, right down the street from you."

"Oh, I don't live here anymore. My mom did, though, back when it was first built in the early forties."

"So you grew up in Brewster?" I asked.

She nodded. "My stepdad passed a few years ago. My mom followed soon after. I live in Boston now."

I took my receipt and went upstairs while Brian put our treasures in the car. There were some lovely crocheted table scarves and a few old flowered tablecloths folded neatly on a bed. Out of the corner of my eye, I noticed a beautiful honey maple box sitting on a dresser. I picked it up, but it was locked. When I shook it, I heard something rattling inside. I couldn't find a price, so I took it downstairs to ask Ally.

On the way down, my fingers traced the faded carvings across the lid. They were dusty and a little sticky, but the box held its own among the other fine pieces of furniture and collectibles.

Ally was out on the porch, quoting a price for some old books.

I waited for my turn to speak with her and then asked, "This box was upstairs, but it has no price on it. How much is it?"

"Not sure of its value nor what's inside. My mother lost the key years ago. She kept it in the attic. I remember she didn't want to break it open; she said it was too beautiful to damage. I honestly don't know what to charge."

I really wanted it, especially because it was locked. My curiosity kept pushing me to take home the mysterious golden box. "Would you take $30?"

"Okay."

"Thank you." I handed her the cash. "If I find anything important inside, I'll let you know. How long will you be on Cape?"

"As long it takes for me to clean everything out."

"Okay, let's exchange cards. We own a gallery down the street. My husband is the artist and we're open almost every day. You should stop by before you leave."

"I just might do that." Ally looked at the card, read the name, and said, "Bye, Nancy."

36

Present Day
VENICE BEACH – LOS ANGELES

DARYL MARCUS switched the Mr. Coffee machine on and laughed at the retro feeling of the small studio that he'd rented, just off the Boardwalk on Venice Beach. It was close enough to catch a few waves, watch the hot chicks roller-skating, and take in a lot of the nighttime action. He kept his cell close, just in case Margaret Cheung needed him.

It was almost sunrise. He grabbed his yoga mat and headed toward the beach to greet the rising sun. Starting his day with meditation kept him focused and strong. His line of work required patience and select skills. He was not very muscular, but he had earned a black belt. Marcus was also an expert in weaponry.

For his morning ritual, Marcus wore nothing but a tiny bathing suit and lay on the mat with his arms crossed against his chest in a mummy position. As the first rays of the sun cast their light across his tanned body, they lit his long gray hair, spread across the mat under his head in a dirty halo. His breath was slow and quiet, his chest barely moving up and down. From a distance, Marcus was so still that he looked dead.

When he was finished with his meditation, he made his way back to his studio. His cell rang.

"Mr. Marcus?" A thick accented voice spoke softly but precise. "I have an opportunity for you."

Marcus kept walking. "What've you got?"

"A very valued and wealthy client is looking for a trustworthy employee."

Marcus opened the door to his studio and poured himself a coffee. "I'm listening." He stored his rolled mat in the tiny closet and sat on the leather couch to hear more. "I'm interested. Text me the location."

Within the minute, his cell alerted him to a text. Marcus liked what he read, packed a few things into a gym bag, and then drove to Hollywood Hills.

A little before noon, Marcus was surprised to see that the gate of the Cannon estate was not closed. He drove down the driveway. The front door opened before he could knock.

A large burly man asked, "How'd you get in?"

Unfazed, Marcus kept his stance. "It was open. I'm here to see Gaylord Cannon."

"Wait here." The burly man started to close the door.

Marcus thrust his foot on the threshold and pushed the door back. "Glad to see you're careful, buddy, but I'm expected." He brushed the man aside and dropped his gym bag on the foyer floor. "You left the gate open, stupid." Within seconds the doorman grabbed Marcus from behind in a headlock and tried to throw him out the door. The two men struggled as Mr. Cannon appeared.

"All right! All right! What's going on here?" He rolled his fingers across the gold eagle on his cane and yelled, "Gerald! That's enough!"

Marcus managed to say a few words as Gerald's arm squeezed tighter around his throat. "I'm Daryl Marcus," he sputtered. "Sent by Margaret Cheung." He continued to try to wrestle free from Gerald's death grip.

Cannon lifted his cane in the air. "Let him go."

Gerald removed his arm from Marcus's neck, stepped back and straightened his Armani navy blue suit, keeping a wary eye on the stranger.

Marcus extended one hand and rubbed his throat with the other. "Nice to meet you, Gerald."

Cannon turned around. "I suggest you two put on some old clothes. There's a little matter that needs to be tended to inside that room." His cane pointed at the wall that hid the secret room. "Gerald will explain." The old man disappeared behind his office door.

Marcus stood and stared where Cannon had pointed. He couldn't see a door. "Well, Gerald, whatever it is, it can't be that bad." He laughed. "So, what's our plan?"

It took Marcus and Gerald half a day to clean Donald's blood off the floor of the secret room. They spent the evening burying his body near the back of the Cannon estate. It was Marcus's idea to use the golf cart to transport everything back and forth. Gerald produced a slight grin of appreciation; anything to make the job easier.

Cannon busied himself with Donald's personal effects. He put the dead butler's cash in his own wallet; then he wrote the current year, plus Donald's initials, on the outside of a gray shoebox. He chortled to himself. It felt good to be back doing what he loved.

After Gerald told him that everything was clean, Cannon carried the box into the secret room. Once inside, he stood to take pleasure in the knowledge that everything surrounding him was all his doing. He ran his fingers across a row of shoeboxes. His first killing in January 1947 was never memorialized for him to remember. He shook his head in disappointment.

As he scanned the display of boxes, Cannon recalled that over the years, with the help of his beloved cocaine, he had rid the world of whores, criminals, and greedy, evil people who'd brought sadness to the good ones. His mother would have approved. Then there were the others: poor souls who had gotten in the way on his heroic path of making things right, like his poor butler, Donald. He placed the butler's shoebox on the bottom shelf.

Cannon returned to his office and picked up the scissors, glue, and markers, to put them away in a drawer on the side of his desk. He pulled on the knob, but it was stuck, again. "Shit." He summoned his two new employees. "Which one of you can handle a hammer?"

Gerald offered, "I killed a man with a hammer once."

"No. That's not what I mean." Cannon attempted to open the stubborn drawer. "Can you fix this?"

"Let me take a look." Marcus moved over to the side and tried to jiggle the drawer, with no luck. He ran his fingers over the front of it. "I'll see what I can do."

Cannon stood up. "Fine. You do that." He turned to Gerald. "I'm going to rest. Let me know when dinner is ready."

Marcus had soon removed the top drawer for a better look inside the stuck drawer. To his surprise, there was a false bottom to it. The drawer had swollen over the years and extended out quite a bit. He took a letter opener and lifted the wood up. Trapped inside were receipts dated from the 1940s. He went to find his boss.

"You found what?" Cannon stepped out of the upstairs bathroom.

"There was a false bottom. The wood had swollen, preventing it from opening."

The two men descended the stairs as they talked.

"You say there were some papers inside?"

"Yes sir."

"Tell Gerald I'll eat in thirty minutes. I first want to see what you found." Cannon closed the office door behind him.

The mahogany desk and the cane were the two things that Gaylord Cannon favored from his father. Now he was curious about this new discovery. A dozen old receipts were lying in a pile on his desk. He sat down to read them. One receipt in particular caught his attention. It was from a Paris jeweler, dated 1946.

The yellowed paper listed two items. One was a yellow diamond set in a gold ring – Value: $40,000. The other was a pearl pouch – Value: $1,000,000.

Cannon counted the zeros that were written next to the pearl pouch's value twice. He sat back and thought of the night his father sent him, Big Paulie, and Jeff to retrieve what Gertie had stolen. He touched the brittle paper again and wondered if that's why his father wanted the pouch returned more than he wanted the ring. If his memory served him right, Gertie Foster and Maggie Foster were cousins. He also remembered he'd returned to Miss Sylvia's, about a month later, and found that the room had been cleaned out. The men who were repairing the building at the time had said they knew nothing of any items that were left inside. Cannon also had discovered there was no evidence that Maggie Foster had stayed around in Hollywood. After reviewing this information for a few seconds, he decided Maggie must have returned to Cape Cod, possibly with the ring and pouch.

After dinner, Cannon met Marcus in the hallway. "Marcus. Are you good on the computer?"

"Yes sir."

He handed him a piece of paper. "I want you to locate this woman. She may be dead by now, but there might be something you can uncover about her life and what happened to her."

Marcus read the scribbles. "No problem, sir."

"Thank you. You may use my computer in the office."

Marcus went to get a beer before he settled in for an evening online with Google. Within five minutes, he began his search on ancestory.com and peoplesearch.com for 'Margaret Foster or Maggie Foster, Massachusetts'.

Gaylord Cannon woke the next morning to a written report from Marcus of what he'd discovered online. According to the U.S. census, which had been taken every ten years, a Margaret Foster, age eleven years old, had lived in Brewster, Massachusetts in 1940. In 1947 she'd married an Edward Grant. They'd remained in Brewster and had one child, Alicia. In 1960, Margaret Grant still resided in Brewster, Massachusetts. A record of her death was recorded in 2014. Alicia Grant was listed as the current owner of Margaret Grant's Brewster house.

Cannon leaned over his desk. Perhaps it was time to revisit his father's request to find the stolen jewelry. The ring might still be around. Given the fact that all of his father's oil wells had gone dry and his own investments had suffered during the recent stock market crash, an influx of money would be just what he needed to restore his wealth. First he'd contact Alicia Grant, and then he'd pay a call on that snoopy lady from New England, Nancy Caldwell. She might know more than she alluded to.

He gazed at a framed photo of his dear mother. Gaylord had made sure his father had suffered in the end. He'd owed that to his mother, since his father had slowly killed her each time he'd boasted to his friends about his affairs with other women, and then had lied to her about them. Yes, the old man deserved to die in such a gruesome manner. Gaylord Cannon blew a silent kiss to his mother.

At dinner that evening, Marcus and Gerald joined Cannon at the table in the dining room. "How would you two like to accompany me on a trip to Cape Cod? I've heard it's beautiful there in early September."

Gerald shoveled his food, but stopped for a second to swallow. "Sounds great, sir. I'd really like to go."

Marcus was quiet.

"What about you, my friend?" Cannon took a sip of wine.

"Well, sir. I don't fly."

"Hmmmm."

"But I do drive and would enjoy a road trip, if that would be all right."

Cannon put down his fork. "It will take a week to schedule a private flight for us, so if you leave tomorrow, we should all arrive together in the quaint little town of Brewster, Massachusetts."

"Thank you, sir. That would be agreeable."

"Marcus, you've handled yourself well since you've been in my employment. It is a bit of an inconvenience for you not to fly with us, but I'll let it go, this time. Besides, transporting some essential items in your car would be advantageous for what needs to be done." Cannon patted his mouth with a linen napkin and stood up. "Now, if you'll excuse me. Marcus, would you please meet me in my office in ten minutes? I like you. I have a feeling you will prove to be invaluable in our future endeavors together."

"Be right there, sir."

Gerald continued stuffing his mouth. Cannon's compliment to Marcus slipped past his attention.

That night, Marcus carried two heavy black suitcases to his car. As he slammed the Audi's trunk shut, he thought that for an old guy, Cannon had quite an arsenal. He laughed to himself and decided that the upcoming trip was going to be fun.

37

Present Day
HOLLYWOOD HILLS – LOS ANGELES

STEPHEN BOUDREAUX was on the phone with Jim Caldwell. "That's all right, Jim. I'm just glad you've been so busy earning a living." He stood up to pour himself some iced water. "No problem. I won't tell your Mom you forgot to call me about the police report." Stephen laughed. "Take care. If I find anything else in my search on this end, I'll tell her myself."

He hung up, sat back down at his desk and rehashed what Jim had told him. Scribbling the name Gaylord Cannon on a big legal pad, he doodled for a few minutes, then threw the pen down, stood up and said, "Shit." He grabbed his shoulder gun and headed for the door. On his way out, Stephen signaled to Patricia. "I'll be gone for the rest of the day. Call me if anything important comes up."

On the drive to Hollywood Hills, Stephen wasn't sure why he was taking the time to revisit the old man, or what he was even going to say to get in to see Cannon again, but now he was curious. The guy said he would call the police on him if he ever returned. Of course, Stephen had a few connections of his own, like his friend Jimmy Fredericks, so he'd be able to talk himself out of any problems with the police. If he did find out something new, it may give him another chance to talk with Nancy.

The estate's gate was open. Stephen drove in thinking there must be something wrong with the security system.

Gerald knew Mr. Cannon was not happy with the current security company and thought the visitor was the company's representative, so he waited at the front door.

As Stephen stepped inside, he asked, "Is Mr. Cannon here? I have an appointment with Gaylord Cannon." He then inched his way over to a large ornate gold-trimmed mirror and pretended to fix his hair. "You're new here. Where's Donald?"

Gerald was quiet as he stood with his legs spread, arms away from his side, ready for anything.

Stephen added, "I'm from the security company. What's your name?"

"Gerald. You wait here." He went upstairs.

Stephen watched him disappear and then hurried over to where Nancy had said there was a secret door. As he felt the wall for a place to open it, he noticed two bulging suitcases near the back of the foyer and a travel itinerary resting on top of one of them. With a quick glance, he saw today's date, Cannon's name, and Boston. It took him off guard, but only for a moment. Probably just a coincidence, he thought. He quickly decided if he wasn't going to get a chance to talk to Cannon, maybe he could come back on his own time. He unlocked one of the windows.

Gerald's feet pounded down the steps. Visibly angry, he yelled, "Mr. Cannon isn't expecting anyone from security..."

Stephen bolted out the front door before Gerald hit the last step on the winding staircase. The burly man kept up a decent pace, all the way out, as he followed the intruder. Stephen leaped into his open convertible and barreled out of the driveway. In his rearview mirror, he could see Gerald pointing a gun at him, but escaped before a shot was fired. He pulled into a small restaurant, a few miles away from the estate, for some take-out food, and then he returned for a stakeout. He parked his car out of sight and began his wait for everyone to leave. After a few minutes, he gave Nancy a call. "Nancy? This is Stephen, from L.A."

"Oh, hello. What's up?"

"You'll never guess what I'm doing right now." He wiped his Russian dressing-stained mouth with a napkin.

"No. I don't think I will." She sounded out of breath. "Listen, Stephen, I'm walking on the beach and may lose my connection."

He sensed urgency in her voice so he spoke quickly. "I just wanted to tell you that I think Gaylord Cannon might be coming to the Cape—"

"Cannon's coming here?"

"There's a good possibility he is. Keep your wits about you." He could hear the wind coming from the phone.

"Uh. Okay."

The phone went dead. "Nancy?" No response. At least he had warned her.

As he finished the last of his Reuben sandwich, Stephen turned his attention back to the black iron entrance gate that was still open. Minutes later, a black SUV pulled out and then the gate closed. He wiped his mouth again. All he needed was a quick look inside that hidden room.

38

Present Day
BREWSTER – CAPE COD

ALLY GRANT looked around the near-empty living room of her childhood home. The sale of the home's contents had been successful. Maybe there was some way she could keep the old house as a summer place and still live and work in Boston. She loved being a lawyer at Smith, Jones, and Wentz. Financially, the little Cape bungalow was probably out of the picture. And yet, it held so many memories.

She grabbed a cup of coffee and settled in at the black-and-white porcelain kitchen table to go through a box of personal papers of her mother's. The old table had been a favorite of Ally's ever since she was little. Her fingers traced the printed black designs that made a checkered pattern across its top. She smiled at seeing a few X marks that she'd drawn inside the little boxes and remembered doodling as a child with a pen across the old-fashioned table. She laughed at what a brat she must have been growing up.

Tired but curious, Ally stared at the cardboard box and then reached inside to lift up a stack of receipts, medical bills, and checking account statements. Underneath them, at the bottom, was a small leather-bound book. The day before the estate sale, she'd emptied her mother's dresser, thinking the papers in the bottom drawer could wait for later, but she'd never taken notice of the book.

Opening it slowly, she realized it was a journal. Ally couldn't recall ever seeing her mother write in it. The first page was dated: *May 15, 1947*. It was a short entry that said Maggie had gone on a trip to Hollywood with a cousin Gertie that didn't end well. Ally never remembered an Aunt Gertie.

After several pages, she discovered that her stepfather, Peter Marshall, had been a big part of her mother's life before she was born. In fact, her mother had been in love with him. So he was not just someone her mother had met in 1961, and then married a year later, which was the story she recalled. Ally kept reading.

Strong emotions began to pour off the page and into Ally's head and heart. Evidently her mother had thought she was pregnant with Peter Marshall's child when he left Cape Cod for California. Was Peter her father? Her mother had then married Eddie Grant. Tears welled in Ally's eyes as she read the despair that her mother had felt when she knew she was destined to marry a man she didn't love only to protect her unborn child.

Why hadn't her mother told her the whole story? It would have made such a difference in the relationship with her stepfather.

By 8 p.m., she'd read a description of Eddie's death and the days after the funeral. Ally felt the fear in her mother's words about the future and being a single parent. Raising a child alone was never easy. But why would Peter and her mother keep their relationship hidden from her as she moved through her young adult years? Ally almost felt cheated. She soothed her feelings with the notion that back then, people just kept more secrets.

Ally dug deeper into the box and found her mother's wedding certificate and compared the dates on it with the date of her own birth, and also when Peter left the Cape. They were all within a nine-to-ten-month time period. Peter must have been her real father. She had to finish reading the journal.

Towards the end of the journal her mother stated that on November 20, 1950, she had sold a ring for $50,000 at an auction house in Dennis. So that's where the trust fund came from! But where did she get the ring? Ally continued reading. On the next page of the journal, her mother thanked Gertie for the ring. It didn't make sense to Ally. No one in the Foster family, including relatives, were wealthy. Where did Gertie get such an expensive ring?

It grew late, and Ally became more exhausted by the minute. She rinsed her cup and, with dazed eyes, watched the water circle the drain. She remembered the honey maple box that she'd sold to the lady from Brewster. She shouldn't have done that, she decided. Her mother's journal had been hidden for all these years, maybe there was more in that box that she should know about. Ally looked for the lady's business card. She'd give her a call in the morning. Maybe she could buy her mother's box back.

39

Present Day
CROSBY LANDING BEACH – CAPE COD

IT WAS A great day for a walk along the dog path, even though a gusty coastal wind swirled the thin beach grasses into little semi-circles against the sandy and rocky terrain. My sunglasses kept the sand particles out of my eyes as I puzzled over Stephen's call. Should I be worried if Cannon was really coming to Cape Cod?

As I approached the dune that led to the ocean side of the path, the wind blew stronger. I decided to turn around and return the way of the protected dog path. It was then that I noticed the long gray silvery outline of an object out on the sandy marsh. It almost resembled a naked body lying on the ground. I hadn't noticed it before, but then my head had been down against the wind. I stepped closer. The object didn't move. I took a few steps further and finally recognized that it was a man on his back stretched across a long narrow board. He wore nothing but a towel draped across his middle. His long, gray hair was splayed like a halo around his head. His arms, crossed against his chest, and his bony but muscular shoulder blades, that protruded up above his neckline, created the image of a mummy. He looked dead.

I doubled back towards the beach so that I could call 911 out of sight of the man's body. I kept turning around to see if he had moved. He hadn't. I stopped walking when I made a connection with the dispatcher. After a detailed conversation, I was finally linked to someone who actually knew where I was and who could help me. "Yes, I'll meet the officer in the parking lot."

I carefully returned along the path, passing the body at a safe distance, to get to the parking lot. He was still not moving.

It seemed like an eternity as I waited at Crosby Landing for the police cruiser. When he pulled up next to my car I recognized him right away. It was Officer Gomes, the investigating officer who, a few years back, had answered my call after I'd uncovered the baby's skull and gold coins at the bottom of the old root cellar in our backyard.

"Mrs. Caldwell. Nice to see you again."

"Yes, the same to you." I began to repeat everything I had told the dispatcher.

There were two other cars in the parking lot besides mine. I offered a question to get the ball rolling. "Maybe one of those cars belongs to the guy in the dunes? You want me to show you where I found him?"

Officer Gomes walked a few feet away to read the license plate of the first car. Then he slowly got back into his cruiser. I tapped my fingertips against the hood of my car as I waited. I assumed he was searching for the car's owner.

He finally got out and said, "This car belongs to a woman from Connecticut."

"What about the other one, over there?" I pointed to the car furthest from where we were standing. It had a California license plate. I grew impatient as I watched him once more walk slowly over to read the plate on the second car and then return to his cruiser to punch in the numbers. I wanted to show him where the man was lying.

"Why don't you show me where the body is?"

Relieved to get going, I started off at a fast pace, but slowed up as Officer Gomes took his time behind me. His black uniform and leather shoes were out of place on the beach. His strides were long, but slow. All the way, I kept apologizing for bothering him and actually calling 911. It was a long walk and I was beginning to feel foolish.

When we reached the area where I'd seen the body, Officer Gomes stopped. "Okay, I see him." He placed one hand on his gun as he took a few steps forward.

I followed right behind with no fear. After all, he had the gun.

"Hello there," the officer called out.

We kept walking closer.

The man moved his arms, sat up, and turned to us. "Can I help you?"

"Well, maybe you can help me." Officer Gomes kept his hand on the gun and stopped a few feet away from the man who was now sitting up on the board.

I stayed where I was, several feet back, curious as ever.

"Would you please stand up, sir?"

"Of course, officer." He took the towel off to reveal that he was wearing a man's Speedo. On top of his chest was also a folded blue denim shirt.

We waited for him to cover himself up.

"Is everything all right, sir?" Officer Gomes asked.

"Why, yes. Everything's fine. I was just enjoying my morning meditation." He looked over to me and then back to the officer. "Have I done something wrong?"

"No," said the officer. "This lady was just concerned for your safety. You weren't moving and looked as if you might be dead."

The semi-naked man laughed. "Well, that's what you look like when you meditate."

"I'm sorry to have disturbed you." I took a few steps closer. "I feel very stupid. Sometimes I'm just a little too curious."

He looked over to the policeman. "If it's all right with you, Officer, may I leave now?"

"Yes, you're free to go."

The mysterious man turned to leave by way of the ocean side. As he passed me, he stared at me in a weird way. Then he said, "Brewster seems to be a bit *too* caring of a town. Good day."

I watched him disappear over the dune that led to the beach until Officer Gomes came alongside me. "Are you going to continue your walk, Mrs. Caldwell?"

"No. I think I'll go home. Sorry again to have bothered you."

"Don't be. We had a bulletin issued for a man with autism who had been missing for 24 hours, and I thought maybe you had found him. He was about forty years old."

We made small talk as we walked back to the parking lot. I felt a little better that I hadn't wasted his time. The California car was still parked in the lot. I stopped and asked one more question. "I was just wondering, what was the name of the owner of the California car?"

Officer Gomes slid back into his car, shut the door and then rolled down the window. "Daryl Marcus."

40

Present Day
BREWSTER – CAPE COD

BY THE TIME I got home from the beach, it was almost dinnertime. Martha had brownies baking in the oven. They smelled delicious. Danny was sitting at the kitchen table playing a video game.

"Where's Daddy?"

"In his studio," he said, without looking up at me.

"Make sure you don't nibble on those treats in the oven. We're going to eat soon."

"*Awww*, please?"

"Maybe just a small one," I said, and kissed the top of his head.

I left the kitchen to find Paul on the computer, checking his email. "Anything interesting?" I said as I sat in the recliner by the window.

"No. But some guy called you. I think it was that private detective from L.A."

"What'd he want?" I was interested to know what Stephen had said, but deep down I wished he hadn't called the house.

"He'll call back if he finds anything at the estate. What's he looking for? And whose estate?"

"Remember I told you about him on the way home from the airport?" I was tired from my walk and felt a little annoyed at having to repeat myself. "The estate belongs to the old Hollywood recluse, Gaylord Cannon." I got up to leave, anxious to check messages on my phone, which I'd left in the house. "I'll be back later."

I assumed Stephen must have called the house when we lost connection on the beach. The fact that he returned to the estate made me wonder if he'd found anything new. He must have uncovered something. As I entered the living room, I heard the house phone ringing. It stopped after a few rings so I assumed Paul had answered. I sat at my desk going through some papers.

Paul came in. "Just got off the phone with Jim."

"How's he doing?"

"He's fine, but he mentioned something that surprised me. Were you with this guy Stephen a lot while you were in California?"

I sat up straight. "We went to eat a few times and spent an afternoon visiting Gaylord Cannon, trying to find out what he knew about Gertie Foster. You know, she's the woman who I thought was buried next to Jim's apartment."

"Yeah, I remember. Jim mentioned that this Stephen had called him about the police report, and then he made a joke that he thought the guy was interested in you."

"What?" I was surprised that Jim would say that to his father, but he was a kidder. It must have been Stephen's note he found back at the Georgian Hotel, the one where Stephen had signed it *fondly.* That's probably what encouraged him to say anything to his dad.

Paul looked serious. "Well, it may have been funny to Jim, but it made me sit up and take notice."

"Well, it's nothing. He's a PI who has connections with the local police. The only real time I spent with him was when we drove to Hollywood Hills. The other so-called dinners happened after my talk at the Treasure Hunter meetings." I resented, again, having to explain myself and probably came off as too defensive, maybe even hiding something. I regretted being snippy.

It wasn't smart of me to react like that, because Paul stood up, and as he left, he said, "I know you love me, Nancy, but sometimes I wonder."

I swiveled my chair around to face the computer. Doesn't he know that I love him and I would never do anything to...but wait, I did do something.

After dinner and the kids were in bed, we both grew quiet. I didn't even want to tell Paul about the incident on the beach from earlier today, with the meditation guy. I wasn't sure if I was punishing myself or keeping it from him in spite. I really wanted to tell him; it was an intense event. A quick kiss between us was all that happened before we went to bed. It was warm outside, but it felt a little cool between us as we said goodnight. My stubbornness took precedence over rationality as I got ready for bed. Guilt took over me as I tried to fall sleep.

41

Present Day
HOLLYWOOD HILLS – LOS ANGELES

STEPHEN GOT OUT of his car and slowly followed the stone wall that guarded the estate until he came to a large section covered with thick ivy. In only two jumps, he'd caught the top of the wall with his fingers while the toe of his shoe landed on a large root. Within seconds he was up and over the wall. He silently ran to the back of the house, to the window he had unlocked earlier. After a quick push on the glass, he crawled inside.

It was still light out, but dusk was slowly moving in. He pulled out his flashlight. The foyer was dimly lit with a single security light. The suitcases were gone. Stephen felt for the secret door. When he entered the small dark room, his hand moved over the wall to find the light switch. As he scanned the room he stared at the three walls of shelves that surrounded him. "Shoeboxes?!"

Moving swiftly, he opened up a box labeled, B/C 1962. Inside were items that belonged to a Betty Crane: a driver's license, pair of pearl earrings, silver watch with a narrow rectangular clock face, and some cash. Before he closed the lid to replace the box back on the shelf, Stephen used his phone to capture the woman's information and the contents of the box. He then lifted the lid of a box labeled: D/B, 2015. It contained a wallet with the driver's license of Donald Baxter, a wedding portrait of a middle-aged woman and a man, who looked familiar. He'd definitely seen the face on the license before, but he couldn't place it.

He inspected ten more boxes; all contained similar personal effects. Stephen recorded the names and dates written on them, plus whatever information he found inside. It was too late to call Nancy. As he drove home to his house in Marina Del Rey, Stephen decided to get a hold of his buddy, Jimmy Fredricks, down at the precinct.

Once inside the narrow 1970, shotgun-styled house, Stephen poured himself a glass of wine and then settled in front of the computer. He opened up the camera on his phone to retrieve the information he'd recorded from the boxes and Googled *Betty Crane 1962*. A missing person's report from Los Angeles Police Department popped right up. Betty Crane, originally from Idaho, had worked as a waitress at the Tropicana Lounge. Last seen at the Roosevelt Hotel, June 13, 1962. Stephen then ran searches for the other names on the shoeboxes. They were all reported as missing persons. He quickly booked a red eye flight to the East coast.

42

Present Day
BREWSTER – CAPE COD

PAUL WAS UP early and out in his studio. I took my time and didn't appear until around 9 a.m. Martha greeted me with, "There was a call for you, Nancy, while you were in the shower."

"Oh?"

"The woman said her name was Ally Grant and that she would call later."

"Did she say what she wanted?"

"Something about a box that you bought at her estate sale."

"Oh, yeah. I bought a box at a house sale this past weekend, when I went with Brian and Patty." I poured some coffee. "Let me know if she calls again."

Paul was photographing a new painting for his files. "Do you know where the box is that I bought over the weekend? The one I asked you to look at to see if you could open it?"

He was quiet.

"Paul?" I waited for a few more seconds before I started looking around the workshop for the box myself.

He stepped away from the tripod. "Sorry. I just needed to get the right light for the picture."

I turned to him. "I know you're busy, but where's that maple box?"

"I put it away so it wouldn't get damaged while I built some frames." He came over, reached underneath the worktable and retrieved the box.

"Maybe you should let it be. Martha said the lady that I bought it from called this morning. I don't know what she wants, but we'd better leave it alone until I talk with her."

"Whatever you say." He sounded disconnected.

I stood at the door. "Are we okay?"

Paul grabbed a stack of mail and walked over to me. "Yesterday's delivery brought a surprise."

"What's the matter?" I started flipping through the letters. My hand stopped on the bill for the lease of our printer. Paul had already opened it.

"We got a late fee. Did you forget to pay it?"

"I'm sorry, I guess I did. I was busy before I left for L.A."

"That's the problem. When are you going to stop all this travelling?" He turned his back to me and returned to the workbench.

"But I like to travel. I enjoy my life as a so-called adventurer, or at least an aspiring one." I smiled at him.

"Well, I'm getting tired of it. I miss you. The kids miss you. And I never know what you're going to get yourself involved in."

I waited to hear him out.

"I love you, Nancy." He turned around and looked me straight in the eyes. "The thought of you getting hurt, or even losing you, makes me sick to my stomach."

"Paul, I'm very careful. I know how to handle myself in almost every situation." I laughed again. "At least, I think I do."

He answered quickly, "It's not funny."

"I'm sorry if you think I'm not capable." His comment upset me so I started to leave.

"Don't go, Nancy," Paul yelled. "We need to talk."

I quickly turned around. "So you think I should just stay home and answer to your every need?" Now I was angry and my words spilled out. "I did that a long time ago. I want something different now. I've always been there for you and the children. I never complained when you wanted to quit your job with that graphic design firm to become a professional artist on your own. We lost all of our security. Do you know how many times I went to bed frightened that we wouldn't be able to make the mortgage payment?" I felt my face turning red.

"You should have told me how you felt."

"I did. And then something would come up and we'd forget about it. I kept everything on an even keel for us. You know how proud I am of you and what we both have accomplished together."

"We seem to be doing okay now."

"Yes, we are, aren't we? With all the bonuses and rewards from my so-called silly treasure hunting, our lives have gotten even easier. But it's my turn now. I like discovering and solving mysteries. I don't necessarily go looking for danger, but it seems to find me."

"Don't you think Molly and Danny deserve the same attention you gave the other kids by staying home with them?"

"Yes, they do. Might I remind you that I'm with them even more than the other kids because I don't have to always be promoting you as an artist? Besides, Martha is here. Thanks to my finder's fees, she's part of our budget now. Martha helps me make sure they do everything they're supposed to do. She's wonderful and very good with the kids."

"I guess I never looked at it that way."

"I'm teaching our children to be independent and to follow their dreams. I don't have to remind you of how important that is."

My cell rang. It was Stephen. I ignored it. "I've got some emails to check on. We'll talk later." I left for my office.

My stomach felt like it was doing flip-flops. Paul and I hadn't had an argument in years, not even during the move to Cape Cod and me getting pregnant again, not once, but twice after I turned forty. I buried myself in aimlessly reading the news headlines online and thinking I should have answered Stephen's call.

Casey came in after a few minutes. "Hey, Mom. I'm taking the kids to the mall tonight after work. I'd promised to take them to see the new Disney movie before I go back to school next week."

"That's good. I almost forgot." I kept reading the article on my screen. A group of underwater archaeologists believed they'd discovered the remains of Captain Kidd's pirate ship in Madagascar.

The group's captain was Barry Clifford, the treasure hunter from Provincetown who'd found the wreck of the *Whydah*. "Going to work now?" I asked. My eyes were glued to the screen.

"Yeah, but I'll be home before dinner so I can take the kids to McDonald's." I heard Casey run upstairs to get her purse.

Stephen called on my cell phone. I ignored it once more to give Casey a hug before she left. I didn't want to talk with him now. By noon, everyone was busy doing his or her own things. I was still sitting in front of the computer when the house phone rang.

I heard Martha pick up. She knocked on the door, "Nancy, I think it's that lady from the sale again."

"Thanks." I picked the phone up. "Hello?" I listened. "Yes, I understand. You're in Hyannis all day? Where shall we meet?" I wrote down the address of a little restaurant in Chatham that she suggested. "At 7:30? I'll bring the box with me."

As I left for the kitchen, the phone rang again. After two rings, it stopped. Paul must have answered it. I found my appetite and began a search for a nice turkey wrap made of lettuce. I grabbed the mayo and mustard jars. While my head was in the refrigerator, I saw Paul out of the corner of my eye.

"So this Stephen called again. Nancy, what's going on?"

"Nothing. What'd he say?"

"That he needed to talk with you and no one else." He got a drink of soda. "Why would he say that?"

"I don't know. I'll call him later and find out. No big deal."

Paul walked away.

I followed him into his studio. He was priming a new canvas when I came in. "I'm sorry, Paul. I'm just a little tired and lost my temper before."

He kept brushing on the white gesso and didn't look up.

"Don't ignore me. You need to understand, I'd never hurt you or the children. I love all of you with my whole heart. I simply like what I'm doing at this moment in my life." I sat down on the workshop stairs. "It seems to satisfy a part of me that I could not achieve if I stayed home all the time. It makes me feel whole. I've been and will continue to be a good and loving mother. You know that."

He leaned the brush on the edge of the paint can and stared out the window.

I stood up. "Well, I guess that's that."

Paul looked at me. His blue eyes grew glassy. I could see he felt hurt. He turned his back to me once more and still said nothing.

"Paul. I'm sorry. It won't happen again, the bills, I mean." After another moment of silence, I left. I held back my feelings until I was upstairs in our bedroom. Then I fell on the bed and cried, torn between what everyone wanted me to be and what I wanted to do.

43

Present Day
ORLEANS – CAPE COD

THE OCEAN COVE Hotel in the small town of Orleans was satisfactory for Gaylord Cannon and Gerald. It was nestled among pine trees and faced a small cove of water that led to the Atlantic. The hotel was very private and had easy access to the Lower Cape. Cannon was reclining in an overstuffed chair when someone knocked on the door.

Gerald looked through the peephole. "It's Marcus."

"Mr. Cannon," said Marcus as he closed the door behind him. "I hope you had a pleasant trip to the Cape. I know I did." He fixed himself a drink from the small suite's kitchen. "Guess who I ran into on the beach yesterday?"

"I don't like to play games. Out with it." Cannon looked disturbed but interested.

"Nancy Caldwell."

He sat up. "How do you know it was her?"

"Back in L.A., when you asked me to find info on that Maggie Foster, I happened to check out the person listed on the business card on your desk. That's who I met yesterday." Marcus sat opposite his employer. "What's she got to do with our business here?"

"When you need to know my business, I'll tell you. You sure it was her?"

"Yup."

"Gerald! I want to leave in about an hour. Make sure the car is ready." Cannon then glared at Marcus. "Transfer that cargo you brought in your car to the SUV."

* * *

The Grant bungalow in Brewster was set back from the road with a long driveway that circled around and behind the house. Gerald stopped the black SUV next to a small sidewalk that led to the front porch. He gave it a quick once over. "Doesn't look like anyone's home."

Cannon peered out the car's window and then rubbed the top of his cane. "Marcus. Get out and see if there's anyone inside."

"Yes, sir." He slid out, followed the little path to the front steps, and knocked on the door.

Cannon watched him peer through the windows that faced out to the porch.

Marcus returned to the car, shrugged his shoulders, and shook his head.

Cannon tapped Gerald's shoulder with his cane. "Drive around back."

Marcus followed the car to the rear of the house. When they stopped in the back, he leaned next to the closed window and yelled, "It looks empty. What do you want me to do now?'

Cannon's window opened. "Get us inside. We'll wait here." The window slowly closed.

Within five minutes, Marcus was in. He first swept the rooms to make sure no one was home and then he went upstairs.

Gerald and Cannon appeared in the doorway.

Marcus came down the stairs. "Just a bed and a few suitcases up there."

All three entered the kitchen. Maggie Foster's Medicare statements, doctor bills, legal documents, and receipts were strewn across the white porcelain table. Marcus and Gerald left to see what was in the basement. Cannon began rifling through the papers.

Maggie's journal was over to the side. He picked it up, saw the first entry, sat down and began to read. He heard Marcus go back upstairs, but continued reading. As he skimmed Maggie's words, he hoped to find a mention about the ring and pearl pouch. Nothing but drivel from a stupid woman, he thought, until…an entry about a trust fund caught his eye. It'd been established for her daughter for thirty thousand. As he read further, Cannon discovered the money had come from the sale of a ring owned by her cousin, Gertie.

Marcus returned with a big smile on his face and threw Nancy Caldwell's business card on the table. "Look what I found upstairs in the suitcase."

* * *

Somewhere over the middle of the country, Stephen tried to sleep on his red eye flight to the East Coast, but the pilot interrupted everyone's peace with an announcement that the plane was being delayed and re-routed to New York instead of Boston. Technical difficulties. All the passengers began to grumble.

44

Present Day
BREWSTER – CAPE COD

THE COOL TOWEL against my eyes felt calming. It was almost 5:30 p.m. I went downstairs. "Martha, don't forget that I'm going out to dinner tonight."

"Is Paul going with you?"

"Not sure."

"Well, let me know. If he's going with you, and the kids are gone at the movies, I'll put the food away for tomorrow."

"I'll go check," I said on my way to the studio. I hoped Paul was not angry with me. I found him laying out another new painting. "Want to go to dinner with me and that lady from the estate sale?"

"I don't think so."

"You sure?" I sensed a chill still lingered between us.

"Tell Martha to put the dinner away. I'm not very hungry."

I could tell Paul was deep in composing the soon-to-be piece of art and knew not to bother him. He would be occupied for the next several hours. "See you later then. Love you."

The Midnight Café was new to the Chatham area. I was glad I'd Googled the location before I left home. There were only a few cars in the lot; not surprising for a new place. I entered the restaurant with the maple box in a canvas bag in one hand and my phone in the other. "I'm meeting an Ally Grant," I said to the hostess.

"Yes. Your party is already seated."

I followed her past several high topped, glossy wooden tables, chairs, twinkling lights, and around ten people at the bar, all chatting and eating. The savory smells of garlic, rosemary, and onion made me hungry. I extended my hand as I placed the bag under the table and sat down. "Nice to see you again, Ally."

"It was so kind of you to meet and agree to return the box to me." She looked down to the floor.

I opened the bag for her to see inside. "When you explained to me that you'd found a secret journal from your mother, I understood your desire to have the box back. Especially since it was locked."

The waitress came over to take our orders.

Ally looked at me. "It was quite a shock to find the journal. I'd never seen my mother write in it. After reading it, I discovered that she had a few secrets before I was born." She sipped her wine.

"Really?" I stirred my herbal tea.

"It seems that she knew my stepfather, Peter Marsh, before she married my father. There was a relationship between them. It got me questioning who my real father is."

"That must have been a shock."

"Well, the dates were right for me to question who did what and when."

I chose not to pursue the possible illegitimate topic. "Did you find any other secrets?"

"Yes, in fact there were a few strange entries from a trip she took to Hollywood with a cousin, a few months before she married Eddie. Not a lot of detail about it, only that she was frightened, cut her trip short, and returned to Cape Cod by herself."

"Sounds like a mystery to me. What was the year she went to Hollywood?"

"1947."

I sat back in my chair. "Did she mention the name of her cousin?"

Our meals were delivered and I began to eat my chicken and quinoa salad.

"I think her cousin's name was Gertie."

45

Present Day
BREWSTER – CAPE COD

PAUL DECIDED TO work on the painting a little longer in his studio. While he concentrated on his brush strokes and composition, he thought about what Nancy had told him, especially her reasons why she should continue to solve mysterious events that just happen to cross her path. She was right, he admitted to himself. She had been there for him when he was struggling with his career, and he probably should be there for her now. Being curious always made her tick. He looked up to the skylight; it was dark outside. Then he noticed the time. Just a little longer, he guessed, eager to finish the details on the porch of a beach house that he was painting.

* * *

Cannon's black SUV left the Grant's bungalow and drove a short distance down the street to the Caldwell's driveway. The three men sat in silence as they observed the dark house.

Marcus turned around to talk with his boss. "Looks like no one's home."

Gerald turned the car off. "There's an outside light on in the back."

Cannon ordered Marcus, "Get out and make sure no one is in there."

"Right away." Marcus got out and slowly walked up the deck to the main door. The inside was illuminated by the tiny glow of blue and green dots from appliances, phones, and cable TV's. He returned to the car. "I don't see anyone. That building over there attached to the house looks like a business or something."

"Do your magic, Marcus. Get us inside." Cannon gripped his cane in anticipation.

Marcus jiggled the door handle and felt around the doorjamb for a key with no luck. Then he noticed a collection of old silverware, odd shaped pieces of driftwood, beach shells, and the vertebrae from some kind of an animal all displayed to the side on a small shelf. These people are beachcombers, he thought to himself. He looked closer and found a small rusted tin box with a key in it.

Once inside, Marcus began his search for signs of life with his flashlight. He started downstairs then went upstairs and through the bedrooms. He returned to the front room, where he recognized the Caldwell woman in several framed pictures on the walls. Her desk was covered with papers and notes. He snickered at a black coffee mug near the computer bearing a skull and crossbones.

* * *

Paul was getting hungry. He washed his brushes and put his paints away. As he closed the skylight, he wondered if it was going to rain. There were no stars in the sky. He flipped a light on from the gallery as he entered the main house through a rear door that connected to the living room. It lit the back area, but the front of the house remained dark. He reminded himself to install a set of little white lights around the ficus tree in the foyer.

As he passed the main door, Paul noticed it was unlocked. He twisted the deadbolt to the side and then approached the dining room. A light flickered in the front parlor. The TV must be on, he guessed. As he neared the parlor's door, he saw the outline of a dark figure. The stranger held a flashlight in his mouth and stood over Nancy's desk. Paul hollered. "Who the hell are you?"

The intruder looked up and then ran towards Paul for his escape. Paul was pushed to the side, fell backwards, and crashed into the floor lamp. Within seconds, Paul got to his feet and took chase after the trespasser. He could see the man fumbling to unlock the foyer door so he grabbed the back of his shirt. "You're not going anywhere."

Marcus spun around and leveled a good punch to Paul's jaw. Paul fell backwards and hit his head against the tiled floor.

Marcus looked down at the sprawled body and pulled out his cell. "Mr. Cannon, you can come in now."

Cannon and Gerald came in the front door and stood next to Marcus. The old man poked Paul's foot with the tip of his cane. "So, who's this?"

"I checked his wallet; Nancy Caldwell's husband."

"This might be a stroke of luck for us. Tie him up. We can use him to our advantage." Cannon looked around the house. "Lovely old place. You don't see many of these in L.A."

"The woman's office is in the front," Marcus said as he examined a telephone cord that connected a phone in the foyer to another at the opposite end of the living room. He yanked it away from the baseboard. "I'll tie him up. Where do you want me to put him?"

"Stick him on the bench there," Cannon pointed to a wooden bench against the wall near the ficus tree. He then disappeared into the dark dining room.

The back of Paul's neck throbbed as he slowly opened his eyes. It didn't take him long to notice that his hands were tied behind his back. "Hey, what's going on here?" He tried to stand up, but a thick hand pushed him back down again.

"Stay put!" someone ordered. The light went on. A huge man stood in Paul's view with his arms crossed against his chest; he held Paul with a menacing stare.

Paul squinted in the light. "Who are you? What do you want?"

The man said nothing.

Another person strode into the foyer. Paul recognized him as the intruder that he had first discovered in Nancy's office. "Listen, there's some money in my wife's top drawer. Just take it and leave me alone."

Then an old man appeared. "So sorry for the situation your wife has put you in, Mr. Caldwell." He sat opposite Paul in a small wingback chair. "Your lovely wife has something that I want."

"Who are you?" Paul sensed the polite but threatening tone in the old man's voice sounded like big trouble. "I don't know who you are and I don't know what you're talking about." He tried to stand up. "What's my wife got to do with this?"

The large man smacked him back down with an open hand across his face. "Shut up! Mr. Cannon's talking."

Cannon, Paul thought, that's the old recluse Nancy met in L.A. He could taste blood from the corner of his mouth. Shit, what's she got herself involved in now? "I still don't know what you're talking about." He grimaced and waited for another slap.

Paul was about to get hit again when Cannon stopped the muscular arm of his assistant with his cane. "That's enough, Gerald." He walked over to Paul and sat next to him on the bench. "I am under the impression that your wife knows the whereabouts of a black pearl pouch...and I want it." He straightened his ascot. "If you don't know anything about it, then where do you think your wife likes to hide things?"

Paul tried to prevent any more pain from the two men in front of him. "Give me a minute to think."

Cannon returned to his seat across from Paul. "Marcus, go find me something to drink in the kitchen. Let's give Mr. Caldwell some time." He stared across the foyer to his captive. "May I call you Paul? It makes me feel more relaxed."

Paul watched Marcus leave for the kitchen. He hated the thought of a stranger rummaging through his refrigerator. He returned a hard stare to Cannon. What a cold and creepy guy the old man was. At the same time, he wracked his brain to remember anything Nancy had told him that might help him.

She had never said anything about a black pearl pouch. The only odd thing was the maple box she'd bought at the garage sale down the street. No, he decided, there's no connection. The cord hurt around his wrists. He stopped twisting his hands because it only made it worse.

46

Present Day
BREWSTER AND CHATHAM – CAPE COD

THE NAME GERTIE made me gulp down the quinoa along with a piece of chicken. I quickly reached for my water. Food was stuck in my throat and I started coughing.

Ally glanced at me. "Are you okay?"

I held my hand up to signal that I was all right. As I tried to swallow, my cell rang. It was Casey.

"Mom?"

I coughed a few more times "Casey. Everything okay?"

"Something's wrong at home."

"What do you mean?" I used my finger to block my other ear so I could hear her better.

"We came home from the movies and Dad's not here."

"Maybe he went to the store."

"No, Mom. Something's not right."

I stood up to go outside. "I'll be right back, Ally." I hurried past the tables and out into the parking lot. "Okay, Casey. What's not right?"

"The door was unlocked. The floor lamp in your office was knocked over."

She sounded scared. "You're sure the cat didn't do it?"

"There was some blood on the bench in the foyer."

"I'll be right home." As I rushed back for my purse, I yelled to Casey, "Get out of the house. Take the kids and get into the car. Lock the doors and call 911."

I handed Ally twenty dollars for my share of the meal. "I need to leave. Family emergency. Maybe we could get together before you leave for Boston?"

"Of course, Nancy."

I pushed in my chair, took the maple box out of the bag, and turned to leave. Over my shoulder, I said, "I'd like to talk more with you about your mother and her cousin Gertie."

It was almost 9 p.m. by the time I reached Pleasant Bay Road going towards Brewster. The muscles in my calf ached as I held back on pushing the gas pedal to the floor. The twists and turns of the old road made speeding not an option. My cell rang and I recognized Paul's number. I slowed down to answer.

His voice sounded timid. "Nancy."

"Paul. What's going on?" I could hear a faint rustling, then I heard a different voice.

"Nancy Caldwell?" It was oddly familiar. "Your husband's fine."

I couldn't breathe. I pulled over to the side of the road by a small beach. "Who is this?"

"Someone you visited when you were in L.A."

"Cannon?" I screamed.

"Well, you are a good detective, aren't you?"

"What do you want?" I opened the window for some air. "I want to talk with Paul."

"Of course, Nancy."

Cannon's politeness didn't fool me. This man was pure evil.

"I'm fine," Paul whispered.

He sounded like he was in pain.

"They want a black pouch or something…" His words trailed off.

I heard a crack and a scuffle. "Paul!"

Cannon's sinister voice took over again. "It seems that your husband knows nothing about what we're discussing. So, you bring me the black pearl pouch and no one gets hurt. Understand?"

"What black pearl pouch?" A sliver of dread and then desperation passed through me. An urgency to get going again pushed me back onto the old winding road.

"Don't play games with me. I'll text you where we can meet. No police. I'm sure you want to see your husband again."

"Wait! You have to give me more information." I almost drove off the road as it turned into a sharp curve. "I don't know what you're talking about."

"Don't lie to me." His voice was calculating and cool.

"Cannon, I don't know anything about a pearl pouch." I took the next curve with a stronger grip on the wheel. "I only uncovered facts about Gertie Foster."

"Ah yes, poor Gertie Foster. Always felt bad about her, but her cousin, Maggie? Now that's a different story. Remember, no police."

The phone disconnected.

My head swam with fear and hopelessness. Then my curious mind took over as I tried to reconcile what Cannon had just told me, and what I already knew.

I could see the police lights flashing as I turned onto our driveway. I jumped out and was relieved to see my old friend, Officer Gomes, talking with Casey. "Thanks for coming," I said and felt calmer, but the feeling was temporary. I leaned into Casey's car to talk to the kids, "You guys okay?'

They looked frightened, but managed some halfhearted smiles.

"I love you guys. Both of you stay here with Casey. I'm going inside with the police. Don't worry." I followed Gomes up the deck to the front door. After a walk through the house, everything checked out exactly like Casey had said. Nothing else looked out of place.

Officer Gomes came over to me. "Mrs. Caldwell, does your husband have any reason to wander off? Any illnesses that would cause him to fall?"

"No, to both questions." My cell buzzed for a text coming in. "It's my son in L.A." I lied. It was Cannon's instructions. I excused myself and went out on the back porch to write them down.

456 Underpass Road near Big Pete's Trailers

#2 Bay

2 hours

No sooner had I written the directions down when I got another call. This time it was from Stephen. I answered. "Hello?"

"Nancy. Where've you been? I've been calling you since yesterday."

"I'm sorry. Something came up that I need to take care of. I can't talk with you now."

"You'd better listen to me. I'm just passing Exit 11 on the Mid-Cape Highway."

"You're on Cape?"

"I've got some important information you'd be interested in. How far away from your house am I?"

I sat down on the wicker chair, but kept my eyes on what was going on in the house. I had to focus on Stephen's words. "About five minutes."

"Good. Now don't get worried, but has Gaylord Cannon contacted you yet?"

"What?" His question threw me, but then I realized that maybe Stephen knew what was going on. I felt some relief, now that I knew he would help me. At least, I hoped he would.

Officer Gomes had me sign his report. "We'll do whatever we can to find your husband. The first 24 hours are the most important. Stay home and let us do our job."

He handed me his card. "This is my personal cell number. Call me anytime." He walked to his car and drove away.

I waved for the kids to come back inside. Molly and Danny quickly threw their arms around me. "Now I don't want you to worry," I said. "Things will be okay." I tried to reassure them again, and then directed everyone into the kitchen to sit at the table. "It's getting late. Tomorrow will be a better day. We'll know more in the morning." Over fifteen minutes had already passed since Cannon's text. I had less than an hour and a half until my deadline. I went into overdrive, but remained calm. "Casey, I want you to get everyone into bed." I looked over to Molly and Danny. "Listen to Casey. I promise things will be okay. You don't have to worry. Your Daddy is very smart. He'll be home before you know it."

I saw Stephen pull up outside. It was good to see him. My fear of him coming between Paul and me took a back seat. Now I needed him. "Someone's here who's going to help us." My stomach relaxed. "I met him in California. He's a private detective and a good guy."

After quick introductions, I hugged the kids one more time and felt relief to see that they took to Stephen right away. He had them laughing as they went upstairs for bed with Casey. When I was sure the children couldn't hear us, I grabbed Stephen's arm and quickly told him what was happening. He then revealed what he'd uncovered back at Cannon's estate and that the people's names from the shoeboxes he'd searched online were all missing persons.

"Oh, my God. I knew that creep was evil. Then what's with this black pearl pouch?" I began to feel a panic attack coming on. Time was of the essence. We only had an hour to meet up with Cannon.

Stephen sat up in his chair. "You said this lady from the estate sale had a mother named Maggie and her cousin was named Gertie?"

"Yes, that's right. She'd found a secret journal from her mother."

Stephen leaned over the table toward me. "And the mother and cousin were in L.A. in 1947?"

"Yes, and she wanted me to return the locked box that I'd bought from her."

Stephen looked right at me. "She was curious about what was in it? Right?" His eyes opened wide as he sat back in his chair. "Well, I'm curious too. Aren't you?" Now he had a glint in his eye and had my attention. "Didn't you say that Maggie Grant's maiden name was Foster? Then her cousin Gertie's last name would probably be the same…"

I got up, grabbed my cell and keys. "You stay here. I'm going over to Ally's house to find out what's in that box."

Before I could count to one hundred, I was standing on the small bungalow's porch. The lights were still on.

Ally opened the door. "Nancy. Is everything all right?"

I could see the box on the kitchen table. I pushed past her. "Do you have a hammer or a screwdriver?"

"Yes." Her actions were hesitant, but she handed the tools to me from a drawer near the sink. "I kept these handy in case I needed any last-minute fixes. What's going on?"

I picked up the maple box and stood it on its side. "Hold this up for me."

"What're you doing?"

"Please trust me. We need to find out what's in this box." I steadied the end of the screwdriver on the lock. "It's a matter of life and death. I'm not joking."

Ally held onto the box and leaned away as I raised the hammer. The lock popped off. I lifted the lid to reveal old postcards decorated with palm trees and orange groves and some familiar photos of Maggie, Gertie, Harry, and Gaylord Cannon. Underneath them lay a black pearl pouch. I checked the time. I now had forty-five minutes. Stuffing the pouch into my jeans pocket, I turned to Ally. "Listen to me carefully."

Ally stood to attention.

"If you don't hear from me in forty-five minutes, I want you to call this man..." I handed her Officer Gomes' card, "...tell him it's an emergency and that Nancy Caldwell wants you to go to the #2 bay, near Big Pete's Trailers, on Underpass. And tell him to hurry! Paul is being held there. Ask him to bring backup."

Ally grabbed a pen and wrote down the address. Her years of reading Nancy Drew mysteries pushed her along in the puzzling scenario without too many questions. She looked unfazed and eager to participate.

As I ran out I said, "I promise I'll explain everything later."

I could hear Ally yell after me, "Not sure what's going on here, but I'll do my job. Be careful." I turned to see her at the porcelain table sorting through the cards and photos from her mother and stepfather.

47

Present Day
BREWSTER – CAPE COD

MY CAR SKIDDED to a stop at the end of our deck. I ran into the house and found Casey and Stephen at the kitchen table.

As I rushed past them to change into my sneakers, I overheard Casey talking to Stephen about her studies at college. I grabbed a flashlight and stood by the foyer. "Stephen. We've got to go."

"Okay." Stephen stood to join me.

"Casey. Stay by the phone. I'll be fine now that Stephen is with me."

Casey hurried over to us. "Where are you going?"

I didn't want to worry her, so I lied. "We're going over to the police station to answer some more questions."

"Okay, Mom. Be careful. I'll stay up until you get home."

"I'll drive," I told Stephen. "I know the roads better."

"Fine, I'll just be a minute." Stephen headed for his rental car.

My car idled while I impatiently waited for him to get in next to me.

"Sorry, let's go." He pulled out a gun and checked to make sure that it was loaded. "What's our plan?"

"We have thirty minutes to get there." I showed him the black pearl pouch. "This is what Cannon was after. I found it in the maple box."

He held it next to the lights on the dashboard. "It's beautiful, but pearls aren't worth killing for." He bounced it up and down in his palm. "It feels heavy."

My eyes stared on the road ahead. "It's empty inside, except for a receipt that's too faded to read."

"Well, pearls are not that heavy. Maybe something's hidden inside the lining."

I held my hand out. "You'd better give it back. I want to have it near me. It's the only thing I've got that might save Paul." I looked at the time. Twenty minutes left. I drove as fast as I could in the dark. Big Pete's Trailers flew by on my left.

Stephen pointed. "Hey, that's where you should've turned."

"I know." I drove up a little further then pulled into the post office, across the street. "Don't you think we should go in by foot?"

"You're right."

I turned the headlights off and parked in the direction of our destination, then grabbed my pepper spray and cell phone from my purse. After a quick run across Underpass Road and up the rutted driveway, we stopped alongside a pickup.

As we crouched against the wheel wells, I could see a black SUV parked in front of the second big door. Smoke trailed into the air from the rear on the driver's side. "Someone's standing by the car near the back. Do you see anyone else?"

"No. But whoever it is, he's not looking this way." Stephen leaned against the pickup's side door and pulled out his gun. "I'm going around the building to see if I can see anything inside. You stay here."

I kept my eyes on the smoke as Stephen disappeared into the darkness. I needed to do something, anything. I duck-walked closer along the edge of the building until I came across a piece of lead pipe. I picked it up.

The man looked like a big guy, but nothing I couldn't handle. When he turned to retrieve something from the trunk I held my breath and watched him lean inside the car. I then followed alongside the SUV, as close to the ground as I could go, to the rear. His backside was still facing out, the rear door opened to the side. I figured I could take a chance and try to knock him out.

I slowly stood up, gripped the heavy pipe with both hands and raised it above my head. With all my force, I swung as hard as I could against his upper back and neck. My weightlifting and racquetball paid off; his body fell forward and into the trunk. He didn't move. I quickly pushed his legs in and over to the side, then I tried to close the door, but it wouldn't shut. His foot was in the way. "Oops, sorry buddy," I whispered as I opened it again to push his huge shoes away from the edge of the top of the bumper. I hoped he'd stay stunned for a while. Just to make sure I sprayed him with my pepper spray. I quietly closed the rear door.

Within minutes, I'd moved up against the building with my make-shift club in-hand. I gripped it tighter as I heard footsteps approaching from inside. The door opened and out came a shorter man.

"Hey, Gerald. Come on in. Mr. Cannon…"

I pounced with another good swing. The guy went down. At that moment, Stephen came around the edge of the building to my side. He stared at me as I looked over my victim. "I did it," I whispered.

Stephen came closer. "Wow! Nobody better mess with you." He sent me a mischievous grin. "Not bad."

"My adrenalin was pumping and it felt good." I took a few deep breaths. "There's another one in the back of the SUV."

Stephen quickly looked in the car to confirm.

My breath was erratic, but I remained calm. "Are there anymore inside? Did you see Paul?"

"Well, there was this one," he said and pointed with his gun to the man on the ground in front of us. "The only other one I could see was the old man, Cannon. I assume the guy tied up in the chair is Paul? His back was to me." Stephen started to pull the man at our feet out of sight.

I looked at Stephen.

He returned another stare.

"What now?" I asked.

"Don't know until we go in. You ready?"

"I guess so."

Stephen opened the door without a sound. Paul was straight ahead of us, tied to a chair. His denim shirt was stained red and his head hung low. On either side of us were rows of dark shelves, like library stacks. The only light hung above a table positioned in front of Paul. Cannon's back was to us.

Stephen touched my arm and signaled that he was going to go to the right, on the far side of the dark shelves, and that I should go down the middle. He gave me a thumbs up. I nervously accepted it as a positive sign. Not sure what I was going to do, I crept slowly toward Paul. I could feel the pearl pouch in my jacket pocket next to my phone as I gripped the pepper spray in my other hand. Cannon was reading something. Just as I was about to speak, my cell went off and the theme to *Pirates of the Caribbean* echoed up into the high ceiling. Paul looked up and saw me. Cannon quickly pushed himself out of his chair and reached for his cane that lay across the table. I fumbled to get the phone out of my pocket, but instead of turning it off, I swiped for the camera app and hit the video, hoping to record, at least, the audio of whatever was going to take place.

Cannon whirled around to face me with his cane extended. He twisted the golden eagle to release a knife. "Nancy Caldwell. It's a pleasure to see you again. Won't you join us?"

I cautiously walked over to Paul, hiding the pepper spray in my hand and replacing my phone into my other pocket. I tried to think of what I should do next.

"I trust you brought the pearl pouch?" Cannon kept the cane pointed in our direction.

"Yes, I have it with me."

Paul looked at me with surprise and fear in his eyes.

I placed my hand on Paul's shoulder and then walked away from him, going a little closer to Cannon. I remembered from my self-defense class that distraction was a key element to disarming a would-be attacker. At the right moment, I would have to try and grab the end of the cane out of his hand. Reaching inside my pocket for the pouch, I tossed it on the table. Cannon lowered the cane slightly to grab the jewelry pouch. He turned it over and over in his bony hand.

I tried to figure out a way to knock the cane away.

"What is so special about this stupid bag?" he asked, as if he wanted me to give him the answer.

Seeing no opportunity to get the upper hand, I decided to play along with him, if only to stall long enough for either Stephen or Officer Gomes to come and save us. "Maybe there's something inside the lining?"

"Well, Nancy, that's very interesting." He lowered his cane to the table, twisted the golden eagle to retract the knife, sat down, and placed both hands on the pouch.

I lunged for the cane, but someone leapt on top of me from behind.

Cannon looked up. "Nancy, I'm not that stupid. I saw Marcus coming behind you." He returned to his task of opening the seam on the black material.

Marcus held my arm behind my back and wrapped his free arm round my neck. My breathing became labored as I focused on Cannon and Paul. I could see the small hole grow bigger as Cannon's fingers frantically worried away at the seam. Paul glanced to the left of the stacks.

Cannon ordered, "Marcus, let her go."

"The bitch hit me with some kind of club." Marcus squeezed my neck tighter.

"Let her go."

As Marcus released his grip, I gasped for a breath and then ran over to Paul's side. He continued holding a gun on both of us while rubbing the back of his neck. As I watched Cannon fiddling with the pouch, I crouched down to kiss and hug Paul.

"Isn't that sweet?" Marcus smirked. "Better get it all in now."

I kept hugging Paul and at the same time started to work the knot on the phone wire tied around his hands. My lips were glued to his. I kissed him until I'd loosened the wire; then I stood up and said to Cannon, "Do you mind if I come closer to see the pouch? Perhaps I can help you." Paul worked to free his hands while the pouch distracted everyone.

"Of course, my dear. Watch your step. You wouldn't want to harm your husband or yourself."

When I picked up the pouch I could see the glint of a diamond inside the lining of the black velvet.

Marcus wiped his nose with his sleeve. "Mr. Cannon. I'm going back outside to see what happened to Gerald."

"Go ahead. I can handle these two."

The old man stared at me as I widened the hole in the black fabric. Out of the corner of my eye, I could see that Stephen was standing at the edge of the shelving, his gun pointed at Cannon's back. I had loosened most of the thread on the seam, but waited for an opportunity to distract the old man even more. I heard the door to the outside slam shut. I saw Marcus hurry toward us.

"Gerald's knocked out cold in the back of—"

I caught Stephen's eye. He gestured that he'd take out Marcus. Before Marcus had a chance to finish his sentence, I threw the pouch to the ground. It burst open and diamonds scattered all over the dirty cement floor.

Cannon pushed away from the table, leaving his cane on top. He got down on all fours to frantically corral the gems. Within seconds, Marcus had reached the table, but Stephen was faster and he hit Marcus on the back of his head with the gun. Cannon looked up from the floor to see Marcus fall. I arched my back to get into a better position to deck the old man as he kneeled upright on the floor. I must have hit his teeth because my hand stung, and yet, it felt so satisfying. Cannon fell forward onto the diamonds.

Paul had untied his hands and ran over to me. "Nancy! Are you okay?"

"Of course I am." I gave him a kiss on his cheek. "I hope you're all right. Sorry about all of this." I massaged my bruised knuckles.

Paul looked over to Stephen. "I suppose this is the PI from Los Angeles?"

I nodded and smiled at the two most important men in my life at that moment.

Stephen extended his hand to Paul after he finished cuffing Marcus's hands behind him. "Nice to meet you, Paul. I've heard wonderful things about you."

I looked at him. "Do you always carry cuffs with you?"

"You never know when you're going to need them." Stephen winked, stood up, and looked around for something to secure Cannon.

Paul offered the phone wire that had been around his hands. "How about this? Make it good and tight."

By the time we'd collected most of the diamonds from the floor, Officer Gomes was walking down the aisle between the shelving. I could see lights from the police car through the opened door. They lit up the night sky.

48

Present Day
HOLLYWOOD HILLS – LOS ANGELES

DETECTIVE FREDRICKS stood on the back patio of the Cannon estate. His men had searched the small private three-hole golf course for the past 48 hours and had uncovered numerous shallow graves.

Stephen appeared at his friend's side, it was almost 3 a.m. "Jimmy. How's it going?"

"Well, it's been busy, but I think we're making progress. You know I don't like to work through the night, but this one's important."

The two men stood on the marble steps in silence.

"What are you doing here at this time of night?"

Stephen rubbed his face. "I just got off a flight from Boston. I was curious."

A bright glow from several police searchlights cast a menacing aura in the dark night. The two men could hear the sound of shovels against dirt, the clicking of cameras, and the occasional somber words, "Found another one, sir."

Fredricks took a call on his phone. "They just identified the remains of a woman, Blanche Jones. She'd been reported missing in late 1947 by her mother in Nebraska. She was in one of the first graves we found."

Stephen kept looking at the macabre sight in front of him. "Did she match with one of the shoeboxes from the hidden room?"

"Yup."

"It looks like you've got a big job on your hands."

An officer approached Detective Fredericks. "We've found some more remains, about 200 yards away from here."

Stephen stared at his friend. "How many have you dug up so far?"

"Close to twenty."

"Holy shit!" Stephen took his phone out to call Nancy. He was sure she would want to know what's going on, no matter what time it was back East.

THE WEDDING

One Month Later – Present Day
BREWSTER – CAPE COD

THE TENT HAD arrived and was set up by noon. Tables, chairs, linens, and portable heaters had also been delivered. We were ready to tie white twinkling lights around the top edges of the tent inside and across to the middle, ending at an old chandelier. It was going to be a beautiful reception. The colorful old plates were all washed, centerpieces had been designed, and the last-minute details were on schedule.

I found Paul in the tent finishing up the electrical connections. "Just got off the phone with Stephen. He'll be able to make it to the wedding after all."

Paul got off the stepladder. "That's great news."

"He wanted to know if he could bring a plus-one. I told him no problem. That makes me so happy; he deserves to have someone in his life again."

"Any more news about Cannon?" Paul leaned against one of the large round tables.

"Nothing since Stephen's early morning call, a few weeks ago. The police have a lot of work identifying all the bodies. I hope the old bastard spends the rest of his life behind bars."

"Take it easy, Miss Ace Detective, I'm confident that he'll get what he deserves." Paul laughed and gave me a hug. "You're quite a woman. I'm glad you're all mine."

I lingered in his arms for a few extra seconds, loving to hear every beat of his heart against mine. "I guess I'd better get back to my duties as the official wedding planner." I left Paul to finish the wiring and returned to the kitchen to organize the set up for the tables. I found Martha talking on the phone with pen in hand. "Of course, Ally. I'll tell her. Take care. See you soon." Martha hung up.

"So...is she coming?" I asked.

My best friend and top-notch nanny said with a broad smile, "Yes, she'll be here."

On the day of the wedding, the ocean calmly lapped against the sandy shoreline at Crosby Landing Beach in Brewster. Brian and Patty's guests lined up on either side of an arbor made of driftwood. The sun was bright and the sky was blue. It was a beautiful Cape Cod day as Paul and I walked Brian down an aisle formed by the couple's loved ones. The highlight of the whole occasion was, for me, that they had asked me to officiate at their wedding. What an honor! As I stood under the old arbor, waiting for everyone else to get into place, I could see all my family, old friends, and several new faces who had become very special to me over the last few months.

Of course, Paul was the most attractive to me, with his grey beard, white hair, and blue eyes. Jim had arrived last night on a red-eye flight. He handsomely accompanied his beautiful sister, Casey, down the sandy aisle. Molly and Danny followed as junior bridesmaid and groomsman.

The stunning and lovely bride appeared from over the dune, walking arm-in-arm with her parents onto the beach. I smiled at the fact that all the Caldwells were included in the ceremony. Patty was an only child, and her best friend wasn't able to make the wedding, so Jim and Casey were wonderful as best man and matron of honor.

The young couple's vows were sweet, endearing, and sincere. Before we knew it, we were all riding on an old wagon, pulled by an antique tractor, from the beach back to our house for the reception.

By 9 p.m., Patty and Brian had snuck off to a lovely inn on the bayside for the night. The few remaining guests were sitting around two tables under the tent, enjoying a final glass of wine or cup of coffee. I could hear the caterers clanging the last of the dishes in their clean-up and laughter from the kids who were watching a movie indoors. Everyone looked exhausted.

I sat with my head leaning against Paul's shoulder. Across from us were Stephen and Valerie, the new person of interest in his life. She was very nice and a good fit for Stephen. To my right sat Ally Foster with Officer Gomes, now known as the newly appointed Detective Tony Gomes. They seemed to have clicked after several meetings concerning the recovery of the pearl pouch and the diamonds. Ally had been pleased to discover she had an Aunt Gertie. Even though Gertie Foster was still a mystery, she was added to the family tree.

Ally sipped her wine. "Isn't it remarkable how we've all connected over the last few months? I think it's great that we're all here, sitting together, at such a happy event."

Everyone agreed.

Jim walked out the back of the house and came into the tent. "Hey, Mom. I forgot to tell you, I got an email from Natalie this afternoon."

I sat up straighter. "What'd she say?"

"When the police had first identified the bones I'd found in my yard as human, Natalie's mother sent away for a DNA test of herself. She forwarded it to the L.A. police and finally got an answer yesterday. Gertie Foster's DNA does match hers."

"I knew it."

"Natalie said that her mom was excited, but sad at the same time, and that it would have been nice to know she'd had a sister as she grew up. She hopes to come visit you with Natalie in the spring."

I turned to Ally. "I hope you'll be able to meet them when they visit?"

"I plan on it." Ally looked straight at me. "It was a miracle that you found those diamonds, Nancy. If you hadn't been such a curious person, and even just plain nosey about my mother and her cousin, I wouldn't have been able to keep my childhood home or start my own law practice and expand into more pro bono work." She leaned over and kissed Tony Gomes on the cheek. "Plus, you also gave me the opportunity to meet this special man."

Tony smiled and kissed her back.

Stephen had his arm across Valerie's shoulder. "Nancy, you're quite a detective."

A feeling of contentment washed over me, even though my eyes were sleepy, and I didn't think I would ever get over my aching feet. Paul and I had helped the kids pull off an outstanding affair, found some missing diamonds, uncovered a serial killer, and reunited a young girl with her long-lost family. I looked over to Ally and Tony and thought what a nice couple they made.

As the night grew later, we all drifted into the house. The last one to leave was Stephen. He leaned in to whisper, "Nancy, Val has a spa appointment before we leave tomorrow. Do you think I could come over?"

"Sure."

"That's good. I have some loose ends to tie up with you about our latest adventure."

The following morning, Stephen stood at the door holding a drink from the Sparrow coffee shop. "Morning."

"Come on in." I led him straight into my office.

He closed the door behind as I sat at my desk. "Why so secretive?"

He sat opposite me and took a sip of his coffee. "Nancy, the police and the FBI were very impressed with you, especially your perseverance in everything that happened with Cannon."

"That's nice to hear." I accepted the compliment, but kept talking. "What ever happened to Marcus and Gerald?"

Stephen quickly answered, "They were charged with kidnapping and aiding and abetting a murder, as in the clean-up of poor Donald. But that's not what I wanted to talk with you about."

I fidgeted in my chair and waited for him to finish.

"The FBI might be contacting you about working with them."

My heart began to race. "The FBI? You're kidding!"

"They told me it wouldn't be full time; just on occasion. You'd be undercover, so your family would never be involved."

I took a minute to consider his words. My stomach flip-flopped.

"Nancy?" He swirled his coffee cup around a few times and waited for me to answer.

"It's a very interesting opportunity, Stephen."

"Sometimes someone like you is needed on a case: a slightly older woman with grey hair who knows how to defend herself and who would not be deterred from a few obstacles thrown in her way. You'd be surprised at the number of historical artifacts that mysteriously go missing."

Is this another compliment or what? I'm not that old, I thought.

"They probably wouldn't put you in real danger. You'd have to go through some training, but nothing you couldn't handle. Besides, I may be partnered with you on occasion." He looked at me with hopeful eyes. "Well, I better get going. Val will be done soon and we have a flight at 4 p.m. Promise me you'll think about it?"

"I certainly will."

Stephen opened the office door to leave, but over his shoulder, he said, "You'd be good at it. Don't you think it could be fun?"

As I watched his car pull out of the driveway, his offer sounded more and more exciting to me. It was exactly what I wanted to do, without bringing more danger to my family. After all, I do love a good mystery. I went to find Paul to tell him what Stephen had offered to me.

*   *   *

The Following Year – Early Spring

Thanks to the generosity of Ally Foster, I received a sizable sum as my portion from the sale of the diamonds that were found in the black pearl pouch. As I sat on my rocker on the gallery porch, I felt blessed and lucky as I watched the security company install the final pieces of one of the top home security systems Paul and I could find. We'd decided it was time to turn our old house into a 'smart' house by utilizing all the latest security technology. No more intruders for the Caldwell family!

Casey was about to graduate from college and make her way in the business world. Molly and Danny were fast approaching their high school years. I shook my head and wondered at how fast they'd grown up. Jim had landed a job in Hollywood with a production company and was very happy, according to his last phone call. The FBI's invitation to come work on special cases was still intriguing, but I hadn't made my mind up yet. They said I could take my time in deciding. Brian and Patty asked me to visit them in Alaska sometime in the summer. I looked forward to seeing the last great frontier.

Paul joined me on the porch and glanced at the security crew. "Are they almost finished?"

"I think so. They're very thorough."

Carolina Wrens sang lovely songs as they flitted around the garden to find the safest place to build their nests and start a family.

Paul held my hand. "I'm very proud of you, Nancy. I always knew you were smart and adventurous. Well, you've proven it, for sure this time."

We took comfort in just being together.

"Do you think the mail came?" I asked as I rocked back and forth on the old oak rocker.

"I'll go see."

I watched my husband retrieve the mail from the box at the end of the driveway. He handed me an interesting looking letter that was addressed to me. The return label said it was from Abigail Ellis Baranov in Rhode Island.

"I wonder who she is?" I glanced up at Paul before I opened the envelope. My breath caught in my throat when a photograph of a familiar blue pattern on a china teacup and saucer fell into my lap.

The End

ACKNOWLEDGMENTS

THE FORTIES continue to be special to me and not just because I was born during that time. There was the music. I love the music of Benny Goodman, Frank Sinatra, and the ballads of love that permeated the airwaves, dance halls, and homes – they still make me want to dance. It was a glamorous time and yet, wild. Hollywood was at its best. Movie stars and the big screen made everyone dream of becoming famous.

When I was a child in the fifties, my parents made every day fun for us. With the advent of television, life only got better. My father was big on gadgets and electronics, especially anything to do with music. He made recordings of my brother, sisters, and me into 78 RPM records. I can see him now, kneeling next to a big wooden record console, holding steel wool on top of an orange spinning disc that was being etched simultaneously by a steel needle. We stood tall as we spoke, sang, or interviewed each other into a large brown stand-up microphone.

There are numerous people and personal memories, kept in my heart, of another time that contributed to the completion of *The Old Cape Hollywood Secret*.

A grand thank you goes to my dear, patient husband, Timothy. To my oldest son Scott, wife Carly, grandson Crosby and my youngest son, Michael, who all live in Los Angeles, a resounding "Wow" and much gratitude is sent for putting up with their unusual mother. My visits to them not only exposed me to Old Hollywood, but present day Los Angeles. When I wanted to visit the LA police station instead of the Third Street Promenade in Santa Monica, they humored me and became my bodyguards. My second oldest son, Tim, wife Jennifer, grandchildren Casey, Madison, and Zack always provide respite for me to craft new stories in the remote regions of Alaska, the location of my next novel.

Daughter Heather, back home on Cape Cod, was my first beta reader – she loved the story. Youngest daughter Annie and her husband Eric were always advising me, especially when there were questions about firearms or what fad the younger generation was into at the present time.

I can't forget my two faithful writer groups, reader Mary Anne Douglas, editor Nicola Burnell, proofreader Cindy Wyckoff, Joan Graham for last-minute editing, and my husband Timothy, Loretta Matson and Tim Graham for their cover design expertise. Two ladies, Jane Stevens and Diane Stephens, filled my head with wonderful stories of when they grew up in the late forties on Cape Cod.

And finally, while staying at the historic Georgian Hotel in Santa Monica for inspiration, I was treated with kindness and attention by two more people, Carlos Tejeda, a very hard working Bell Valet; and an extremely polite policewoman on the Santa Monica pier.

My life is a series of adventures and thanks to all of the above, I am continually surprised with what each day brings. Thank you!

ABOUT THE AUTHOR

INTERNATIONALLY best-selling author Barbara Eppich Struna is fascinated by history and writes a blog about the unique facts and myths of Cape Cod. Her published books are *The Old Cape House* and *The Old Cape Teapot*; her third novel in the Old Cape Series is *The Old Cape Hollywood Secret*.

Besides being a storyteller at heart, she is currently president of Cape Cod Writers Center, a Member in Letters of the National League of American Pen Women, a panelist at the International Thriller Writers - Thrillerfest 2016, and a member of Sisters in Crime and two writing groups.

ALSO BY BARBARA EPPICH STRUNA

The Old Cape House (Historical Fiction) – Nancy Caldwell relocates to an old sea captain's house on Cape Cod with her husband and four children. When she discovers an abandoned root cellar in her backyard containing a baby's skull and gold coins, she digs up evidence that links her land to the legendary tale of Maria Hallett and her pirate lover, Sam Bellamy. Using alternating chapters between the 18th and 21st centuries, *The Old Cape House* follows two women that are lifetimes apart, to uncover a mystery that has had the old salts of Cape Cod guessing for 300 years.

The Old Cape Teapot (Historical Fiction) – Nancy Caldwell returns in this second novel in a series of adventures. The story is told using alternating chapters between centuries. After finding an old map on Antigua, she leads us on a journey across Cape Cod filled with danger and lost treasure.

Made in the USA
Lexington, KY
28 September 2018